Sign up for our newsletter to hear
about new and upcoming releases.

www.ylva-publishing.com

Other Books by Jae

Happily Ever After 1&2

Standalone Romances:
Bachelorette Number Twelve
Just a Touch Away
The Roommate Arrangement
Paper Love
Just for Show
Falling Hard
Heart Trouble
Something in the Wine
Shaken to the Core

The Hollywood Series:
Departure from the Script
Damage Control
Just Physical
The Hollywood Collection (box set)

The Oregon Series:
Backwards to Oregon
Beyond the Trail
Hidden Truths
The Complete Oregon series (box set)

Fair Oaks Series:
Perfect Rhythm
Not the Marrying Kind

Portland Police Bureau Series:
Conflict of Interest
Next of Kin

The Shape-Shifter Series:
Second Nature
Natural Family Disasters
Manhattan Moon
True Nature
Enemies by Nature
Shifting Nature

The Vampire Diet Series:
Good Enough to Eat

Unexpected Love Series:
Under a Falling Star
Wrong Number, Right Woman
Chemistry Lessons

THE SHAPE-SHIFTER SERIES #8

SHIFTING NATURE

JAE

Author's Note

Dear reader,

Thank you so much for picking up *Shifting Nature*, the second part of Tala and Faith's story!

I assume you've already read part one, *Enemies by Nature*, but if you haven't, let me strongly urge you to read it first—and by *strongly*, I mean with the persistence of a shape-shifter who's caught the scent of their prey.

Tala and Faith's story is really a two-book saga, so to fully understand and enjoy *Shifting Nature*, you need to have read *Enemies by Nature* first.

Go ahead and read it. I'll wait.

If you have already read it, high five! I'm thrilled you liked it enough to want more, and I did my best to deliver a payoff you'll enjoy.

As always, happy reading and warm regards,
Jae

P.S. The glossary of shape-shifter terms is available at the end of this book and on my website:

www.jae-fiction.com/glossary-of-shape-shifter-terms/

CHAPTER 1

Faith gazed through the passenger-side window and watched the rolling hills of northern Virginia pass by in a blur.

She and Tala had been driving east, toward DC, for twenty minutes, and now the mountains were slowly fading into the background.

Her head was still spinning with everything that had happened this weekend.

Less than forty-eight hours ago, she had accompanied Tala to her brother's engagement festivities as her pretend mate, while secretly having only one goal: spying on Tala's pack for her father, who was convinced the Wrasa were hatching sinister schemes against humanity.

And she had found out a lot: that the average Wrasa family could bankrupt any all-you-can-eat restaurant; Tala made an excellent heating pad for period cramps; and, most importantly, Tala's pack had nothing to do with her mother's death.

Her father wouldn't be happy with any of that information, and she dreaded telling him she hadn't gone through with his plan to plant a bug in the Petersons' home.

After the warm welcome most of them had given her, she could no longer justify it.

Another twenty minutes went by, and neither of them had said anything.

Tala was just as quiet as Faith. Her gaze was locked straight ahead, and she seemed to be a million miles away.

After the constant lively chatter of the pack, the silence felt strange.

Faith had thought she would be relieved, even eager, to leave Silver Falls, to escape Tala's pack and the need to pretend to be her mate.

And she did feel relieved, but more about finally being able to stop spying on Tala.

Yet Tala's silence gnawed at her, eating away at her relief. It was so different from the night before, when they had freely shared painful secrets from their pasts.

Was Tala trying to process everything that had happened this weekend, as Faith was, or was something else going on?

Was she angry with Faith for telling her off in front of her entire pack during breakfast?

When she couldn't stand the silence anymore, Faith cleared her throat. "I feel like I should apologize."

"You already did," Tala said. "Twice."

"Well, they say the third time's the charm," Faith quipped to lighten the mood. But this time, she wasn't actually apologizing for following Tala's pack into the woods—and alerting her father, who had sent two members of his anti-Wrasa group after them.

Before she could explain what she was apologizing for, Tala glanced over. "I don't need a third apology. I'm not saying what you did was great, but now that I've had some time to think about it, I get why you followed us."

"You do?"

"Yeah, I mean… Finding out that our ritual spot is in the exact same location where your mother died all those years ago… That must have seemed suspicious, especially since your father keeps telling you we're all evil monsters."

Faith's heart beat faster as she remembered the shock of seeing the red pin on the map, pointing at the spot where her mother's body had been found. She hadn't wanted to believe that Tala's family had anything to do with her mom's death. The better she had gotten to know Tala and her pack, the more she had started to doubt her father's convictions about the Wrasa.

But she hadn't been able to rule it out—not without following them so she could see what was going on with her own eyes.

"That and you were pretty secretive about what would happen during that ritual taking place in the middle of the night and about why I couldn't come with you," Faith added. "It made the entire ritual seem like something you were trying to hide from humans."

"We were," Tala said quietly.

Faith tamped down the old instincts to immediately assume nefarious intentions. "But…why? You freely shared all the other engagement traditions with me. What made this one different?"

"The name of the ritual—yasi makamar—translates to *night run*," Tala said. "The packs of the two people getting engaged meet at the more powerful pack's ritual spot, where they shift shape and run together in their animal forms."

Faith nodded. "I figured that out." A shiver went through her at the memory of a Syak pack—wolves with eerily glowing eyes—charging toward her, their howls echoing through the dark forest.

All her nightmares seemed to have come true. She hadn't known they were Tala's family. How could she when Tala had failed to mention her relatives were wolves, not foxes? Thank God she had tried to run instead of squeezing the trigger on the gun her father had smuggled into her suitcase!

Tala glanced away from the road and gave her a worried look. Her fingers twitched on the steering wheel as if she was suppressing the urge to reach over and touch Faith. "You okay?"

"I'm fine." Faith wanted to move forward, not linger on that night. Both of them had contributed to it by keeping secrets, so now it seemed important for her to know the full truth. "So why's that a secret? I mean, you're shape-shifters. Humans already know you can turn into animals."

"Yeah, but what humans don't know is…" Tala hesitated. She tugged at the collar of her shirt, and Faith noticed that she wasn't wearing her ID tag, as if she was delaying putting it back on until the very last second. "When humans saw Kelsey shift on TV, they were stunned and entirely focused on the end result of the transformation—the powerful creature she turned into—not the transformation itself. But the truth is, during those moments, my kind is very vulnerable. All of our bones, joints, muscles, and organs rearrange themselves, and our senses change too, leaving us disoriented."

Tala was right. Faith had focused on the wolf in that recording, not on how defenseless a creature would naturally be while their body rearranged itself.

"That's the reason shape-shifting is part of the engagement ritual," Tala added. "The two packs show that they trust each other like family."

"That's why you didn't tell me anything about the yasi makamar." It all came down to trust—or the lack of it. "Thank you for telling me now. I swear your secret is safe with me."

"I wouldn't have told you if I thought otherwise," Tala replied.

Silence fell again, but this time, it wasn't awkward.

"Um, by the way, that wasn't what I meant when I said I feel like I should apologize," Faith finally said.

Tala glanced at her again, then back to the road ahead. "So what did you mean?"

"I wanted to apologize for telling you off in front of everyone during breakfast," Faith said. "That's probably not something a Syak mate would do to the future leader of the pack, is it?"

"No, it's not." Tala tapped her fingers against the steering wheel. "But you weren't completely wrong."

Faith pressed a hand to her chest in faux shock. "Wait... If I translate that into non-alpha language... Are you admitting I was right?"

Tala shrugged. "While I stand by my assessment, rating your looks against Mirella's to one-up my brother was an asshole thing to do."

"Yes," Faith said. "I mean, I probably should have told you in private, but it didn't sit right with me, especially since Lasandra was right there."

Then she paused and mentally repeated what Tala had just said. *I stand by my assessment...* A flush warmed Faith's body. Did that mean Tala really did think Faith had been the hottest woman in the room, even compared to her brother's gorgeous fiancée, and hadn't merely said it to outdo Rey?

She pushed the thought away to focus on the conversation.

"Lasandra?" A frown marred Tala's face. "What does she have to do with it? I didn't even mention her."

For someone so clever, Tala could be pretty clueless when it came to relationships sometimes. "Exactly. You told your brother his fiancée was the second-hottest woman in the room, implying that I'm the hottest. That means Lasandra didn't even rate second place in your book. Since she's your ex, that's just...ouch."

"What? That's not what I... Damn." Tala thumped her fist against the steering wheel. "I owe her another apology, don't I?"

"Another?" Faith asked.

"Mm-hmm. I apologized earlier for breaking things off the way I did, without much of an explanation."

Faith turned in the passenger seat to study her, but Tala's focused expression gave nothing away. "Do you still love her?" she asked quietly.

Tala was taking much too long to contemplate the question.

The muffled roar of a truck speeding by emphasized the silence in the car.

"Yeah," Tala finally said. "I do."

The seat belt seemed to tighten around Faith, squeezing her chest and making it hard to breathe.

"I mean, she's family and an amazing person," Tala added. "But I'm not *in love* with her, and if I'm completely honest, I'm not sure I ever was."

The pressure on Faith's chest eased.

"I thought I was, but maybe I was merely in love with the idea of being with a Syak because I thought that would make me more of a true wolf." Tala sounded as if she had only now figured it out herself. "I know it might be hard to understand, but—"

"No, not at all," Faith said. "I get it."

Tala turned her head toward her. "You do?"

"Yes." Faith fiddled with the edge of the bandage on her palm. "If I'm perfectly honest, I think I'm in the same boat. Don't get me wrong, I loved Jon. I mean, what's not to love? He's a wonderful father and gets along great with my dad. But I'm no longer sure if I was ever in love with him or just the idea of having a complete family again."

Deep down, she had known it for years, yet she had never told anyone, not even her best friend, Sabina. But she sensed that she could tell Tala without having to fear being judged.

A soft chime from Tala's side of the car interrupted before she could say anything.

"I bet it's my mom," Tala said with a grin. "She probably noticed that you 'forgot' to take the leftover skiyo with you."

Faith shuddered at the memory of the Wrasa dish and its earthy taste.

Then Faith's phone chirped too.

"You got your phone back?" Tala asked.

"Oh, yeah. I forgot to tell you. Arnold found it in the forest."

Tala let out a low whistle. "And he gave it back? That's as close to an apology as you'll ever get from him."

The phone in Faith's back pocket chirped again, followed by a chime from Tala's. Apparently, someone was trying to reach both of them.

Faith pulled hers from her back pocket and unlocked it.

She had two new messages, both from the same unknown number. Quickly, she tapped to read them.

This is a message from Jeffrey Madsen's office, it said. *The council speaker wanted you and Tas Peterson to be aware of this, in case the press reaches out to you for a statement. He'll be in touch with you later today.*

The second bubble held only a link.

"What is it?" Tala asked.

"Your boss sent us a link. You probably got the same message."

Faith tapped on it.

An article from a news website came up.

The headline declared: *Peter MacAllister Speaks Out Against Interspecies Marriage.*

With a sinking feeling, Faith started to read the article.

As debates about the proposed Wrasa Rights Act intensify, Peter MacAllister, leader of HASS (Humans Against Shape-Shifters), voiced his staunch opposition to interspecies marriage in a recent interview with WNN.

The Wrasa Rights Act, if passed, would be the first federal law to recognize Wrasa as having equal rights, including the right to marry humans.

Though human/Wrasa partnerships currently remain rare, attitudes appear to be changing, especially among younger people, who no longer view interspecies relationships as taboo.

MacAllister, who has long opposed the Wrasa Rights Act, took a hard stance against what he calls a "dangerous threat to families and our society's moral fabric."

He asserted that "marriage should be a sacred union between two humans, not between a human and a shifter. If we let this so-called Wrasa Rights Act pass, we'll be undermining the sanctity of marriage. What kind of world are we leaving our children if we allow such unnatural unions?"

There were more quotes, but Faith couldn't bear to read them. Her stomach churned.

Tala glanced over as if sensing her distress. "What's wrong?"

"My father." Faith sighed. "He gave an interview. I'll spare you the details, but he spoke out against the Wrasa Rights Act and interspecies marriages."

Tala's knuckles whitened on the steering wheel, yet her expression remained impassive. "That's not exactly new, is it?"

"No. He's said similar things before. I never agreed, but back then, it didn't feel so…personal." Then she realized how that sounded and quickly added, "Not that you and I will really get married, but it's only a tiny step from not allowing interspecies marriages to banning Wrasa from marrying at all. To think that your brother and Mirella or any of your relatives could have that right taken away…"

Tala nodded grimly. "No doubt your father will advocate for that next."

If Faith was honest, she couldn't rule it out. She stared at the last paragraph of the news article.

MacAllister's daughter, Faith, has recently been revealed to be engaged to a shape-shifter. Ms. MacAllister has not publicly commented on her father's statements. As the debate over Wrasa rights and interspecies marriage heats up, her silence speaks volumes.

Faith worried her bottom lip between her teeth. The journalist who had penned that article was painfully accurate. The world thought she was engaged to a Wrasa, while her father fought to keep her from having the right to marry one. And still, she acted as if she had the privilege to remain apolitical and stay out of that debate.

But if she spoke up, that would have grave consequences.

She could lose her father and her amicable relationship with her ex-husband. If she sided with the Wrasa, they would see that as a personal betrayal. It would become impossible to keep Chloe out of it because her entire life would be affected.

Was she really ready to risk it all?

CHAPTER 2

It had been a quiet ride back to DC.

Faith had been deep in thought since she'd read her father's interview. She had felt Tala's questioning gaze on her several times, but Tala hadn't pressured her to reveal what was on her mind.

Very unlike the pushy Saru she'd been when they'd first met.

Or maybe Faith was paying more attention, and that was why she caught glimpses of Tala's considerate side more often.

Once they passed the Waterfront Center, Faith pointed to the right. "Take a r—"

Tala had already flicked the indicator on and guided the SUV into the steep, narrow street that led to Faith's town house.

Faith sent her a startled look. Tala had picked her up at the hotel after work on Friday. Why was she familiar with Faith's neighborhood? "How did you…?" She bit her lip. "Let me guess. That was in the brief the council gave you too?" Even though she was no longer convinced the Wrasa were evil, it still felt like an invasion of her privacy.

"Um, no, not exactly." Tala hesitated.

"No secrets, remember?"

Tala sighed. "I staked out your den…um, your neighborhood before I approached you."

Faith put two and two together. "That's how you knew which coffee shop I frequent. You didn't just coincidentally show up there."

Tala stared straight ahead, avoiding her gaze, and nodded.

A shiver crawled up Faith's spine. For a second, that old view of the Wrasa as sinister beings with evil plans reared its ugly head. Forcefully, she pushed it down. While the Wrasa hadn't approached it in a straightforward way, she wanted to believe they'd done it with good intentions.

Tala parked along the street and shut off the engine.

For a few moments, they sat in silence, neither of them getting out.

"Why?" Faith finally asked. "Not just the not-so-coincidental coffee shop meeting. Why did you approach me to be your fake girlfriend? I mean, you couldn't know I'd agree to that ridiculous scheme because my father wanted me to spy on you."

Tala glanced down to where she was making grooves into the fabric of her pants with her fingernails. "I want to tell you, but I need Madsen's okay for that. I already told you more than I should. Can you give me some time?"

Faith reached over and stilled her hand before Tala could shred her jeans. Then she realized her hand was basically resting on Tala's thigh, and she quickly pulled her fingers away. "Um, yes, of course."

Tala brushed her hand over her leg one more time before she climbed out of the car.

Faith followed her to the back of the SUV and tried to take her suitcase from Tala, but Tala didn't relinquish it.

"What kind of fake girlfriend would I be if I didn't carry your suitcase all the way to your door?"

Faith chuckled. "By all means, carry it, then."

"Oh, wait!" Instead of closing the hatch, Tala lifted the panel of the spare tire compartment and reached inside. "Here. Your father would become suspicious if he didn't get this back."

Faith stared at the object Tala had pressed into her hand. It was her father's gun.

Heat shot into her cheeks as the memory of following Tala's family into the forest with the weapon flooded back. She knew Tala returning it was a sign of her trust, and that made her feel even more ashamed.

Quickly, she unzipped the front compartment of her suitcase and slid the weapon in before zipping it back up.

Tala watched her without saying anything, but her eyes held no trace of anger.

Side by side, they climbed a set of half-hidden stairs that led from the street into a tranquil courtyard. The afternoon sun made the brick facades of the town houses appear to glow. Faith had instantly fallen in love with the historic buildings when she had first seen them. More than a hundred years ago, they had belonged to a paper mill before they'd been converted into town houses.

Tala's nostrils flared as she inhaled, and Faith imagined that she might still be able to detect a hint of paper pulp lingering in the air.

But whatever Tala smelled didn't seem to be something pleasant.

"Humans lying in wait!" Tala jerked her head at the bushes to their left and pushed Faith behind herself. "Could be reporters…or HASS goons!"

Faith's heartbeat sped up as she stumbled backward. She gritted her teeth. Surely her father wouldn't dare send more of his group members?

Before she could reach for the gun in her suitcase, four guys jumped out from behind the bushes.

Faith's gaze flew to their faces. She'd never seen them before. They clearly weren't part of her father's group.

Camera flashes went off, making Faith squint against the sudden brightness. She raised her arm to shield her face.

"Ms. MacAllister, how does it feel to be in a relationship with a shifter, knowing how your father feels about them?"

"Did it cause a rift between your father and you?"

"Did he disown you?"

"Do you regret getting involved with a shifter?"

Relentless questions rained down on Faith, who flinched back.

A menacing growl rose from Tala's chest, raw with fury. "Back off!" She kept her own body between the paparazzi and Faith. Her fingers curled into claws as if she was barely holding the instinct to shift at bay.

"No, Tala!" Faith gripped the back of Tala's shirt. Even through the fabric, she could feel the tension rippling through Tala's body. A single fox couldn't possibly take on four humans—and even if she could, the resulting photos would condemn the Wrasa.

Tala whirled around, gripped Faith's elbow, and urged her toward the town house.

The paparazzi followed, now leaving more space between them and Tala, as if sensing they had pushed her dangerously close to losing all self-control.

"Hey, is that a wound on your face?" One paparazzo rushed around them and snapped several close-ups of Faith's face. "What happened?"

Faith lifted her hand and touched her cheek. It was still tender.

When she winced, more flashlights erupted.

White spots danced across Faith's vision.

Once again, Tala leaped between her and the paparazzi with a growl.

Faith shrank behind her. "It's…nothing."

As soon as she'd said it, she knew it had been the wrong answer. The paparazzi didn't know why she was so reluctant to reveal the truth, so now they were jumping to all the wrong conclusions.

A glint entered the paparazzo's eyes. He looked like a shark scenting blood in the water. "Did you two get into a fight? Is there trouble in paradise?"

"Is the wedding off?" another asked.

"Did she hit you?" a third one shouted, each word cutting deeper.

"What? No!" Fury gripped Faith. How could they think something like that of Tala? But then again, a month ago, she would have been ready to believe the most sinister things about her too.

Her upper lip lifted into a snarl, Tala advanced on the nearest paparazzo, who immediately staggered back.

Faith latched on to her shirt. "Tala, no! You'll only make it worse." She circled around Tala so she was the one in the front. "It was an accident," she told the paparazzi. "Just a branch that hit me while we took a walk through the forest."

They traded skeptic looks. "Accident. Right."

Oh God. This was getting out of hand, and nothing she said seemed to make any difference. They had naively thought they could control the tabloids. But now Faith could already see tomorrow's headlines: *Evil revealed: Faith MacAllister spotted in tears after her shape-shifter girlfriend's violent attack!*

"It was!" Faith tried to reason with them calmly, but her voice came out strangled with desperation. She needed to make them see Tala wasn't the violent monster they believed her to be. "Everything is fine between us. Wonderful, in fact. Tala would never hurt me."

More doubtful looks from the paparazzi. Her denial only fueled their twisted fantasies.

This was spiraling out of control. They had to do something before the tabloids painted Tala or even all Wrasa as domestic abusers. "She's the most tender lover I ever had," Faith added. She turned toward Tala, gripped her hand, lifted it to her mouth, and pressed a gentle kiss to the inside of her wrist.

Tala's pulse was pounding a wild staccato beneath her lips, and her skin was even hotter than usual.

Flashes went off around them.

Ooh. Photos of tender kisses clashed with the domestic abuse story, yet they had still pressed their shutter buttons.

The paparazzi couldn't care less about what had really happened between Faith and Tala. They weren't after the truth—they were after money. They would sell whatever pictures they could, and the tabloids would write a matching story.

So if we give them scandalous photos of a different kind…

A daring plan formed in an instant. She reached for Tala's other hand too and tugged her closer.

Tala went willingly, probably trying to shield Faith with her own body.

But that wasn't what Faith had in mind. How could she give her at least a heads-up, warn her that she was about to do something unexpected, without giving her plan away to the paparazzi?

An idea popped into her panicked mind.

It was silly. Completely outlandish. But it was the only thing she could think of, so she did it anyway.

She winked at Tala.

Tala blinked. Had Faith just…winked at her?

Humans don't wink, Faith had told her repeatedly.

And yet she had. Clearly, she was using it as a warning, the way she had when Sabina had wanted to go bowling with them and Faith had sent her a bunch of winking emojis. But what exactly was she trying to tell her?

She searched Faith's eyes. Her pupils expanded, making her eyes appear even darker, like black holes pulling her in.

Faith slid one hand up Tala's arm, to her shoulder, setting off goose bumps, then tugged her forward. Her breath, quick and ragged, washed over Tala's mouth.

Great Hunter! She's going to—

Then Faith's lips were on hers.

Tala had expected the same whisper of a kiss they had shared in the bowling alley, but this was different.

Heat flooded Tala's body, and surprise instantly gave way to desire.

She cupped the back of Faith's neck to hold her in place—for believability's sake, of course—and returned the kiss.

Faith's lips were as soft as she remembered and cool at first, but they warmed against Tala's within seconds.

The paparazzi's voices faded into the background, replaced with the thrum of Tala's own thundering heartbeat…or maybe it was Faith's, pounding wild and fast against her own as their mouths moved against each other.

Tala traced Faith's full bottom lip with her tongue.

When Faith's lips parted, Tala grazed her tongue with the tip of her own while caressing the back of Faith's neck with her fingertips.

A low gasp escaped Faith, making Tala's pulse trip even faster. She clutched at Tala's shoulders with both hands and surged forward until her body was flush against Tala's.

The press of Faith's breasts against her own made Tala bite back a moan. She couldn't think, couldn't do anything but pull Faith even closer and deepen the kiss.

Fireworks went off.

Tala had always assumed things like that happened only in human romance novels, but now star-shaped bursts exploded behind her closed lids.

Closed? Wait! She forced her eyes open and struggled to pull herself back to reality.

It wasn't fireworks. Camera flashes went off all around them.

With a growl, Tala broke the kiss.

The paparazzi were taking photos of the hottest kiss Tala had ever experienced!

Which was probably exactly what Faith had intended, Tala realized when her brain started to function again.

"Did it work?" Faith whispered into her ear while pretending to nibble it.

The brush of her lips against her earlobe sent a flare of arousal down Tala's body. "Oh yeah, it definitely did," Tala whispered back, her voice hoarse. She cleared her throat. "Um, I mean, yes, they bought it."

Then a realization struck her. This was what Jorie had seen in her dream vision—the two of them kissing while the cameras flashed around them!

The paparazzi stared at them. One of them let go of his camera with one hand to fan himself. "Man, I think I don't need payment for this job," he said with a husky laugh. "This was reward enough."

"See? No trouble in paradise, boys." Tala smirked at them. "Now get out of here before I call the police and have them delete the photos!"

The guy closest to them snapped one last picture, then they ambled down the path and disappeared around the building across from Faith's home.

Within seconds, Faith and Tala were alone.

Faith took a wobbly step back, away from Tala. "Um, sorry for ambushing you like that," she said, her voice low so no one could overhear. "It was the only thing I could think of."

"Oh, no, no. Brilliant improvisation." Tala waved her hand dismissively, as if sexy kisses were part of the strategic warfare curriculum at the Saru Academy.

"Thanks," Faith said with a small smile. She lifted her hand and touched her lips, which were reddened from their kiss.

Great Hunter, don't do that. It made Tala want to surge forward and kiss her again, and this time, there were no paparazzi around to give her a reason.

"Um, I'd better go after them and make sure they're gone." She waved in the direction the paparazzi had disappeared in.

Faith nodded.

Tala's feet felt heavy, every muscle protesting as she walked away from Faith and crossed the courtyard. She took several deep breaths and tried to get her rebellious heartbeat under control.

A single fake kiss shouldn't leave her this rattled. But then again, nothing about it had felt fake.

One of Faith's neighbors sat on a bench in front of her house. She scowled as Tala approached.

Usually, Tala's sharp senses were on high alert, scanning her surroundings, but her brain was still dazed. The only thing she could focus on was reliving the feel of Faith's mouth, the softness of her body against her own, so she needed several seconds to make out what the blonde was wearing: a *Moms Against Shape-Shifters* T-shirt.

"Disgusting animal!" the woman shouted, her voice cutting through Tala's daydream like a knife. "Leave your dirty paws off human women!"

Tala's kiss-stunted reflexes had no time to react as an object arced through the air toward her.

Pain exploded through her temple. Tala stumbled back. She lifted her hand to her pounding head, and her fingers came away bloody.

Fire flared along her skin. She pulled back her upper lip in a wild snarl, revealing teeth she could already feel lengthening.

No! She couldn't let it happen. Not here, out in the open, with the paparazzi still nearby. She fought to stay anchored to her human form, but the fox clawed at the edges of her self-control, threatening to break free.

"Tala! Oh my God!" Faith rushed toward her—Tala sensed it without having to turn around.

Tala could barely hear her because every cell in her body pounded along with her head, getting ready to shift and tear into her attacker before the woman could harm her mate too.

Her vision blurred. The fire beneath her skin burned hotter and hotter. She couldn't fight it much longer.

A surge of adrenaline cut through the haze of desire clinging to Faith's brain. On legs that had felt wobbly only seconds ago, she sprinted across the courtyard.

"What the hell is wrong with you?" she shouted at Camille. She couldn't believe her neighbor had thrown an unopened soda can at Tala!

Camille pulled out her phone and started to film Tala. "Wrong with me?" she shouted back. "Asks the woman sleeping with this monster!"

Fury hit Faith like an avalanche of lava that boiled up from deep within her. Her vision went a hazy red, and her nails bit into her palms. The pain wrenched her back from her focus on Camille.

She wasn't important—Tala was.

Faith skidded to a stop next to Tala, who stood bent over, clutching her head. "Tala! Are you okay?" She grabbed her shoulders and guided her to straighten up so she could see.

Blood trickled from a gash on Tala's temple.

Faith sucked in a sharp breath. "Tala!"

Tala's eyes instantly locked onto hers. They were wild and unfocused, and her pupils had elongated into vertical slits, like those of a fox.

Oh shit! Tala was about to shift! Pain could do that to them, she remembered Tala telling her.

"Stop filming!" She lunged at her neighbor, trying to wrench the phone out of her hand, but Camille was taller and lifted the device out of reach. "You have no right!"

Camille kept recording. "I have every right to show the world what a monster she really is!"

"The only monster the world will see is you!" But as clear as that was to her, she knew the Wrasa haters wouldn't see it the same way.

If she didn't do something to prevent it, the video of Tala shifting and possibly attacking the can-throwing Wrasa-phobe would go viral on social media.

"We need to get you inside. Now!" She pulled Tala's arm over her shoulder, hooked an arm around her waist, and dragged her toward the house.

Tala leaned heavily against her and staggered along. Heat radiated off her in waves.

They stumbled up the six steps to the front door.

"Hang on," Faith repeated again and again, her voice urgent, as she fumbled with the keys, trying to find the right one. "Don't shift. Focus on me."

Finally, she shoved the key into the lock and turned it.

But as she tried to pull Tala inside, Tala dragged her feet. "Are you sure?" she gasped out.

Faith tugged on her arm to urge her forward. "What?"

"You said…no one gets through…your front door until you're…you're ready to introduce them to Chloe." Tala's voice was hoarse and guttural, each word scraping from her throat as if it cost her tremendous effort.

Faith gaped at her. She couldn't believe Tala remembered what she had said what felt like eons ago—especially in the state she was in. "You're bleeding and barely hanging on! Come in!" Chloe wasn't home anyway, and even if she were, that would have been the least of Faith's worries right now.

The door swung open, and they staggered through.

Faith kicked the door shut behind them, and they both slumped against it, breathing hard, with Tala's arm still across her shoulders.

"Kalyani, nemi," Faith whispered soothingly. "Everything's okay. You're safe now."

Tala blinked and stared at her. Gradually, her pupils returned to normal.

"I'm so, so sorry. I can't believe she threw that can at you!" Faith pulled her phone from her back pocket and swiped to unlock it.

"What are you doing?" Tala asked, sounding as if she was still struggling to form words.

"Calling the police, what else? She attacked you!"

Tala gripped her hand, stopping her from calling 911. "No. That rarely ends well for us Wrasa."

Before Faith could answer, Tala raised her upper lip and let out a sharp, menacing growl—but not at Faith. Her attention locked onto something in the hallway.

Faith jerked her head around.

They weren't alone! Jon stood in the hallway, glaring at Tala. "What the heck, Faith?"

With another growl, Tala tried to protectively step between Faith and her ex, but Faith didn't let go of her waist. She gave a soft squeeze and whispered, "Let me handle this, please."

A subvocal growl still vibrated against Faith's side, but finally, Tala gave a reluctant nod.

Once Faith had made sure Tala could stand on her own, she let go to face Jon.

He pointed at Tala as if he wished his index finger were a gun. "What is she doing here?"

"What are *you* doing here?" Faith shot back. "I gave you a key for emergencies only, not so you can snoop around when I'm not home!"

"I didn't snoop! Chloe had bad dreams all night, but she refused to take a nap unless we came here so she could nap on the couch with her glow-in-the-dark dinosaur blanket."

As if hearing her name, Chloe ran over from the living room. "Mom! You're back!"

"Hey, sweetie!"

When Chloe curiously glanced in Tala's direction, Faith quickly blocked Tala's bleeding temple from Chloe's view.

Jon caught their daughter before she could reach Faith. "Chloe, go to your room."

Chloe's bottom lip trembled. "But Mom is—"

"You can say hi to your mom in a minute," Jon said. "I have to talk to her first. Alone."

"It's okay, sweetie," Faith said in the same soothing tone she had used with Tala. "I'll come upstairs as soon as we're done here, okay?"

Chloe nodded, whirled around, and ran up the stairs to her room.

Faith strode toward Jon. "What the hell, Jon? You come to my house without so much as letting me know, and now you think you get to call the shots and send Chloe to her room when I haven't seen her in three days?"

"I'm protecting her, okay?" Jon shot back. "Or do you think it's good for her to see her mother clinging to a shifter who's dripping blood all over the floor? No wonder she has nightmares!"

Faith wrestled down a wave of anger at his tone when he talked about Tala. He was right about the blood; she had to give him that. A quick glance over her shoulder confirmed that Tala was, indeed, still bleeding. "Why don't you go tend to the wound?" she said to Tala. "The bathroom is upstairs, first door to the right, and the first aid kit is in the cabinet beneath the sink. I'll be right up to help."

"Are you out of your mind? I'm not letting her go upstairs, where Chloe is!" Jon blocked her access to the stairs.

Tala pressed her shirtsleeve to the gash. "Save your breath. I'm not going upstairs. I'm not leaving her alone with you for even a second, asshole."

"You pretend I'm a threat to Faith? That's rich, coming from you, shifter!"

Faith had heard enough. "Stop it! Both of you." She whirled toward Jon. "Tala can barely stay on her feet! She needs medical attention, and she needs it now! Unless you intend to help her, move out of the way and let her go upstairs!"

A vein in Jon's temple pounded. His gaze flicked between Faith and Tala, who stood her ground, despite the blood staining the sleeve she pressed to her head.

The air seemed to crackle with the tension between them.

Finally, Jon stepped aside.

Tala hesitated, clearly unwilling to leave her alone with him.

"Please, Tala," Faith said, her voice softening. "Go. He won't hurt me."

"Fine." With one last growl at Jon, Tala stalked past him.

His jaw clenched, and for a second, he looked as if he would tackle Tala from behind, but beneath Faith's warning glare, he didn't.

He and Faith watched as Tala disappeared around the corner, then listened to the creak of the stairs. Twice, Tala paused—either to steady herself against the banister or to listen and make sure Jon was staying civil—then the bathroom door clicked shut behind her.

Jon turned back toward Faith. He squinted, then crossed the hall toward her. "What did she do to you?" He reached out as if to touch her cheek.

Faith turned her head away. "She didn't do anything. I wasn't paying attention and ran into a branch; that's all."

"I'll kill her with my bare hands!" Jon ground out as if he hadn't even heard her. His fists bunched.

"Would you stop it? I said she didn't harm me. She and her family spoiled me the entire weekend. The only harm they did was to my waistline."

"She's manipulating you. It's what they do." Jon started pacing next to her.

"Stop it!" Faith said more forcefully. "It's this kind of fear-mongering and hateful tirades that got Tala hurt. This is the consequence of what you and Dad are doing." She pointed at the droplets of blood dotting the hardwood floor. With trembling fingers, she pulled a tissue from her pocket, bent down, and wiped at the spots as if that would fix what had happened.

Jon stopped pacing and studied her as if she were a stranger. Slowly, he shook his head. "You're worried about her."

Of course I'm worried, she wanted to shout, but then snapped her mouth shut and straightened. He hadn't gone through the process of getting to know Tala and her family, hadn't caught rare glimpses of the mischievous fox beneath the tough wolf. He didn't understand.

"In fact," Jon leaned closer, as if scrutinizing her under a microscope, "I'm starting to think you're faking your feelings for her a little too convincingly."

Heat swept up her chest and into her cheeks, and she knew she was blushing. She turned away under the pretense of tossing the blood-dotted tissue into the trash can. *Great.* Now Jon would jump to all the wrong conclusions.

But maybe they weren't completely wrong. She hadn't felt *nothing* when she'd kissed Tala. Despite the camera flashes going off all around them, she had lost track of why they were kissing and had been swept up in the sensation of Tala's lips on hers.

Faith shook off the thought. One crisis at a time. First, she had to deal with Jon. She turned back toward him. "You're seeing things that aren't there. Not just between Tala and me, but with the Wrasa in general. They're not monsters. Most of them are good people."

"I'm not going to stand here and let you pretend they're human."

"I never said they were." Faith struggled to stay calm. "But that doesn't mean they're evil."

He still looked at her as if she were the one who didn't understand. "Your ignorance will get you killed—and Chloe too. I'm not going to let that happen to my daughter."

"*Your* daughter?" Faith repeated with an incredulous laugh. "I seem to remember giving birth to her. She's *our* daughter, not just yours."

"Then act like it!" Jon thumped his fist against the side of his thigh. "Right now, I seem to be the only one taking responsibility for her safety!"

"She is safe with Tala!" Faith paused.

Her words seemed to echo through the house.

Wow. She'd never thought that she would ever say that—and mean it with absolute conviction. All this time, she had been so determined to keep Chloe out of their scheme, to never let her daughter meet Tala or any other Wrasa, but now she realized how ridiculous her fears had been.

Jon stared at her. "What happened to you?" he whispered, his voice rough, and this time, he clearly wasn't talking about the welt on her cheek.

Faith lifted her chin. "I started to think for myself instead of letting you or Dad shape my view of the Wrasa."

"Fine." His tone said something different, though. "Believe whatever you want. You're an adult. But Chloe isn't. If you won't see reason, I'll get her out of here."

He took one step toward the stairs, but Faith quickly grabbed his arm and held on. "No! You leaving is a good idea, but Chloe stays here. There were four paparazzi out there not even ten minutes ago. They might still be around. Camille definitely is, ready to film you the moment you set foot outside the house. Chloe's picture will be plastered all over social media and the tabloids if you take her with you."

"I'm not leaving as long as that monster is in the house!" He stabbed his finger in the direction of the upstairs bathroom.

"Stop calling her a monster—and stop pretending you're protecting me! I spent the entire weekend with her and several dozen members of her family, and I even—" Just in time, Faith caught herself before she could add, *Shared her bed.* That wouldn't help calm Jon down. "I even went into the forest at night with them. You were fine with me staying with them when it served your and HASS's purposes. And now you want to play protector?"

"I—"

"No, Jon. I'm done letting you and Dad make the decisions. This is my house, and you're leaving—right after you give back the key to it." She held out her hand.

Jon trembled with agitation. "You're making a big mistake, Faith."

Faith was done discussing this. She waved the fingers of the hand she held out. "Give me the key, Jon."

"Your father will think so too," he added, his tone threatening.

Faith closed her eyes for a second. She knew he was right. "Let me worry about that."

Finally, Jon's shoulders slumped. "You'd better protect her, Faith. If something happens to Chloe, I'll never forgive you." His voice cracked with raw emotions.

Faith lightly touched his shoulder, for a moment getting a glimpse of the deep-seated fear beneath his anger. "I promise she's safe."

His gaze seared into hers before he nodded stiffly and pulled out his keys. The jangle as he fumbled with the key ring echoed in the entryway. Finally, he slipped the silver key off the ring and clenched his fist around it before reluctantly handing it over.

"Thanks," Faith said quietly as she pocketed it.

Instead of heading to the door, he tried to walk around her to the stairs.

"Hey!" Faith grabbed his arm. "Where do you think you're going? Didn't we just agree you were leaving?"

"Not without saying goodbye to Chloe," Jon said.

Faith shook her head. "You can call her later. If I let you go upstairs, you'll pick another fight with Tala."

"I won't," he answered. "Not with Chloe around."

She searched his eyes and finally gave in, hoping she still knew him well enough to trust his word. "All right."

Together, they headed up the stairs.

CHAPTER 3

Tala stared into the mirror above the sink and tried to make out how deep the gash on her temple was, but her reflection blurred before her eyes.

The pounding pain told her it wasn't something that could be healed with one of the *Hello Kitty* Band-Aids from Faith's first aid kit or a healing kiss from the woman who usually kissed Chloe's boo-boos better.

The thought immediately brought back the sensation of Faith's lips against her own. She still couldn't believe how easily Faith had unraveled her with a single kiss.

The fine hairs along her forearms tingled—partly due to a lingering effect of Faith's touch and partly a warning as she struggled to keep her fox leashed.

Scents and sounds hailed down on her overly acute senses, and reliving the kiss only added to the sensory overload.

"Stop thinking about it!" She snarled at her reflection and resolutely stuffed the first aid kit back where she had found it. "You're supposed to be pretending, remember?"

The words sounded slurred, as if her mouth was already stretching into a snout.

She paced the bathroom like a caged animal and strained to make out what was going on downstairs. Voices drifted through the door, and she could make out Faith's but couldn't understand the words.

Being forced to leave her with Jon was a worse kind of agony than the head wound. Every fiber of her being rebelled against staying in the bathroom. She wanted to rush back downstairs so she could protect Faith.

A burning ache spread through her joints and bones.

Groaning, she kicked off her shoes, which suddenly felt too tight.

Her fox clawed to the surface, and holding her back sapped all of Tala's energy.

It was tempting…so tempting to let go of her rigid control.

And maybe she should. A quick shift into her animal form and back would take care of the wound. Then she could rush downstairs to avoid leaving Faith alone with her asshole ex-husband for too long.

Plus if she healed the gash by shifting, Faith wouldn't have to take care of it. She would not need to step close to her in the tiny bathroom, gently touch her face, and—

Tala cut off the thought with a growl.

Avoiding temptation by not letting Faith play nurse was definitely a good idea.

With trembling fingers, she unzipped her jeans.

Faith took up position in front of the closed bathroom door, feeling like a bodyguard as she waited for Jon to come out of Chloe's room.

She tilted her head toward the bathroom, trying to make out any sounds from within.

Was that a moan?

A shiver of concern raced through her. "Tala?" she called. "You okay?"

No answer came.

Before she could check on Tala, the door to Chloe's room opened, and Jon stepped out. "Promise me you won't let your guard down with the shifter for even a second," he said. "Call me if she makes you even the slightest bit uncomfortable."

Faith didn't move an inch. "The only one making me uncomfortable right now is you, Jon."

"I'm just trying to keep you safe. I hope it won't be too late by the time you realize that." He studied her for a few more seconds, then shook his head and clomped down the stairs.

The moment the front door closed behind him, Faith sprang into action.

"I'll be right with you, Chloe," she called toward her daughter's bedroom.

A quick knock and she wrenched open the bathroom door.

Clothes were strewn all over the floor. There was no first aid kit anywhere—and no Tala. At least not in her humanoid form.

A fox stood next to the tub.

Before Faith could recover and close the door, it dashed past her and escaped the bathroom.

Faith lunged and tried to grab the fox by its ruff, but it let out a playful yip and agilely jumped out of reach. It…she turned toward the stairs, pricked her ears in that direction, and sniffed the air, as if making sure Jon was gone.

When Faith tried to take advantage of her distraction by sneaking up on her, the fox danced out of reach again.

Tala whirled around, cocked her head at Faith, and regarded her with a foxy grin.

"This is not a game, Tala." Faith put both hands onto her hips and gave Tala the kind of look that had worked on Chloe even when she'd been going through her toddler tantrum phase.

Apparently, it didn't impress foxes. Tala let out an excited bark, stretched out her slim forelegs in front of her, and lowered her body, with her rump still raised high and her bushy, white-tipped tail wagging.

It was clearly an invitation to play.

Faith didn't have time for that. She stepped forward to capture Tala, but the fox dashed to the side again.

"Tala!" Faith stomped her foot.

The door to Chloe's room creaked open a few inches, and Chloe peeked through the gap.

"No! Chloe, go back into your room and close the door!"

But it was too late. Chloe had already seen the fox.

Her face lit up, and she threw the door open. "A corgi!" She shot out of her room, launched herself at Faith, and threw her arms around her. "Thank you, thank you, thank you, Mommy! I've always wanted one!"

Faith stood frozen and hugged her daughter close. "Um, no, sweetie. She's not a corgi." A giggle escaped her. She could easily imagine the indignant look on Tala's face if she'd heard that. Her fox form was longer and taller than a corgi, but admittedly, not by that much. "This is Tala. Do you remember her from the parade?"

Chloe let out a squeal that made Faith wince and the fox twitch her ears. "Tala!"

"Shh, sweetie. Not so loud or you'll scare her."

"Tala," Chloe repeated in an awed whisper. Her eyes widened as she stared at Faith's cheek, then the bandage on her hand. "You're hurt!"

"Just a few scratches. I didn't watch where I was going and ran into a tree." Faith mimed bouncing off a tree trunk to make her daughter giggle and wipe that concerned expression off Chloe's face.

It worked.

"I'll kiss it better," Chloe announced and planted kisses on her palm and then next to the welt on Faith's cheek.

"Thanks, sweetie." Faith caressed her daughter's messy curls. "It's all better now."

"Good." Chloe slid from Faith's arms and walked toward the fox, her hand outstretched.

Faith's heart beat faster. She hurried after her and pulled her back. "You can't just walk up to her like that, Chloe. She's not a pet. We don't know if she wants to be touched." Despite what she'd said about Tala not hurting her or Chloe, could she be sure the same was still true when she was in her animal form? Tala had told her the Wrasa didn't think like humans once they shifted. Would Tala understand that Chloe was only a child and not out to hurt her?

Chloe's face fell. "But, Mom, she knows me! She won't be scared." She bent forward to be closer to the fox. "Hi, Tala. It's me—Chloe! We met at the parade, and you jumped really high and rescued my balloon when it flew away! Do you remember?"

According to Tala, the Wrasa didn't understand human language while in their animal form, but the fox swiveled her ears in Chloe's direction and cocked her head as if listening attentively. Carefully, she stretched her neck and stuck out her pointed snout.

"Oh, she's trying to sniff you. Hold still, Chloe."

Both of them held their breath.

The fox's long, catlike whiskers fanned forward as she sniffed Chloe's leg. Whatever Chloe smelled of seemed to meet her approval. Tala made a low warbling sound and rolled onto her back like a puppy begging for pets.

"Aww!" Chloe knelt next to the fox and glanced up at Faith. "See? She remembers me!"

"Apparently, she does." Faith exhaled sharply. She knelt too so she could supervise as Chloe petted the fox.

Gently, Chloe touched the white bib extending down the fox's chest, then ran her fingers over Tala's exposed belly. "Ooh! Her fur is so soft! Like Mr. Snugglefluff!"

Faith bit back a chuckle at the comparison with Chloe's stuffed bunny.

"Feel it, Mom!"

"Um, I…"

When Faith hesitated, Chloe took her hand and guided it to Tala's fur.

Barely breathing, Faith touched the russet pelt along Tala's flank. When the fox just looked at her with those expressive golden eyes, she slid her fingers along the white fur on her belly.

Ooh. Chloe was right. She was incredibly soft!

The fox's lips curved back, revealing sharp teeth, but before Faith could pull back her fingers, happy chitters drifted up from Tala's chest. It sounded almost as if she were laughing!

Chloe giggled along with her.

Their sounds were so joyful that laughter burst from Faith too.

Tala squeezed her eyes shut like a contented cat and let Faith stroke a spot beneath her white chin.

Chloe looked up at Faith, her gaze full of wonder. "She's beautiful, isn't she?"

A lump lodged in Faith's throat. "Yes, she is." Even though Tala's animal form was beautiful too, Faith wasn't talking about the fox. But Chloe didn't need to know that. Faith stared down at Tala and struggled to reconcile the cute fox with the woman she had kissed.

God. This would take some getting used to.

Not that she expected to ever kiss Tala again.

Chloe petted behind one of the black ears, then froze. "Mom, she's hurt!" She pointed at the blood-matted fur at the side of Tala's head.

Faith used her fingers to gently part the fur around the wound.

The fox lay still and let her do it, regarding her with trusting eyes.

Faith had been sure the gash would require stitches, but now she could see it had closed and was no longer bleeding. While it wasn't completely gone, it had the appearance of a much older, almost healed wound.

"No, look, she's fine."

"But there's blood!"

"She was hurt, but now she's fine," Faith said. "That's why she shifted into her animal form, sweetie. The Wrasa can heal small injuries when they shift shape." So far, she had always avoided discussing the Wrasa with Chloe, but now she could see how ignorant that had been. The Wrasa were part of the world Chloe lived in, and Faith would make sure she had accurate information.

Chloe's eyes went round. "Like Max!"

"Um, Max?"

Chloe gave her a "duh" look. "Max, the unicorn from *The Magical Forest*. He can heal people with a touch of his horn."

"Oh, that Max." Faith chuckled. "Yeah, kind of. But the Wrasa aren't invincible like Max. They can get injured, and if they do, they hurt just like us."

"I'll be very gentle with her, Mom," Chloe said, a solemn expression on her face.

"Good. I'm sure Tala appreciates that." Faith rubbed behind Tala's ear. The sensation was soothing, and she could almost feel her adrenaline level dropping.

Something seemed to ripple beneath her fingertips.

Faith glanced down and froze mid-stroke. The russet fur was receding!

It took her a moment to fully comprehend what was happening, her brain struggling to catch up with what she was seeing.

Tala was shifting back!

"Chloe, can you get me my robe from the bathroom?" Faith said quickly. "Tala is ready to shift back into her human form."

"But I want to see!"

"No." Faith made her voice firm. She stood from her crouched position to give Tala some space and block Chloe's view of Tala's body with her own. "It's like bath time, Chloe. No one is allowed to see your body without your permission. Tala deserves her privacy."

"Okay," Chloe grumbled. Unenthusiastically, she trudged to the bathroom and came back just as the fox's limbs had turned into arms and legs.

Faith took the robe from her and covered Tala's body with it, trying hard not to sneak a glance at all the bare skin on display.

"Mom, you're looking!" Chloe said. "You said we're not allowed to look!"

Faith's cheeks burned. Had she just been caught checking Tala out by her six-year-old? "I'm not! I only peeked to see where I need to put the robe."

"Look all you want," Tala drawled as she sat up, slipped her arms into the sleeves of the robe, and tied the belt. She rose from the floor and sent Faith a confident smirk. "I don't mind."

The burning in Faith's cheeks intensified. Quickly, she redirected her gaze to the floor.

Chloe hopped up and down, clearly oblivious to Tala's innuendo. "Yay! Next time, I get to watch her shift!"

When Faith looked up, she noticed how tightly Tala's hands gripped the belt of the robe. Tala wasn't as casual about the entire incident as she pretended. Her flirty bravado masked a hidden layer of emotion.

Of course! Faith nearly slapped her own forehead. Tala probably felt very vulnerable—not because she'd been naked in front of them but because they had seen her in her fox form when she was still more comfortable being seen as a wolf.

Maybe she even remembered rolling over and showing her belly for scratches like a pet. By now, Faith knew Tala well enough to understand how embarrassing that might be for her, so she decided not to say anything.

She would just let her pretend it was no big deal at all—even though they both knew otherwise.

Tala fought against the urge to pull the fluffy, light-pink robe up to her nose and sniff it. The terry cloth smelled like Faith's milk-and-honey scent, and it wrapped around her like a soothing embrace. To distract herself, she reached up and touched her temple to check on the wound.

Good. The gash was all but gone.

"That's so cool," Chloe whispered. "Look, Mom! It's all healed. Why can't humans do that? I had to go to the hospital when I fell off my bike and hurt my knee! That's not fair!"

Her indignant face made Tala laugh, which felt good after running on adrenaline and mutaline for what felt like hours.

"Humans have other skills that we Wrasa don't have," Tala said when Chloe kept looking at her, clearly expecting an answer.

"Like what?" the girl asked.

Tala feverishly tried to think of something. "Like…uh…"

"Modesty, apparently." Faith poked her in the shoulder.

Her playful attack didn't trigger any of Tala's defenses. How strange. The touch was casual, like that of a pack member who'd known her for years, yet it sent a spark though Tala. *Damn.* Her guard was slipping, and it wasn't just because she was hungry and exhausted.

Chloe burst out laughing, even though Tala wasn't sure she had fully grasped the banter.

"Well, if you think it's so easy, then *you* name something humans are better at." Tala flashed her a challenging grin.

"Lots of things," Faith said, her chin proudly lifted. "Like…um…"

"Yeah?" Tala drawled.

An answering challenge flashed in Faith's brown eyes.

For a second or two, Tala thought Faith might say, "Kissing." And, honestly, she wouldn't have objected, because damn, Faith could kiss!

"Like…making a salad," Faith finally said.

Tala lifted her eyebrows. "Making a salad? That's your answer?"

Faith nodded sagely. "Your family obviously thinks potatoes with two pounds of bacon and about five thousand calories' worth of mayo make a light salad."

"Sounds about right." At the mention of food, Tala's stomach let out a noisy rumble. She pointed at her middle. "And that sounds like I'd better get myself home to feed the beast." Not before she had thoroughly combed the neighborhood to make sure Jon, the Wrasa-hating neighbor, and the paparazzi were gone, of course.

Chloe giggled.

Tala walked toward the bathroom to get dressed. Truth be told, the thought of returning to her much-too-quiet apartment didn't hold much appeal after spending the last three days with her pack.

The pack. Yeah. That's who you'll miss. Right.

"Um, Tala?" Faith called.

One step from the bathroom door, Tala turned. "Thought of something else humans are better at?"

"Actually…yes. Ordering pizza. Care to give Chloe and me a chance to prove it?"

Tala searched her face. She hadn't suggested she go home only so she could raid the fridge; she had wanted to respect Faith's wish to keep Chloe out of their scheme, which likely meant Faith would want to limit the time Tala spent around her daughter. "Are you inviting me to dinner?"

"Yes!" Chloe shouted before Faith could answer.

But Tala continued to look at Faith, waiting for her reply. The decision whether to invite her in had been taken from Faith earlier, but now Tala wanted her to have a choice.

"Yes, I am." Faith sounded sure of herself. "In fact, I think you should stay the night."

Heat flickered through Tala. *Stop it. Her pup is right there! She didn't mean it like that…or did she?*

Faith's cheeks flamed a charming red. "Um, I mean, the paparazzi might still be around, and we don't want them to spread rumors if they realize you're not sleeping over. Plus you might have a concussion and shouldn't be alone."

Right. That made sense. Well, not the concussion part because even if she'd had one, it would have been healed or at least on its way to healing after she'd shifted. But they definitely didn't want the tabloids to print a "trouble in paradise" story.

"You're right." She gave Faith a nod. "Staying the night is the reasonable choice."

"We're having a sleepover? Yay!" Chloe started an excited victory dance. "Can we have a giant blanket fort in the living room and all sleep there?"

Faith firmly shook her head. "You wouldn't sleep a wink if we did that, and you've got school tomorrow morning. No blanket fort. Everyone is sleeping in their own bed, and Tala will sleep on the couch."

On the couch. Was that a message for her? Of course, Tala hadn't expected an invitation to share Faith's bed.

"Sorry," Faith said with an apologetic shrug. "I don't have a guest room, but I swear the couch is super comfy."

No guest room? Faith's home was beautiful and cozy, but it wasn't as large or luxurious as Tala might have expected for Peter MacAllister's only daughter. Apparently, she had bought the house with her own money instead of relying on her dad's.

Tala's respect for her grew.

"But Tala can sleep with me, Mom!" Chloe piped up.

"No, Chloe. Your bed isn't big enough for an adult."

"She can shift and curl up into a ball and sleep at the foot of the bed, like Mr. Whiskers when I'm staying over at Grandpa's," Chloe replied.

Um… The kid hadn't just seriously compared her to a kitten, had she? Tala straightened and squared her shoulders to show how much bigger she was.

"No, Chloe, that's not a good idea," Faith said.

"But why?"

Faith sent Tala a look that pleaded for help.

"Because shedding season has started," Tala said. "I'm losing my winter coat and would leave chunks of fur all over your bed."

A grin dashed across Faith's face, and she gave Tala a hidden appreciative nod.

"I don't mind," Chloe declared. "I could brush you."

"Uh, thanks, but the couch is fine." Tala turned back toward Faith and gestured discreetly at the dried blood on her face. "Do you mind if I take a quick shower while you prove your pizza-ordering skills?"

"No, of course, go ahead," Faith replied. "There are fresh towels on the shelf next to the shower."

"Thanks." Tala escaped into the bathroom, glad to have a few minutes to herself to collect her thoughts and rein in her emotions.

She turned on the shower and let Faith's robe slide off her shoulders. A contented rumble vibrated through her chest as she stepped beneath the gentle spray and let the warm water wash away the blood and the tension of the day.

Beneath the coppery tang of blood were two much more pleasant aromas. Faith's scent and that of her pup were all over her.

Tala dimly remembered them scratching her behind the ears and chin and running their fingers through the fur along her belly—and she had rolled onto her back, lain still, and let them do it as if she were an obedient family pet!

So much for being a tough, scary alpha!

It was embarrassing. Or at least it should have been. Instead, the emotions the hazy memory evoked were more complex.

Letting Faith and her pup touch her like that felt strangely right, as if that was the way things were supposed to be. She found herself reluctant to scrub their scents off her skin.

The bathroom door creaked open. A wave of cool air hit Tala's wet skin, making her shiver and tense.

The familiar milk-and-honey scent tickled her nose, and she instantly relaxed.

Her senses prickled, and she was acutely aware that just a thin, white shower curtain separated them. For a moment, her imagination ran wild, showing her flashes of Faith pulling back the curtain, running her heated gaze over Tala's naked body, then tearing off her own clothes to step beneath the spray with her. She could almost feel Faith's wet skin pressing against hers as steam swirled around them.

"Tala?" Faith's voice was soft, barely audible over the sound of the water, but it was enough to wrench Tala from her fantasy.

Great Hunter! She had to get a grip! She was a Saru, not a teenaged pup ruled by hormones. Where had her rigid self-control gone?

"Yes?" Tala replied, trying to sound normal.

"I brought you some fresh clothes," Faith said. "Yours had bloodstains all over, so I threw them in the wash. They'll be all clean for you in the morning."

"You really don't have to do that," Tala called over the patter of the water. She didn't want to admit how good it felt to have Faith take care of her that way.

"It's the least I can do after my neighbor attacked you." Faith sighed, and the bitter notes of guilt and regret mingled with her fresh scent. "I'll leave the clothes on the counter. Hope they fit okay."

"I'm sure they'll be fine," Tala said, although wearing something that carried Faith's scent probably wouldn't help her rein in her damn libido.

Faith lingered for a moment, as if she wanted to say something else. Then she cleared her throat. "All right. I'll let you finish up. The pizza should be here soon."

The door clicked shut behind her, yet her scent still lingered in the steamy air.

Tala closed her eyes, lifted her face into the spray, and turned the water to cold, hoping the chill would help clear her head.

Faith bustled around the kitchen, getting plates and glasses out of the cabinet so they could eat as soon as the pizza arrived. She tried not to let her mind wander to Tala taking a shower, to the way the warm, soapy water ran down her flat belly and athletic legs…

The creak of the stairs announced Tala coming downstairs.

Faith snapped the cabinet shut, as if that would help keep a lid on her wayward thoughts. Tala was no longer her enemy; she was an ally and quickly becoming a friend she trusted, but getting involved with her for real would mean entering uncharted, dangerous territory. It could blow up her entire life in ways she wasn't ready for.

A few seconds later, Tala stepped inside the kitchen as if sensing that was where Faith would be.

Faith turned around to face her.

Because of the aura of confidence and authority surrounding Tala, she always appeared larger than life, and Faith kept forgetting that Tala was actually three inches shorter and thinner than she was.

The sight of Tala wearing her clothes felt intimate…and unexpectedly sexy. The sweatpants Faith had given her hung low on Tala's slim hips. She had rolled up the legs, adjusting for her shorter stature. The T-shirt—which said *Chaos Coordinator* across the chest in a quirky font—draped loosely over her lithe body. It slipped off one shoulder, revealing a tantalizing glimpse of smooth skin. Her short, auburn hair, still damp from her shower, clung to her skull in tousled waves, emphasizing her high cheekbones and her piercing golden eyes.

Faith's mouth went dry. She swallowed hard, and the sound was much too loud in the silence of the kitchen. "Feeling more human now?" Faith asked to sound casual.

Tala chuckled and crossed the kitchen toward her. She moved with the confidence of a supermodel wearing custom-tailored clothes. "I feel more like myself. But even the most amazing shower in the world won't make me human."

A blush stung Faith's cheeks. "I didn't mean…" God, why was she suddenly as clumsy and awkward as a teenager? "It's just a figure of speech. I'm fully aware you're not human."

Tala was so close now that Faith could feel the heat emanating from Tala's body. "Is that a bad thing?" Her voice was low and intimate.

Faith's heart raced with Tala's closeness. For a moment, she didn't know what to say, caught off guard by the question and the intensity of Tala's gaze. "No," she whispered hoarsely. "I—"

The doorbell rang.

Saved by the bell. Faith blew out a breath as the charged atmosphere between them dissipated.

"Pizza!" Chloe ran over from the living room, where she'd been coloring the picture of a fox.

A few minutes later, they sat at the table in the dining area, with three large pizzas.

Chloe was chattering away as if she had known Tala for years, telling her about her favorite books, her friends, and her recent visit to the zoo and peppering her with a thousand curious questions.

"Chloe, slow down," Faith said for the third time. "Your pizza is getting cold."

Her daughter took a big bite of her slice. A bit of tomato sauce dribbled down her chin. "What's your favorite pizza, Tala?" she asked around a mouthful of pepperoni pizza.

"Don't know if I have a favorite." Tala popped a piece of pepperoni into her mouth. "I've never met a pizza I didn't like."

Faith laughed. "You've never met *any* food you didn't like."

"Not true. I can't stand Brussels sprouts."

"Me neither!" Chloe bounced in her seat as if excited to find something they had in common. She finished her slice and then fully focused on Tala. "Where does your tail go when you turn into a human?"

"Um, sweetie…"

Tala reached over and lightly touched the side of Faith's thigh, sending a rush of heat up Faith's leg. "It's okay." She widened her eyes and craned her neck as if trying to get a glimpse of her own butt. "Oh no! You mean it's gone?"

A belly laugh erupted from Chloe. She turned toward Faith and said, "She's joking," as if Faith didn't already know.

Faith decided to just sit back and watch them interact. It was interesting to see Tala's goofy side come out, yet what amazed her even more was Chloe.

Her daughter had never had a shy bone in her body, but this was remarkable even for her. Faith especially marveled at how easy it seemed to be for Chloe to switch from treating Tala like a favorite pet to an adult she clearly admired—as if she didn't struggle at all to accept both of Tala's forms equally.

Maybe kids like Chloe really were the future. Faith hoped so.

"Rhino Hero card!" Chloe shouted and pointed at the symbol on the roof card she had just placed on top of the two-foot card tower. "You have to place Rhino Hero on the dot!"

Human pups were loud! After several rounds of this card game, Tala was starting to get used to Chloe's volume. Or maybe she was losing her hearing in the ear closest to the girl.

"That's tricky," Faith murmured, studying the tower.

"Nah." Tala reached into the card structure, deftly pulled the rhino figurine from the lower story, and put it on top of the tower before building her own walls and adding a roof card with a flourish. "Not if you have nimble fingers."

When she turned to flash Faith a triumphant grin, she found Faith's gaze fixed intently on her fingers.

The lighthearted banter they had kept up throughout the game was gone—replaced by something that sent a rush of heat through Tala's body.

Her hand tingled, and she fought the urge to reach out and cup one of Faith's flushed cheeks.

"Mom!" Chloe's impatient voice cut through her daze. The girl sounded as if she had repeatedly tried to get her mother's attention. "It's your turn!"

Faith blinked. Her gaze snapped back to the card tower. A shy smile tugged on her lips as she peeked at Tala out of the corner of her eye, then quickly away.

Tala's heart was still racing as she watched Faith carefully place her wall cards. A light tremor ran through her fingers as she put a roof card on top.

The flimsy card tower wobbled, then collapsed.

"Yes!" Chloe shouted. "You lose!" She turned toward Tala. "How many roof cards do you have left?"

Tala held up her last remaining card.

"Me too! Yay, winners!" Chloe held up her hand for a high-five, and Tala gently tapped it.

"All right," Faith said. "Now that you two have completely humiliated me…again, I think it's time for bed."

Chloe's face scrunched up into a frown. "But I want to stay up with Tala!"

"No, Chloe. It's past your bedtime. You'll see Tala tomorrow morning," Faith said, but Chloe still pouted.

When her mother didn't relent, she looked up at Tala with a hopeful expression. "Can you come read me a bedtime story? I have one with a fox, just like you!"

Tala stiffened. Lately, she hadn't minded as much when someone referred to her as a Rtar. People could assume whatever they wanted. But Chloe and her mother weren't *people*. She needed them to understand who she was.

Great Hunter, what was happening to her? Chloe was a six-year-old mini human. Tala shouldn't care what she thought.

"Um, sweetie. Tala is a Syak," Faith said before Tala could decide whether she should let it go. "A wolf-shifter."

"Nuh-uh. I saw her, Mom. Don't you know what a fox looks like?"

"What people are goes beyond what they look like, Chloe," Faith said. "Tala is adopted, like your friend Isabella. You remember what that means, right?"

"That her mommy didn't grow her in her belly, but she loves her just as much!"

"Exactly," Faith said. "It means Tala is now part of a new family, who shaped her as much as her mother and father did."

A tiny wrinkle formed on Chloe's forehead as she seemed to think about it. Then she nodded eagerly, as if that made total sense to her. "And they're wolves?" She glanced from Faith to Tala.

"Yes," they said in unison.

"Scary ones?"

Tala waited for Faith to answer that one. No doubt the memory of the entire pack charging toward her in the dark forest was still giving Faith nightmares, so Tala wasn't sure what she would say.

"Well," Faith said, "she's got a grumpy uncle and a very strict grandmother, and one of her brothers can be a bit of a brat…"

Chloe giggled.

"But they also bought breakfast ingredients just for me, patched up my hand when I fell, and included me in a very special family celebration," Faith continued.

Tala released a long breath. It filled her with unfamiliar warmth that Faith remembered the pleasant moments from this weekend, not only the scary ones.

The corners of Faith's mouth tugged up into a grin. "Oh, and one of them brought me a mouse."

"Aww, mice are so cute!" Chloe squealed, obviously assuming it had been alive.

Tala kept a neutral expression. "What can I say? It's a gesture of hospitality among my kind."

"So they're nice?" Chloe asked.

Faith nodded. "They're nice."

Tala couldn't keep up her impassive mask. She stared at Faith. She knew Faith had made huge strides in overcoming her deep-seated mistrust of the Wrasa, but this? Telling her daughter that Tala's pack members were decent people—that they could be trusted—was monumental!

"Good," Chloe said in a "so that's decided, then" tone. "Can we go visit them next weekend?"

Tala and Faith stared at each other, exchanging a "shit, how do we get out of this?" look.

If Tala introduced Chloe to the pack, things would get complicated. As her mother had said, most of the family would immediately adopt the human pup. Everyone would start to form relationships, which would end abruptly when their scheme concluded and they officially split up.

For the first time, Tala began to understand why Faith hadn't wanted to involve her daughter in any of this.

"It's not that easy, Chloe," Faith finally said. "Syak are really private. We can't just invite ourselves."

Chloe's face fell. "But I want to meet them," she mumbled with her bottom lip jutting out.

"I know, sweetie." Faith lovingly swiped back a strand of hair that had fallen onto Chloe's face. "I promise we'll do something fun next weekend, okay?"

"Okay," Chloe said unenthusiastically. "Can Tala come read me a bedtime story? Please, Mommy!"

Faith held up her hands. "You'll have to ask Tala."

The girl turned toward Tala and looked up at her with big puppy dog eyes. They were the same color as Faith's, so Tala instantly had a hard time saying no to her. "Please?"

Tala had never been tasked with reading a bedtime story to her nephews, her niece, or any of her younger cousins because her job often kept her away from the pack. But she was a decorated Saru and had figured out the most complex of missions, so how hard could it be? "All right. Lead the way."

Eagerly, Chloe grabbed her hand and led her up the stairs, her fingers small and cool against Tala's.

Faith followed them and made sure Chloe brushed her teeth.

Once they had entered the girl's bedroom, Chloe went to her bookshelf and pulled out several books until she found the one she wanted. She carried it over to Tala and handed it to her.

Tala had expected a story about a fox, as Chloe had requested, but instead, the cover showed a cartoonish illustration of a wolf pup, its amber eyes big behind its glasses. Bold, yellow letters stretched across the top, spelling out the title *The Wolf Who Loved to Read*.

Chloe tapped the cover. "This is Winston. He's a wolf, like you, and he loves to read."

Maybe Tala had inhaled some of the fur she must have shed while shifting. It was the only logical explanation for that huge lump that lodged in her throat. "Winston?" she croaked.

Faith laughed. Her eyes twinkled in the low light of the lamp on the bedside table. "Not macho enough for a wolf?"

"Depends," Tala said. "Is he an alpha?"

Chloe's brow furrowed. "What's an alpha?"

Tala searched for the simplest way to explain it in a way a human pup would understand. "He or she is the leader of a wolf pack. The one who makes sure everyone is okay, safe, and well-fed."

"Like Mom?" Chloe asked.

Tala hadn't expected that reply, but it made her look at Faith with a smile, which broadened when she saw Faith's stunned expression.

"No," Faith said, "more like Ta—"

"Yes," Tala replied, thinking of the way Faith had stood up to her grandmother, her uncle, and the rest of the pack. "Kinda like your mom."

Chloe scratched her nose. "I don't know if Winston is like that."

"Well, then let's find out." Tala carried the book over to the bed.

CHAPTER 4

Faith glanced back to make sure Chloe was asleep before quietly closing the door behind them.

When she turned, Tala hovered silently next to her.

Putting Chloe to bed together had felt as intimate to Faith as sharing a bed. Had it felt that way to Tala too?

The floorboards creaked as Faith shifted her weight. "Thank you for being so patient with Chloe."

"My pleasure. She's a great kid." Tala's golden eyes glowed with intensity. "And you're an amazing mother."

Faith sighed. "Sometimes, I'm not so sure." Some days, she felt as if she was barely keeping it together, juggling work, chores, and trying to give Chloe everything she needed.

Tala's gaze never left Faith's. "I am. Chloe is clearly happy, well-adjusted, and compassionate. That doesn't happen by accident. It's because she has a good alpha."

They smiled at each other.

The warm glow in Tala's golden eyes and the sincerity in her voice soothed the raw edges of Faith's insecurity. "Thank you," she whispered.

Tala reached over, took Faith's hand, and gave it a soft squeeze. "You're very welcome."

Instead of letting go, their fingers tangled together. They stood in the hallway, staring at each other.

Faith was suddenly very aware that they were alone for the first time since the fake kiss that hadn't felt fake at all. Well, other than that moment they'd shared in the kitchen. But Tala hadn't touched her then. The gentle pressure of Tala's hand on her own, her heat seeping into her skin, made Faith's heart beat faster. Could Tala hear it? Was she feeling this too?

Finally, Tala dropped her gaze to their joined hands. She shifted her weight, and a floorboard creaked.

It startled them both out of the intimate bubble they'd been wrapped in. They let go at the same time.

"Um, let me get you some sheets for the couch." Faith took a step back and tried to steady herself as she walked to the linen closet. The sensation of Tala's fingers touching hers lingered, but she did her best to ignore it. She grabbed a set of sheets, a blanket, and a pillow and led the way downstairs, with Tala following closely behind.

They worked together in silence. Faith spread the sheet over the couch, and Tala bent down to tuck in the edges. When Tala ran her palm over the sheet to smooth out the wrinkles, her hand trembled slightly.

"Are you okay?" Faith asked.

Tala looked up. "Yes, of course. I shifted twice, so by now, my head is as good as new."

"That's great, but what about…mentally and emotionally?" Faith asked quietly.

"I'm a soldier, remember? We're trained for situations like that. Even though I admit my reaction probably didn't seem like it." Tala grimaced.

"I wasn't just talking about the attack. I meant—" Faith hesitated, trying to muster the courage to talk about what was going on between them but chickened out. "Are you okay with Chloe and me seeing you in your animal form? That probably wasn't as easy for you as you pretended."

"Oh." Tala blinked as if she had expected Faith to say something else. She plopped down on the couch, now covered with a fresh sheet, and directed her gaze to the spot where her fingers drew patterns over the fabric. "It was a bit weird. Yesterday, in the forest and afterward, I didn't have time to think about it, but…"

Had it really been only yesterday that she had followed Tala and her pack into the forest, convinced that they were doing something sinister? So much had happened since then…so much had changed that it felt as if the yasi makamar ritual had occurred weeks ago.

Tala was still painting patterns on the sheets. "You're actually the first human who ever saw me in my…my fox form." She peeked up as if to watch Faith's reaction.

Faith sank next to her onto the couch. "I'm the first?" she got out in a whisper.

Tala nodded.

Warmth spread from Faith's chest to every inch of her body. "Wow. That's… I'm really honored. Thank you for trusting me. I know you didn't have a choice in the forest, but you had one today, and you even let me touch you in your fox form. That means a lot, especially after everything I've—"

Tala gently laid her index finger against Faith's lips. "That's in the past."

Faith's breath caught. She couldn't have said anything, even if Tala hadn't stopped her from speaking, because the gentle touch had turned her vocal cords into wobbly goo, along with her limbs. Dazed, she nodded.

When Tala lifted her finger away, Faith's lips still tingled. She searched for something to say to fill the silence. "It's a bit strange for me too," she blurted out. "Seeing you in your fox form."

Tala's jaw muscles clenched. "Is it strange because I see myself as a Syak, yet I don't shift into a big, impressive wolf but instead turn into this small—?"

Now it was Faith who pressed her finger to Tala's lips. She didn't want Tala to think for even a moment that she was seeing her for anything but what she was: a captivating, powerful, fiercely loyal person whose true self shone through, no matter what form she was in.

Tala's lips were warm and incredibly soft, and Faith had never wanted anything more than to stroke her finger along their full curve just once.

God, what was she doing?

Faith wrenched her hand away. "No," she said quickly. "Not because of that. This weekend and the past month since we met, I let go of a lot of preconceived notions I've had about the Wrasa. Compared to all of the other assumptions I had to overcome, accepting that you're a Syak whose animal form isn't a wolf was easy. If I'm honest, I really like it."

Tala blinked rapidly as if she couldn't believe Faith would view it as something positive. "You do?"

"Yes," Faith said firmly. "For one thing, it was scary enough to have my six-year-old walk up to a fox. Letting her pet a wolf would have given me a full-blown panic attack."

"Then what was so strange about seeing me in my animal form?"

"I know you're a Wrasa and that you can turn into a fox. But knowing it, and watching the woman I…" Faith stopped mid-sentence. Now she had maneuvered herself into a dead end. But maybe it was time to grab the bull by the horns—or was it the fox by the tail?—and talk about the kiss.

Tala's eyes widened.

Crap. Had Tala thought she'd been about to say, *Woman I love?* Of course, that hadn't been what Faith had intended to say. "Woman I kissed," she blurted. "It took me a minute to wrap my head around the fact that the fox I was petting was also the woman I had kissed just minutes earlier."

"Oh," Tala said. "I understand why that takes some getting used to. Um, I mean…" She waved her hand. "You getting used to my dual nature. Not to kissing me." She tried to flash a confident grin, but it turned into an awkward half smile that revealed her insecurity.

They both stared at the little dents in the sheet between them.

"About that…the kiss…" Faith finally said. "I'm sorry I ambushed you like that. I tried to warn you and let you know what I was about to do, but…"

"I got that you were trying to tell me something, but how was I supposed to make the connection?" Tala asked.

"Um, well, on our first date…fake date, I told you humans only wink in romance novels, and there's usually also a lot of kissing going on in those novels, so I thought if I winked at you, you'd connect the dots and realize…" *Great.* She was rambling. Faith snapped her mouth shut.

Tala regarded her with a faint grin playing around her lips. "That you were about to kiss me?"

Faith's cheeks burned. "Um, yeah. Sounds pretty ridiculous, now that I'm saying it out loud." She grabbed the pillow and covered her face with it. "But it made sense to me in the moment."

The sound of Tala's laughter filled the room. "Sorry to say it made no sense to me at all. I had no idea what you were about to do."

"No?" Faith peeked out from behind the pillow, then lowered it to her lap. "Well, you played along beautifully anyway. That kiss was very…" *Hot, sizzling, passionate, alluring…* She mentally flicked through the *Thesaurus of Sexy Words* and dismissed them all. Finally, she settled on, "Convincing."

"Yeah," Tala said, her voice a full register lower than usual. "It certainly was. Very, very convincing." Her gaze dropped to Faith's lips, her golden irises like smoldering flames.

One of them groaned.

Faith thought it might have been her. The sound seemed to echo in the charged space between them. Before she could draw another much-too-fast breath, their mouths were on each other.

It was like striking a match in a room full of fireworks, igniting something wild and urgent within Faith.

The pillow dropped to the floor as Tala cupped Faith's face with one hand, careful to avoid her injured cheek, and drew her closer.

Intoxicatingly close.

The touch might have been meant to ground Faith, but instead, it sent her senses spiraling. The heat of Tala's palms against her skin, the taste of her lips, the soft but insistent press of her body were a heady mix.

Tala closed her mouth over Faith's bottom lip and gave it a gentle tug that made desire ripple through Faith's body.

When Tala slid her tongue inside, Faith eagerly met it with her own. Moaning, she gripped Tala's shoulders and curled her fingers into the shirt Tala had borrowed from her.

The kiss grew more urgent.

Before Faith knew how it had happened, they ended up stretched out on the couch, with Tala half on top of her, their lips never separating for even a second.

Faith lost her sense of time and place, lost every bit of reason as they continued to kiss. She ran her hands up Tala's back, feeling the heat emanating from her through the thin fabric, and then buried her fingers in Tala's hair to keep her mouth exactly where it was.

Tala's weight on her was delicious, and Faith arched up against her with a low moan.

It took her several seconds to realize that the vibrations in her back pocket weren't another effect Tala's kiss had on her body.

Her freaking phone was ringing!

No one called her after Chloe's bedtime unless it was important.

"Wait," Faith gasped against Tala's lips and pulled away, the kiss ending as abruptly as it had begun.

Tala rolled off her. Her breathing was as ragged as Faith's, her cheeks flushed, and her hair tousled in the sexiest way.

"My phone is ringing," Faith hurriedly explained. She didn't want Tala to think she had pulled away because she regretted their kiss.

Do you?

Faith had no time to think about it.

She fumbled until she managed to pull the phone from her pocket.

The word *Dad* flashing across the screen was like a bucket of ice-cold water being dumped on her overheated body. "It's my father. I need to take this."

An impenetrable mask settled over Tala's face, snuffing out the sizzling passion Faith had seen there only seconds ago. "Go ahead," she said in a carefully neutral tone.

Faith swiped a trembling finger across the screen and lifted the phone to her ear. "Hi, Dad." She tried to sound casual, as if she hadn't just been kissed senseless by someone her father considered a sworn enemy, but her voice came out husky and strange.

"What the hell happened?" her father shouted, making her flinch and move the phone away from her ear.

"Uh, I… I don't know." She stared at Tala's reddened lips, then realized her father wasn't talking about the kiss. He didn't know about that, thank God. "What do you mean?"

"Jon said you got hurt!"

Jon. Of course. He had run straight to her father. Faith sighed. She pointed at the phone with her free hand and mouthed, "Be right back."

When Tala nodded stiffly, Faith climbed the stairs and closed the door to her bedroom behind her. "Like I told Jon, I wasn't watching where I was going and ran into a branch. It's just a few scratches; that's all."

"So it has nothing to do with you taking that monster home with you?"

"What? No! Tala didn't hurt me. She was the one who got hurt! My neighbor hit her in the head with a can of soda, and she was bleeding badly."

"So?" Her father sounded baffled, as if he honestly didn't understand why that would matter. "That's no reason to drag her inside, where your innocent, defenseless daughter was!"

Faith bit her lip to avoid telling him that Tala being hurt was plenty of reason or that Tala would never do anything to harm Chloe. She knew he wouldn't listen. It would only lead to a shouting match. "Let's talk about it tomorrow, okay? This isn't a good time. Chloe is asleep in the next room, and, um, Tala is…she's still here."

For a moment, there was only silence.

Shit. She shouldn't have told him that.

"What?" Her father's voice boomed through the phone. "Why would you let her stay, especially with Chloe being home? Don't you get that she's dangerous?"

Faith hadn't wanted to have this discussion now, but she couldn't let him keep saying things like that about Tala. "You're dead wrong about her, Dad. I got to know her really well this weekend, and she's loyal and compassionate;

she has a playful streak that she's trying to hide around most people, and she's got the patience of a saint when it comes to kids."

"What happened in Silver Falls?" he asked, a suspicious tone entering his voice. "I know you didn't tell me everything."

"I will. I promise. Tomorrow." Okay, maybe not *everything*. She would finally have to tell him she was done spying on the Wrasa, but she couldn't reveal she'd kissed Tala—not only to trick the paparazzi but because she'd wanted it…wanted her.

Her father would never understand. If her relationship with Tala ever turned into something real, he wouldn't accept it. He would do what he hadn't when she had come out as bisexual: threaten to cut off contact if she didn't come to her senses, forcing her to choose between him and Tala.

It was an impossible choice because she wasn't choosing only for herself but for Chloe too. Since Jon's parents had died a few years ago, he was the only grandparent Chloe had. She couldn't do that to her daughter.

"Please don't do anything before we have a chance to talk, okay? Don't send Noah or Violet or anyone else. Can you promise me that—and really mean it this time?"

"You expect me to leave you and Chloe alone with a shifter in the house?"

"I expect you to respect my wishes," Faith answered firmly. "The last time you ignored them, you put me into more danger than the Wrasa ever did. Please, Dad. Please promise me you won't send anyone."

He let out a long sigh. "All right. But if this monster harms one hair on your head, I'll hunt her down and—"

"She won't."

For a few seconds, silence stretched between them like a chasm.

"I have to go, Dad," Faith said, her voice hoarse. She had to explain to Tala that a kiss like the one they'd just shared, as breathtaking as it had been, could never happen again.

As Faith's footsteps faded down the upstairs hallway and a door clicked shut behind her, Tala flopped back onto the couch.

What in the Great Hunter's name just happened?

She could still feel Faith's lips on her own, her gentle curves pressed against her body.

Her mind was a mess of conflicting emotions and unanswered questions. The only thing she could tell for sure was that Faith clearly felt attracted to her too. And, if Tala was honest with herself, it was starting to go beyond purely physical attraction. Unless she was completely misjudging the situation, she wasn't the only one feeling that way. Faith felt it too. Tala couldn't—or maybe didn't want to—put a label on it, but she knew it was something deep and powerful that she hadn't felt in a long time, if ever. Even her fox seemed to sense it, treating Faith like her mate.

Tala had no clue what to do with that knowledge, how to navigate the shift in their dynamic. This wasn't supposed to happen, and she still couldn't explain why it had. There was just something about Faith and the way she looked at her—really saw her.

She knew what she wanted to do: kiss Faith again as soon as she walked back through the door.

But this was about so much more than only the two of them and what they wanted.

Faith was a mother; she was Peter MacAllister's daughter, and she was a human who had no idea what the Saru...what Tala had done. She was a woman who could strip Tala of all defenses with a single glance—at a time when she couldn't afford to be vulnerable.

There were a thousand and one reasons why she shouldn't get involved with Faith...and yet they had all disappeared the second their lips had touched.

With a growl, she jumped up from the couch and reached for her phone, which Faith must have pulled from her bloodstained pants and left on the coffee table.

Ruminating about Faith and their kiss wouldn't get her anywhere. She needed to call Jeff Madsen and get him to send a Saru unit to protect Faith and her daughter.

Instead of an assistant, the council speaker himself answered after two rings. "Report," he barked without wasting time on pleasantries.

"I need a Saru unit to patrol Faith's neighborhood tonight," Tala said.

"What happened?" Madsen asked.

What *hadn't* happened? "A bunch of paparazzi lay in wait for us when we returned."

"Not surprising," Madsen said. "I expected something like that after MacAllister's interview."

"Yeah, but what I didn't expect was a woman wearing a *Moms Against Shape-Shifters* T-shirt trying to take me out with a can of Coke."

For a few seconds, only silence stretched between them, as if Madsen needed to process that mental image first. Then he let out a growl. "Did you get hurt?"

"Nothing a quick shift couldn't cure, sir. I'm not worried about myself. But Faith's daughter is in the house, and we need to protect her—both of them—at all costs."

"You would think HASS would take care of that," Madsen mumbled, "since they're always going on and on about protecting humankind."

"I wouldn't be surprised if MacAllister sent his goons. Faith is on the phone with him right now, and I hope she talks him out of it. I'd prefer if they didn't show up at Faith's house, adding to the chaos." Tala hesitated. If she told him she was staying the night, he might jump to all the wrong… or maybe the right…conclusions, and it hadn't been that long since a relationship between a Wrasa and a human had been strictly forbidden.

There is no relationship, she told herself. *It was just one kiss.*

Plus the Saru would notice her car parked outside anyway.

"I don't think MacAllister's people would appreciate me staying the night," she said, then realized how that might sound and quickly added, "To protect Faith and her daughter and to make sure the paparazzi are buying the fake-relationship story."

"Right," Madsen said. "Good thinking. I'll send out a unit and tell them you're on the premises."

Tala quietly released the breath she'd been holding and sank onto the couch. "While I have you on the phone, sir… There's something else we need to talk about. Faith wanted to know why we asked her to play my pretend mate and why we were confident she'd agree to it. Do I have your permission to tell her?"

Madsen hesitated uncharacteristically long. "You realize that would mean we have to tell her about Jorie and the dream seers?"

"Yes, sir."

"Are you sure we can trust her with that sensitive information?" Madsen asked. "She's MacAllister's daughter."

She was so much more than that, but Tala couldn't explain that to the council speaker.

"How do we know she won't tell her father?" Madsen continued. "If she does, he'll happily use it against us, making us sound like a weird cult."

"You know I'm not one to trust easily, but I trust her," Tala said firmly. "She lied to her father to protect us, and she told me the truth about trying to bug my apartment. She has respected every custom and tradition I've introduced her to so far. She'll respect us seeking guidance from dream seers too."

"Hmm." Madsen scratched his cheek. It sounded as if he needed to shave. "That's not my decision to make—it's Jorie's. But let's wait until you've had a chance to check in with Mirella tomorrow. I ordered her to do a bug sweep of your parents' house and the entire property, just to make sure Ms. MacAllister didn't lie about not planting a bug."

Blood roared through Tala's ears. She had thought he would let her talk to Mirella and make up an excuse about why they needed her to do that. "Oh Great Hunter! Please say you didn't tell her why!" She couldn't keep her voice from rising in volume and pitch.

"Calm down, Saru!" Madsen growled.

Tala barely kept herself from growling back. "You don't understand, sir. Mirella is my brother's mate. If she tells him, my entire pack will find out."

"Mirella is also a Saru. I gave her an order, and she'll follow it without questioning my reasons—like any Syak would."

Was that a dig at her? Tala chose to ignore it. "So you didn't tell her Faith and I aren't actually a couple?"

"That's what we agreed on—to keep Operation Make-Believe Mate on a need-to-know basis. Besides, I'm not in the habit of explaining myself to subordinates." Madsen waited a beat before finally adding, "I didn't tell her anything, just told her to get it done."

Tala eased up her tight grip on the phone. Okay, she could work with that. She would tell Mirella she'd caught a whiff of Noah's and Violet's scents at the edge of the property and wanted to make sure they hadn't managed to bug the house while the pack hadn't been home. "All right, sir. I'll check in with her tomorrow."

"Good." Madsen's tone indicated that he was about to dismiss her and end the call.

"Oh, sir?" Tala said quickly. "What about…the First Law?"

"What about it?"

Tala strained her ears to make sure Faith was still upstairs before she whispered, "Will we ever tell Faith what the Saru…what we did to keep our existence hidden? Not now, of course, but maybe in a few years, when we know we can fully—?"

"Are you out of your mind?" Madsen shouted so loudly that a ringing sound started in Tala's ear. "That secret is the one thing keeping us safe! Other than Jorie and Rue, no human can ever find out."

She's not just any human, Tala wanted to say. But she knew he was right. They couldn't risk it. The potential consequences were too devastating. "Right," she said quickly. "Of course." Her shoulders slumped.

"You'd better not let your feelings cloud your judgment, Commander," Madsen snarled. Then he was gone.

Tala's hand with her phone dropped to her lap. She stared at it. Had he just said…*feelings?* How on earth had he known?

She firmly shook her head. There was nothing to know.

Whatever was happening between her and Faith, she had it under control. She could easily put a stop to it and re-erect the boundaries that had started to blur.

And that was exactly what she would do.

Faith lingered on the stairs, trying to steady herself before walking back into the living room. When she took that last step, it felt like jumping off a cliff.

Tentatively, she peeked around the corner.

Tala sat on the edge of the couch, her posture stiff and her expression unreadable.

Faith cleared her throat, then realized that Tala with her acute senses had probably heard her breathing on the stairs for the last three minutes.

A flush swept up her neck, but she ignored it as she walked over.

"You okay?" Tala searched her face. The neutral expression wavered, for a second replaced with one of concern.

Faith nodded.

"Are you sure? I could hear your father shouting at you through the phone."

A sigh escaped Faith. "He's really not happy with me right now. He can tell something's going on; he just isn't sure what."

Tala's gaze veered away, and a heavy silence settled between them.

Come on. Say it. "Um, about that…" Faith fidgeted with the hem of her shirt as she struggled to find the right words. "About what happened earlier…"

Tala looked up, and Faith lost her train of thought as she met those golden eyes.

She wasn't sure what she saw in them. Was it a glimmer of hope? A hint of sadness? Maybe both?

Then the Saru mask settled back on Tala's face. "You don't have to say it." Finally, it was Tala who broke the silence. "We both know it's a bad idea."

"Oh." So Tala had come to the same conclusion. That was good, right? It would make things between them much less awkward. "I mean, oh yeah, totally. It would only complicate things. My father already won't like what I'll tell him tomorrow, but he won't do much to stop it as long as he thinks it's all fake and I'm just doing it out of misguided compassion for the Wrasa. He'll try to make me see reason, but that's it. However, if you and I became involved for real, there's no telling what he would do."

Tala let out a growl. "He wouldn't hurt you, would he?"

"No, never." Faith firmly believed that. "But he would hurt you—all Wrasa. He would fight against interspecies marriage and the Wrasa Rights Act even harder."

Tala nodded grimly. "He would stop at nothing to make sure I'll never lay a paw on his only daughter and possibly taint his precious human bloodline."

Faith found herself smiling despite the heavy feeling that had settled in the pit of her stomach. "You're a woman. Even if you 'laid a paw' on me, the 'tainting his bloodline' part wouldn't happen."

A sly grin curved up Tala's lips. "Are you sure?"

"I'm sure," Faith said. "I had an A+ in biology."

"Not in Wrasa biology, though."

Faith squinted at her. Tala was joking, right? Wrasa women couldn't really—? She shoved away the thought and the accompanying image of Tala's naked body pressing against her own. "It doesn't matter," she said loudly. "Because this"—she waved her hand back and forth between them, then to the couch, which she would never be able to look at again without thinking of their kiss—"won't happen again."

"Right," Tala said, just as loudly. "If I ever kiss you again, it'll be because the paparazzi have their cameras trained on us, not because your lips are incredibly soft and you taste like honey."

The unexpected words sent a tingle through Faith's lips. Her gaze dipped to Tala's mouth, and she couldn't help reliving how it had felt to kiss her. "Exactly," she said, trying hard to keep any kind of wobble from her voice.

"And if I kiss you back, it'll be because we want to convince an audience, not because there would be a much bigger push toward interspecies marriage if humans only knew what amazing kissers Wrasa are."

Tala smiled, but her eyes remained serious. "All part of our evil plan for world domination."

Faith stood next to the couch for a few more seconds. She searched for something to say to further lighten the mood but came up blank. Finally, she gave herself a mental nudge. "I should let you get some rest. It's been a long day."

Tala glanced at the clock on the wall, but she didn't point out that it was only half past eight.

"Do you need anything else?" Faith asked. "A second pillow? A glass of water?"

Tala shook her head. "No. I don't need anything."

A knot settled in Faith's chest. "Good night, Tala."

"Night, Faith."

Faith forced herself to turn and walk away without looking back.

It was the right choice. But then why did it feel so wrong?

CHAPTER 5

WHEN HER ALARM WENT OFF the next morning, Faith let out a long groan. Despite going to bed early, she had barely slept. She shut off the alarm, then lay there for a moment, unwilling to get up and face the day... or, more specifically, face Tala.

But she knew she couldn't afford to linger in bed.

Chloe often dawdled and was easily distracted in the morning, so getting dressed and having breakfast seemed to take forever, and making it to school on time was a challenge.

Faith forced herself out of bed, took a quick shower, and hurried through her routine. Dressed in her work uniform, which always made her feel more composed, she went over to Chloe's room.

Her daughter's bed was empty. Only Mr. Snugglefluff, the stuffed bunny, was propped up against the pillow. Chloe must have been too excited about their overnight guest to stay in bed.

Somehow, Faith wasn't surprised.

In her pantyhose-covered feet, she headed downstairs. Her attention was immediately drawn to the couch, where Tala had slept. The place where they'd kissed.

It was empty. The sheet and blanket were neatly folded.

Had Tala left already...without a goodbye? There was no note on the coffee table.

The sting of disappointment was much sharper than Faith would have expected.

But then she became aware of a heavenly scent and voices drifting over from the kitchen—Chloe's curious tone, followed by Tala's amused one.

"Can you talk to animals?" Chloe asked.

"Kind of," Tala replied patiently. "It's mostly reading their body language. Like if I did this"—she let out a low snarl—"it means: stop stealing the blueberries!"

Chloe giggled and snarled back.

Faith couldn't help smiling as she walked over. She paused in the doorway and took in the domestic scene.

Chloe sat on the counter, already dressed, dangling her legs as she peppered Tala with questions.

Tala stood at the stove, seeming surprisingly at home in Faith's kitchen. She was wearing her own clothes, which Faith had washed for her the previous night. She had rolled up her shirtsleeves, and the muscles in her arm flexed as she expertly flipped a pancake, every motion precise and controlled, with a coiled power lurking beneath. Her black jeans hugged her legs, showing off their sinewy strength. The sun was rising outside, and its light streaming in through the kitchen window made the color of Tala's hair seem to shift from burnished copper to rich cinnamon. The ends curled slightly, framing her angular face and softening her fierce appearance as she glanced over at Chloe.

Her nose twitched, and she turned toward Faith as if she had caught her scent. Her smile, which had been relaxed and carefree with Chloe, turned into something more guarded. "Morning." Tala's gaze traced the lines of Faith's crisp white blouse, then veered down to her pencil skirt.

The intensity of her attention made Faith's pulse race.

"Hope you don't mind," Tala murmured huskily.

Truth be told, Faith didn't mind Tala looking at her at all. *Oh. She means her using the kitchen. Of course.* She quickly shook her head and smoothed her hands down her skirt. "No, it's fine. More than fine, actually. Thank you for making breakfast."

It had been just her taking care of all the morning tasks for what felt like forever, and it was nice to have someone else take over.

"I helped," Chloe declared.

Faith lifted her eyebrows. She knew what her kitchen looked like when Chloe helped with the cooking—and the spotless counter was not it.

"She added the blueberries," Tala said. "At least the ones she didn't eat." She turned toward Chloe. "How many pancakes do you want?"

Chloe held up one hand with all fingers spread wide.

"How about we start with two?" Faith said quickly before Tala could deposit five pancakes on Chloe's plate.

They carried their plates to the table in the dining area, and Chloe forgot her curious questions as she dug into her pancakes.

Faith didn't have much of an appetite. Her stomach twisted itself into a pretzel at the thought of the conversation she'd have to have with her father later, so she just picked at her pancake.

Tala plowed through her stack within minutes, probably still hungry after shifting the night before, then eyed Faith's half-eaten food. "Not a fan of pancakes? Do you want me to make you something else?"

"No, I'm not hungry. Here, you have it." Faith slid the plate across the table.

Tala sliced off a piece of the offered pancake with her fork and eagerly popped it into her mouth. She chewed twice, then froze. Her pupils widened.

Chloe's fork clattered onto the table. "Mommy, quick! She's choking!"

Tala frantically shook her head. She looked as if she was about to spit out the bite but then swallowed it with an audible gulp. "I'm fine. I just forgot that we're not…um…that we're no longer with my pack."

It took Faith's sleep-deprived brain several seconds to understand. Tala had accepted food off her plate even though they didn't have an audience! A nervous chuckle escaped her. "Guess we just got used to it."

Chloe scratched her head as if they were speaking a foreign language. "Huh?"

"Um, Wrasa don't usually share their food or accept food from anyone else's plate," Faith said but decided not to tell her daughter about the only exception.

"Oh." Chloe gave Tala a concerned look. "Are you in trouble because you ate Mom's pancake?"

The tension fled from Tala's face as she gave her a reassuring smile. "No."

Chloe's gaze darted to Faith. "Is Mom in trouble?"

"No, Chloe," Faith said. "No one is in trouble. It's just not usually done."

"Can I have your pancake, then?" Chloe pulled the plate toward herself before Faith had finished nodding.

A few minutes later, they carried their plates to the kitchen. As Faith rinsed the dishes and put them into the dishwasher, Tala pointed at her hand. "Careful. Your bandage is coming loose."

Faith glanced down. The self-adhesive gauze pad barely clung to the heel of her hand. It had probably gotten wet in the shower earlier. "It's fine. I'll put a new one on later, once I'm at work."

"My sister would never let me live that down," Tala said. "I'll change it for you. Come on. It'll only take a minute."

The thought of having Tala touch her, even just to change the bandage, made Faith's breath catch, so maybe that wasn't such a good idea. Keeping her distance was safer. "That's really not necessary."

"Let me help," Tala said softly but with quiet insistence.

It came as close to pleading as Faith had ever heard from her, and she found herself unable to say no. "Okay." She closed the dishwasher.

"Chloe, go get your school bag and get ready," she told her daughter before leading Tala upstairs.

Tala got the first aid kit out from beneath the sink and pointed at the tub. "Sit."

"It's a half-healed scrape, Tala," Faith said with a smile. "I won't pass out or get wobbly knees."

"Sit."

"Yes, ma'am." Faith gave a playful salute and sank onto the edge of the tub.

Tala stepped closer. Her larger-than-life presence filled the bathroom, making it seem to shrink around them. The small space felt almost suffocatingly intimate. Tala's leg brushed Faith's knee through the thin layer of pantyhose. The contact sent a jolt through Faith's body. Maybe sitting down had been a good idea after all because her legs didn't feel too steady.

She held her breath as Tala reached for her injured hand.

"Hold still," Tala murmured—a warning that was completely unnecessary because Faith couldn't have moved even if she'd wanted to.

Tala's fingers were warm against her skin and her touch gentle as she carefully peeled away the old bandage. She studied the scrape with intense focus.

Faith peered down too, mostly to distract herself from Tala's closeness. A scab had formed, and the scrape didn't appear infected, yet Tala's lips pressed into a tight line as if she were faced with a mortal wound.

"Sometimes, I forget how fragile humans are."

"I'm not fragile," Faith said, but her voice was just a faint whisper.

"I know."

They both glanced up at the same time.

A lingering look passed between them until Tala directed her attention back to the task at hand. Gently, she placed a new bandage over the wound.

With the pad of her thumb, she traced a tender line along the edge of the dressing, sending goose bumps up Faith's arm.

Faith couldn't hold back the low gasp that escaped her.

Tala's gaze darted to her face…to her lips. The heat of her leg against Faith's nearly bare skin seemed to increase.

"Tala…" It was her voice, but Faith had no idea what she wanted to say. Was she warning Tala to back away or beckoning her closer?

The sound of her name seemed to jerk Tala from her daze. She stepped back, giving Faith room to breathe. "All set," she murmured, her voice husky.

"Thanks." Faith got up from the tub and smoothed down her skirt with trembling hands. "We need to get going, or Chloe will be late for school."

"Right. Let's go." Tala whirled around and marched out.

As Faith followed her out of the bathroom, she stroked her fingers along the edge of the bandage, where she could still feel Tala's touch.

She couldn't help wondering whether she had lied to Chloe earlier. Maybe she was in trouble after all.

Tala left the town house first. She paused in the courtyard and sniffed the cool morning air. It carried the scent of magnolia trees and city life, but the biting aroma of aggression was absent.

Her gaze swept over the bushes and surrounding buildings. No paparazzi. No HASS members. No Wrasa-hating neighbors. Nothing seemed out of place.

Not that she had expected it. The Saru unit had already checked the neighborhood twice this morning and texted her an "all clear," but Tala refused to take any chances when it came to keeping Faith and her daughter safe.

Tala turned back toward the house and gave Faith a wave, indicating that it was okay to step outside. She walked them to Faith's car, which was parked in the underground parking garage that belonged to the town house community.

Chloe skipped ahead with the energy of a six-year-old, while Tala kept a watchful eye on their surroundings.

The day before, Faith's neighbor had managed to catch her off guard. No way would she allow something like that to happen a second time, no matter how distracting Faith's presence was.

When they reached the car, she checked it out to make sure no one had messed with it before she allowed Chloe to climb in.

But instead of doing that, Chloe flung her arms around Tala's waist and clung to her in a tight hug.

"Uh…" Tala stiffened for a second, caught off guard by the open trust and affection Chloe's scent revealed. She hadn't expected to ever meet Faith's daughter, much less to have Chloe bond with her the way she had.

What surprised her even more, though, was that it wasn't one-sided at all. She'd always liked pups well enough, but she had never craved having her own. They were too loud, too unpredictable to have them around for longer than a few hours.

But even with her never-ending questions, Chloe hadn't gotten on her nerves for even a second.

Finally, Chloe pulled back and looked up at her, her brown eyes pleading. "Will you come have pizza with us again next weekend?"

"Um, I'm not sure yet." Tala wasn't sure of much right now, not even the next steps of their mission—probably getting Faith to speak up for interspecies marriage or Wrasa rights in general, but Madsen hadn't shared the details of his plan yet. She also didn't know if Faith would even want her to hang out with Chloe again.

"We could have something else," Chloe said quickly. "Maybe ice cream!"

In the face of the girl's enthusiasm, Tala couldn't say no, but she didn't dare say yes either. "We'll see, okay? In the meantime, take good care of your mom, okay?"

Chloe nodded as if she had every intention of protecting Faith as fiercely as Tala would. She waved and climbed into her booster seat in the back of the car.

Tala watched her for a moment, then blinked and tried to shake off the weird feeling that gripped her.

Faith stood just a few yards away, and Tala's breath caught as she turned toward her.

The sight of Faith in her hotel uniform wasn't helping at all. Tala had nearly dropped the frying pan when she had first seen her in the kitchen earlier.

A tailored navy-blue blazer hugged Faith's gentle curves, and a formfitting pencil skirt of the same color ended right above her knees, showcasing her shapely legs.

Her chestnut hair was swept up into a top knot that gave her a bit of a sexy librarian look.

The professional outfit made her seem untouchable, and that only made Tala want to touch her more. Her fingers itched with the desire to brush aside the purple neck scarf tied neatly at Faith's throat and caress a line from her neck to her collarbone, which peeked out from beneath her crisp white blouse.

She curled her fingers into fists. *No,* she firmly told herself. *No touching.* They had agreed to keep this strictly professional—on a make-believe mate level only.

That left her with no idea how to say goodbye to Faith, who seemed equally hesitant.

"So…" they said at the same time.

After spending nearly every second of the last three days together, it felt strange to go their separate ways.

Tala shuffled her feet—which she had never done in her life. Great Hunter, this was all supposed to be fake. How had she gotten so tangled up in this…in them?

Before she could decide on an appropriate goodbye, the heels of Faith's black pumps clicked on the concrete as she closed the distance between them.

Her arms slid around Tala's shoulders in a short but heartfelt embrace. "Thank you," she whispered into Tala's ear. "For introducing me to your family. For…everything."

The by-now familiar aroma of hot milk with honey on a rainy day swept over her, making her eyes flutter shut. Today, the fragrance seemed even more enticing than usual, and it took everything Tala had not to bury her face against Faith's neck to inhale the scent or to lean up and kiss her.

She forced her eyes open and quickly stepped back. "You know," she said, aiming for a casual tone, "now that we're back and no longer trying to fool my family, you don't have to use so much mate scent perfume. Since you don't need it to mask your emotions at work, just a dab is enough." Keeping things on a strictly pretend basis would be a lot easier if Faith kept the use of the perfume to a minimum.

"Oh crap!" Faith pressed a hand to her mouth. "I forgot to put on the perfume! I haven't unpacked yet, and it's at the bottom of my suitcase."

Tala stared at her. It took a few moments for the words to sink in. Faith hadn't applied any perfume? How was that possible?

She inhaled deeply, filling her nostrils with the intoxicating blend of their scents.

It wasn't the perfume she smelled on Faith. It was the real deal. Mate scent—hers and Faith's, and it smelled even richer and more irresistible than the perfume ever had!

No way. That was impossible. There had to be another explanation.

But as much as Tala tried to find one, the tornado of thoughts tumbling through her mind spun too fast to cling to any even remotely plausible reason.

"Tala?" Faith's voice sounded as if she were underwater—and that was how Tala felt…helplessly drowning. "You okay? You look like you've seen a ghost."

"Wrasa don't believe in ghosts," Tala replied. Neither did they believe in two people developing mate scent when they weren't even a couple! She forced a smile. "I'm fine."

Faith searched her face as if attempting to decipher the emotions Tala was desperately trying to hide. "Are you sure?"

"Yes," Tala said, sounding less than convincing, even to herself. "You have to go, or you'll be late."

"Right." Faith fiddled with her car keys, her gaze still on Tala. "What about the perfume?"

"You'll be fine without it for a day. Now that we hugged, my scent is all over you, and there probably aren't too many Wrasa at the hotel anyway."

Faith's cheeks flushed a deep pink. "Okay." Finally, she opened the driver's side door and got in.

When the car pulled away, Tala stood there for several minutes, her entire body frozen in shock, staring after them.

CHAPTER 6

Somehow, Tala found herself in her own car, without remembering how she had gotten there. She sat in the driver's seat in silence, gripping the wheel but not starting the engine.

Her mind raced as she tried to make sense of what had happened, but the mate scent clinging to her skin made it hard to think clearly.

Mate scent. She and Faith had somehow developed real mate scent.

How was that possible? It wasn't supposed to happen. Not with a pretend mate. Not with Faith MacAllister. And definitely not this quickly!

They had only shared one kiss. Okay, two. Three if you counted the brush of their lips in the bowling alley.

Usually, even Wrasa couples didn't develop mate scent this fast. For some, making love for the first time triggered the process that changed the way they smelled, while it took months for others—and sometimes, it didn't happen at all. She and Lasandra had been together for more than a year without ever forming a chemical bond like that.

Tala hadn't been sure it would ever happen to her with anyone, but now it had—with Faith.

The ringing of her phone cut through the silence.

Tala jumped, hitting her knee on the steering wheel. She mumbled a curse in the Old Language and pulled the device from her pocket.

Unknown caller flashed across the screen.

Tala let it go to voicemail. She wasn't in the mood to talk to anyone.

A few seconds later, a text message from the same number appeared. *This is Jorie Price. Would you call me back?*

Oh wolf poop! Their only remaining dream seer had never called her before. Now Tala fumbled with the phone in her haste to call her back.

"Maharsi?" she said as soon as Jorie accepted the call. "This is Tala Peterson. Sorry for not picking up. I didn't recognize your number."

"No worries," Jorie replied. "Jeff suggested I call you."

Tala almost asked, *What Jeff?* Just in time, she realized Jorie was talking about Jeff Madsen. No one else she knew called the council speaker by his first name. He and Jorie probably worked together more closely than Tala had realized. "Yes. Right. The situation with Faith MacAllister has changed a little. I think she's really on our side now and could make a wonderful ally—if we show some trust in her in return."

"You want to tell her about my dream vision involving the two of you." It sounded like a statement, not a question.

Had Jorie guessed, had Madsen told her, or had she seen what Tala would ask in another dream? "Um, yes. I think it would help her to fully trust us. Maybe it would give her that one last nudge she needs to publicly come out in support of Wrasa rights."

"You might want to wait a few more days, just to be sure, but if you're confident she's ready, then you have my permission to tell her."

Tala raised both brows. That was it? She'd been prepared for a drawn-out back-and-forth in which she had to work hard to convince Jorie.

Jorie's chuckle interrupted the stunned silence. "Did you expect a 'we can't trust humans' speech? I'm human too, you know?"

"I know that, of course," Tala said quickly. "I just…"

"Forgot for a moment?" Jorie finished for her, still sounding amused. "I'll take that as a compliment. I know it's still mind-boggling for most Wrasa that a human could turn out to be a dream seer."

"And develop mate scent," Tala muttered.

"That too." Jorie paused. "Is there something else you wanted to talk about?"

The question sent a shock wave through Tala's body. Her heart thudded in a fast staccato against her rib cage. She should say no and end the call as quickly as possible.

But who else was she supposed to talk to? Even ignoring the fact that Madsen had ordered her not to tell anyone about the fake-relationship scheme, she'd never been one to talk about personal problems or ask for advice. She'd always been a bit of a lone wolf—strong, independent, and in control, never taking the time to make close friends. Talking to her family wasn't an option either, because they all assumed she and Faith were a happy couple, so they wouldn't understand what was so shocking about the mate scent.

The only person who could help her make sense of this mess was Jorie.

"Maharsi, if I may ask a personal question…"

"Go ahead," Jorie said, her tone neutral. "And please call me Jorie."

Tala gripped the phone more tightly. "When did you first notice you and Tas Westmore had developed mate scent?"

An affectionate chuckle reverberated through the phone. "We didn't notice. Griffin's pride did. Her sister even went to the doctor because she was convinced there was something wrong with her sense of smell."

"How far into your relationship was that?" Tala asked, then quickly added, "If you don't mind me asking, Maharsi…um, Jorie."

There was a brief pause on the other end. "Are you really curious about my relationship, or is there something else going on?"

Tala squeezed her eyes shut and leaned her head back against the driver's seat. "The vision you had about Faith and me kissing surrounded by paparazzi… It happened exactly like that." She hesitated, then forced herself to add, "Well, maybe not exactly like that. Please keep this to yourself and don't tell Manark Madsen, but…there wasn't, um, a lot of acting involved."

"You're falling in love with her," Jorie said, her tone calm and knowing, without even a hint of surprise.

"You knew that would happen?" Tala blurted. Then her brain caught up with what Jorie had said. "Uh, I mean, I didn't say I'm in love, but there's something about Faith that draws me to her in a way that is utterly…" She cut herself off, not wanting to lay bare all her emotions.

"Confusing?" Jorie finished for her. "Infuriating? Unsettling? Irresistible?"

"Yes." The word slipped out before Tala could stop it. It was all of the above.

"I know that feeling," Jorie said. "Falling in love with a six-foot-two liger-shifter who'd been sent to kill me was all that and more."

Tala furrowed her brow. Why did Jorie insist on repeating that phrase—falling in love—to describe the parallels in their circumstances? "I'm not sure how it happened and if it's even possible, but…" Her voice got quieter and quieter with every word until she finally whispered, "Unless I'm hallucinating, I think we've developed mate scent."

"Ah," was all Jorie said. Her tone didn't give away whether she'd already known that or not.

Rumor had it she'd been a professional poker player, and Tala had a feeling she had raked in more than her fair share of winning pots, bluffing the other players.

"What am I supposed to do? Ignore it and hope it'll go away? Will it?" So far, Tala had told herself that her attraction to Faith would fade in time. But now she was starting to doubt it. Even her body chemistry was telling her that Faith was her mate!

"I can't tell you that," Jorie answered.

"Because you don't know or—?"

Jorie sighed. "The future isn't set in stone, Tala. If I tell you too much or the wrong thing, it could change the course of events in a way that would be catastrophic for the Wrasa."

Tala thumped the steering wheel with the side of her fist. "But isn't that your role as a maharsi? Guiding us with the wisdom you gained through your dreams?"

"It is," Jorie said quietly. "And to be perfectly honest, I still struggle with it. I wish there was a Wrasa maharsi left who could help me deal with that massive responsibility, but unfortunately, I'm all you have."

Great job, Tala. Now she had insulted their only dream seer! Tala bit her lip. "I didn't mean to imply that you're inadequate in any way."

"It's all right. I get your frustration," Jorie said. "Dream seeing isn't exactly a science. Half of it is interpretation and guesswork, and many of my visions only become clear in hindsight. So when there's a lot on the line and my dreams don't give me all of the details, I've learned to be more cautious about what I share. The last time I wasn't, I almost got Kelsey and Rue killed because I misunderstood a vision. It ended with—"

"I know exactly how that situation ended," Tala growled because she couldn't bear to hear it.

Jorie went quiet for a moment. "You're not blaming yourself for Kelsey outing the Wrasa on national TV, are you?"

"It doesn't matter," Tala mumbled.

"I carry as much responsibility for that as you do. Probably more. But it can still work out in the end."

How? Tala wanted to ask but knew Jorie wouldn't or couldn't answer, so she remained silent and stared through the windshield without seeing any of her surroundings.

"I can't tell you what to do," Jorie finally said. "All I can tell you is that it'll all work out if you have faith in Faith."

The words made Tala's lips twitch, but she was too tense to fully smile. "Faith in Faith," she repeated.

"You're a tracker, right? Griffin tells me that means you've always relied on your instincts. Trust them now."

Tala tried to rein in her frustration. "All right. Thanks. And please keep this between us. As it is, I don't have the easiest standing with Manark Madsen, and if he found out about Faith and me… I'm not sure he'd be as understanding as you are."

"Got it," Jorie said. "And feel free to save my number as a contact. Just in case."

Tala hadn't expected that. "Thanks, I will."

They ended the call, and Tala saved Jorie's number, then dropped the phone onto the passenger seat.

Trust my instincts… She tapped the steering wheel. *Trust Faith.* What did that mean? Was she supposed to pursue a real relationship with Faith? Because earlier, all of Tala's instincts had screamed at her not to let Faith go.

Okay, maybe that had been her libido, not her instincts.

Perhaps Jorie had meant her protective instincts, sharpened by a decade as a Saru who had guarded the Wrasa's secret existence.

She wouldn't figure it out sitting in her car, staring at the tiny smudges left by flies on her windshield.

Time to check in with Mirella. It was just a formality, but at least it was one thing she could check off her to-do list so she could finally tell Faith about the dream seers.

"Did you sweep the house for bugs?" Tala asked as soon as Mirella accepted the call.

"Hello to you too, serska," Mirella said, using the word for *sister-in-law* in the Old Language. "Your brother and the rest of the pack are fine, thanks so much for asking."

Tala let out a growl. After discovering the mate scent, her patience was running thin. "This isn't a social call, Mirella. I'm calling as a Saru commander, not as your future sister-in-law."

"Fine," Mirella said. "If you're not interested in the well-being of your pack… Yes, I did complete the sweep."

"Good. Did you let Manark Madsen know there were no bugs?"

A sudden hush fell.

Had they been disconnected? "Mirella?"

"Um, who said there were no bugs?"

Tala froze in place. She even stopped breathing. If Mirella said anything else, she couldn't hear it over the frantic pounding of her heart and the roaring of blood rushing through her ears. "What?" she finally got out. "You found bugs in the house?"

"One," Mirella answered.

"Where?"

"In the kitchen."

Tala shook her head, trying to put together the pieces of a new reality that no longer made sense. "It had to be the two HASS goons. Somehow, they made it into the house, probably when most of us were at the yasi makamar." But even as she said it, she knew how weak that explanation sounded.

"Impossible," Mirella said. "If they'd planted the bug, their stink would have been all over the kitchen. But it wasn't. The only human scent in the house was Faith's."

No. Tala didn't want to believe that Faith had planted the device. "What are you implying?" Tala's voice was as sharp as a blade.

"I'm not implying anything. I know she's your mate, and you love her, but…" Mirella hesitated. "She's a MacAllister. Are you sure we can trust her?"

"Of course I'm sure!"

"Honestly, I'm not. At the time, I thought I was imagining things because…well, Rey wasn't too thrilled about you bringing a human home, and I admit I let his opinion color my perception of Faith, but… The night of the feast, your mother and I caught her in the kitchen."

"Caught her doing what?"

"I'm not sure, but she was really jumpy and behaving weirdly," Mirella said. "Like we'd caught her doing something she shouldn't."

Tala remembered waking up that night with Faith gone from the bed. Faith had said she'd gone downstairs to look for a heating pad. Had that been a lie?

The thought hurt like a stab to the chest. She rubbed the heel of her hand over her breastbone. "No," she said loudly, both to herself and to Mirella.

That night had ended with her playing heating pad for Faith. It had been a moment of trust and tenderness. None of it had felt like a lie.

The next night had brought them even closer, and they had made each other a promise: no more bugs.

Yeah, but you also promised her no more secrets—and you couldn't keep that promise either. Tala ignored the little voice in the back of her head.

"No," she repeated, trying hard not to show how shaken she was. "It must have been HASS. Maybe they sprayed lavender or chemicals to hide their scent on their way out. God knows they're always coming up with something new they can use against us."

"Maybe," Mirella replied, but her tone said she didn't believe it.

Tala did, though. At least she wanted to.

Have faith in Faith, Jorie had said. Their dream seer couldn't be wrong.

But then again, Jorie had told her dream seeing wasn't an exact science. Sometimes, she was wrong.

"Don't call Madsen," Tala said, using her fiercest alpha tone. "I'll update him myself. And don't breathe a word of any of this to the pack, not even to Rey, or I'll make sure the only Saru mission you'll ever be sent on will be cleaning latrines for the next year!"

She jabbed her finger at the *end call* button without waiting for a reply and rested her head against the steering wheel, hoping it would ease the pounding behind her temples.

A thousand questions tumbled through Tala's mind.

She needed answers. She needed to talk to Faith.

Maybe there was a logical explanation for everything. Faith had told her she'd brought a bug with her but hadn't gone through with it after realizing her father had been wrong about the Wrasa. Perhaps she had accidentally dropped the bug without noticing when Mirella and Tala's mom had nearly caught her planting it.

It was possible, right?

The seasoned, cynical Saru commander she'd been a couple of months ago would have laughed at her.

Was she being naive, letting her feelings cloud her judgment, as Madsen had suggested?

She didn't want to believe it, but she'd have to tread carefully.

Telling Faith about the dream seers was off—at least for now. Instead, the next time she saw Faith, she'd have to find out if she was still spying for her father.

Maybe she could convince Jeff Madsen to jump ahead to phase two of Operation Make-Believe Mate—having them attend political events and fundraisers together so Faith could show her support for the Wrasa.

This weekend was a charity luncheon raising funds for adding new departments to hospitals, with staff and equipment dedicated to treating Wrasa patients. Tala knew because she had repeatedly donated to the project. It was near and dear to her heart because it would prevent pups from suffering the way Rey had.

It could be a test for Faith's loyalty. If she was still working against them, spying for her father, he would never allow her to publicly voice her support. He might tolerate Faith playing Tala's girlfriend as long as he thought it was serving his own purposes, but he would draw the line at her openly condemning his hateful rhetoric. Instead, she would either come up with an excuse for why she couldn't attend the luncheon or refuse to give a quick statement of support for the cameras.

It was a brilliant plan any Saru would have been proud of—and Tala hated it. As Faith had said in Silver Falls, she and Faith felt like a team now—partners who worked together against the rest of the world.

Testing Faith like that felt like a betrayal, and every fiber of Tala's body screamed at her not to do it.

But what if her feelings were clouding her judgment? Could she risk the future of her entire species just because of her own growing attachment to a human?

Tears of frustration threatened to rise, but she forced them back. No time for weakness. She needed to do something. Remaining inactive was what had led to Kelsey shifting on TV, outing the Wrasa, and Tala couldn't afford to make the same mistake twice.

Her own heart might be on the line, but so was the fate of her people.

CHAPTER 7

FAITH HAD NEVER BEEN ONE to take advantage of the fact that she was the boss's daughter. Today, though, she was running a few minutes late because they had lingered at the breakfast table, and Chloe clearly hadn't wanted to say goodbye to Tala.

Okay, truth be told, Faith hadn't been eager to see her leave either.

After three days with Tala and her pack, being back in her everyday life felt unexpectedly…weird. It was like wearing a wrong pair of glasses—nothing looked quite the same as before.

She shook her head at herself.

Faith's heels clicked on the polished marble floor as she entered the hotel's lobby.

The low hum of conversation and the scent of freshly cut flowers greeted her.

She waved at the concierge, then stepped to the left, out of the way of guests leaving, and paused to survey the lobby.

Checkouts seemed to be running smoothly. Even the new front desk employee who had just completed his training assisted a guest with a confident smile.

The floral arrangements on the low tables in the seating area all looked beautiful, but one of the pillows on a leather couch had a coffee stain. Faith made a mental note to let housekeeping know.

A commotion near the bell desk drew her attention.

A portly guest in an expensive suit gestured animatedly, shouting at one of the bellhops.

Faith recognized him instantly. It was Jasper, the only Wrasa on staff.

He stood with his eyes downcast, letting the guest rant without defending himself.

For as long as he'd worked in the hotel, he had always been the quiet type—working efficiently but rarely interacting with the rest of the staff.

Faith had never bothered to learn more about him. She didn't even know what subspecies he was. God, she really had been ignorant when it came to the Wrasa.

She strode over, her polite director of guest experience mask firmly in place. "Good morning. Is there a problem, sir?"

"Yes, there is!" The guest whirled around to face her. "He damaged my suitcase! I've observed him before, and he's incompetent and careless!"

Jasper's gaze flicked up to meet hers before he dipped his head in deference. The ID tag around his neck clinked with the movement. The engraved letter W identified him as a wolf-shifter. He reminded her of Tala's youngest brother and her submissive cousins. "I promise I handled it very carefully, Ms. MacAllister."

Faith eyed the piece of luggage between the two men. It was a luxury rolling trunk that likely cost more than Jasper had made in the past two months. The brown leather was smooth and looked brand-new, without a single scratch on it. "I'm sorry, but I don't see any damage," she said to the guest. "Could you point it out to me?"

"Someone like him shouldn't be allowed to handle expensive luggage!" he ranted instead of showing her the perceived damage.

Someone like him? Then sudden clarity hit Faith with the force of a punch to the gut: He wasn't just complaining about the service. It was Jasper's presence in the hotel…his very existence that didn't sit right with the guest!

"I picked this hotel because Peter MacAllister owns it," the customer continued. "I thought I wouldn't have to deal with *their kind* here." He wrinkled his nose as if Jasper were a stain on the hotel's otherwise pristine reputation.

Her father hadn't hired Jasper. His policy had always been clear: no shape-shifters in his hotels.

Somehow, Jasper must have slipped through the cracks. Maybe their previous general manager had hired him before retiring.

He'd been a practical man who might have pointed out the advantages of employing someone who could handle the long shifts without complaint, lift heavy loads—and be paid less than minimum wage since Wrasa had fewer legal protections.

Faith gritted her teeth. Her gaze darted to Jasper.

His shoulders were hunched, and a fine tremor ran through his lanky frame, as if he were struggling to maintain his composure. Faith couldn't make out his features because he had his head lowered. Either it was his natural reaction to a confrontation, or he was fighting not to shift and trying to hide the first signs of the transformation.

A protective fire flared up in Faith. Her professional mask slipped for a moment. "Sir," she began, her tone much too sharp. She caught herself and continued, carefully navigating the tightrope between firmness and politeness: "I assure you all of our staff members are trained professionals who handle our guests' luggage with the utmost care and respect. Jasper in particular has been nothing but exemplary in his duties. My father and our management team stand by him."

"Your father?" the guest asked.

Faith nodded. "Peter MacAllister." She reached into her blazer pocket and handed him one of her business cards. "I'm Faith MacAllister, director of guest experience. If you have any specific concerns about our service, I'm here to address them."

The guest looked back and forth between her and the card. His mouth opened and closed twice before he finally muttered, "Well, I suppose the damage is minimal, so I'm willing to let it slide this time. But I still think—"

"Thank you," Faith said. "Clearly, it was all just a misunderstanding."

His face went firetruck-red, and he sent her a disgruntled glare.

Faith held his gaze, refusing to back down. She could only hope her father never found out she had stood up to a guest like this, especially because of a Wrasa employee. He had drilled his "the guest is always right" principle into her, but this time, she couldn't take that stance.

"I guess so," the guest finally muttered. He grabbed the handle of his suitcase and pushed past Jasper on his way to the sliding glass doors. One of the trunk's metal corners hit Jasper in the shin, and he let out a startled growl.

"Jasper!" Faith took another step toward him. "Are you okay?"

Jasper glanced up. Heat radiated off his body in waves. Something wild flared in his eyes—something Faith had seen before, when Tala had been attacked by her neighbor and struggled not to shift.

Oh crap. If Jasper lost control and turned into a wolf in the middle of the lobby, chaos would break out. Even if no one got hurt, her father would fire him on the spot.

"Calm down," she said, keeping her tone as soothing as she could. "He's gone. Everything is okay. Kalyani, nemi."

The words had seemed to soothe Tala and help her regain control.

But unfortunately, they appeared to have a different effect on Jasper.

His eyes widened, but at least they lost that wild, unfocused expression. "W-what did you just say?"

"Kalyani, nemi? Did I pronounce it wrong? Is it Kalyani, nemmi?"

Jasper ducked his head and looked around as if he was trying to make sure no one had heard her. "Um, you might not want to say that."

"Why? It means 'everything's okay,' right?"

"*Kalyani* means 'it's okay,' but *nemi*…" He lowered his voice to a whisper. "It means 'jewel' or 'treasure.' It's our most intimate endearment—one we only ever use with our mate."

"Oh, I'm so sorry." That explained his reaction. "I learned the phrase from my mate and repeated it without knowing she tacked an endearment on."

Jasper looked as if purple aliens had landed their spaceship in the middle of the lobby. "You…you have a mate? I thought you were just wearing a new perfume."

"You haven't heard? Every tabloid and gossip site in the country has been writing about it, and I know the staff is talking." She had assumed the gossip had spread through the entire hotel…around the whole world by now. "You don't talk to the other employees a lot, do you?"

He lowered his gaze. "No, I don't. I heard rumors, but I thought they couldn't be true."

Was he being discriminated against by the staff? Or was it his choice not to socialize? Faith vowed to keep an eye out for him. "Anyway, I'm sorry you had to deal with that." She nodded toward the sliding doors the hateful guest had disappeared through. "Are you okay?"

"I'm fine." Jasper managed a strained smile. "I'm used to it."

"You shouldn't have to be," Faith said firmly. "You're part of our staff and deserve the same respect as everyone else. If you don't get it—from guests or colleagues, please let me know, and I'll handle it."

"Thank you. I appreciate it, but it's really fine." His face was calm. He had managed to resist the urge to shift, and his polite bellhop expression had returned.

He didn't believe she would always be on his side, Faith realized. She had been part of a management team that had looked the other way for too long. Now she would have to earn his trust—and she was determined to do that.

"My door is always open." She smiled at him. "And I promise not to call you *nemi* again."

That elicited a nervous chuckle. "Thanks." His nostrils flared as if he were taking in her scent. "Judging by your mate scent, your mate is not someone I want to make jealous."

Wait…mate scent? She hadn't put on any of the perfume today, so how could he smell it on her? Was he really fooled by the trace of Tala's scent that might still cling to her clothes?

Before she could ask, Jasper hurried off to help another guest with several suitcases.

She stared after him.

Now that she had a moment to think about it…

Tala had murmured that soothing sentence—kalyani, nemi—when the grief about her mother had hit Faith and she had cried on Tala's shoulder. They had been in Tala's old bedroom, completely alone, with no other Wrasa in sight.

There had been no need to pretend, no reason to use endearments.

Unless…

Faith sucked in a breath. Unless it had been a Freudian slip of the tongue…or whatever the Wrasa equivalent was.

Was it possible the mate scent was real…and Tala's feelings for her were too?

Twenty minutes later, Faith sat at her desk, her mind only half on the guest arrival lists for the week, which she was checking for VIPs, while the other half was replaying scenes of last weekend and this morning—each one featuring Tala.

The door to her office swept open without a knock, shaking Faith from her thoughts. Her father stormed in. A glossy magazine landed on her desk with a slap and slid across the wooden surface toward her.

"Please tell me the tabloids pulled this shit out of their asses, and you didn't actually…" His voice broke as if he couldn't bear to say the words. "I didn't want to believe it when Jon told me, but then I saw this…"

Faith set her lists aside and took a look at the magazine article.

The headline screamed in bold letters: *HASS leader's daughter reveals intimate details about her forbidden affair with a shifter: "She's the most tender lover I ever had!"*

"Tell me it's not true," her father whispered, his voice strained with desperation. He gripped the back of her visitor's chair with both hands. His complexion was ashen, and dark shadows beneath his eyes indicated that he hadn't slept.

His stance against the Wrasa was wrong, based on nothing but prejudice, but the agony in his eyes was real.

A twinge of compassion stirred in Faith's chest. "No, Dad. It's not true. I didn't sleep with her. I just said that because the press was about to paint Tala as a domestic abuser."

His iron grip on the chair eased. "But you kissed her." With a trembling finger, he pointed at the magazine.

Beneath the sensational headline was a close-up of her and Tala kissing.

In the picture, Tala gently cupped Faith's neck, and Faith was clutching Tala's shoulders with both hands, eyes closed, body pressed against Tala's, completely lost in the heat of Tala's embrace.

Faith stared at the photo. Their kiss looked as real as it had felt. She hadn't wanted to admit it, not even to herself, but the undeniable truth had been captured vividly in the picture.

"Why would you do that?" her father whispered. He sounded heartbroken.

Anger sparked deep within her. "Why would I do that? You were the one who suggested I pretend to be Tala's girlfriend! Of course I had to act like it. What did you think would happen?"

Her father's ashen face turned red. "You coming home with plenty of information we can use against the shifters, not you consorting with one of them!"

"I did find out plenty of information about the Wrasa, but you don't want to hear any of it. I found out they're loyal and caring. They love food and their kids and their mates...spouses, and the only thing wicked about them is their sense of humor."

"That's exactly what they want you to think. They spent a lifetime hiding. They're master manipulators."

"No, Dad. I no longer believe that. I saw how hiding their existence harmed them."

"No one forced them to hide!"

"Actually, we did," Faith replied as calmly as she could manage. "During the Inquisition, we burned many of them at the stake, nearly driving them to extinction. They hid because it was necessary to survive, not because they had evil intentions. We—humans—are just as likely to lie and manipulate."

He thumped his fist against the padded top of the chair. "Nonsense! Unlike them, we have values and decency!"

"Really? Because I spent the entire weekend lying to Tala's family. As a thank-you for them welcoming me into their home, I manipulated them so I could plant a bug. I risked getting some of them hurt…or even killed… during their sacred engagement ritual." She felt worse with every word; her stomach churning as it once again hit home what she had done.

"And? Did you?"

Faith frowned. "Get them hurt?"

"Plant the bug! Last I checked, it wasn't transmitting."

Faith stared at him, her heart plummeting. "That's really all you can think about, isn't it? I never should have agreed to help you spy on the Wrasa. I thought I was being a supportive daughter, but all I did was enable your obsession."

"Obsession?" His voice spiraled out of control. "I was trying to keep you—all humans—safe and catch the killers who murdered your mother!"

"Do you remember what you told me when I was a teenager and afraid you'd start dating again, remarry, and replace me and mom's memory with a new family?"

His grim face softened. "Of course I remember. I told you you'd always come first. And I kept my word."

"You did. You canceled important business meetings to go to my PTA meetings, bake sales, and school plays."

"Of course I did. You're my daughter, and I meant what I said. You'll always come first. You and Chloe."

"But in the past year, ever since the Wrasa revealed their existence, you haven't done that. You put your hatred first. You put me in danger with your obsessive need to prove that the Wrasa are evil."

He roughly massaged his temples with one hand, covering his eyes in the process for a moment. "And I regret it. I never should have had you pose as a shifter's girlfriend to spy on them, and I certainly shouldn't have sent you to spend an entire weekend alone with a bunch of them. I don't know what I was thinking, but I promise it'll never happen again."

"That's not what I meant. Having me spend time with the Wrasa isn't what put me in danger. Your hatred is. You gave an interview on how modern civilization will end if we allow interspecies marriage, fanning the flames of people's fears and hate, even though you were fully aware everyone assumed I was engaged to a Wrasa! You had to know there would be a backlash against me!"

He sank into the visitor's chair as if his legs had lost the strength to hold him up. "I swear I'll keep you safe. That interview was ill-timed; I admit that, but it was about those monsters, not about you."

"That's part of what you don't understand. It *is* about me. I…I've made friends among the Wrasa. Tala's mom treated me like her own, making me tea in the middle of the night because I was having cramps." Faith struggled to fight back tears. "I never had that."

Her father stared at her. The mask of his anger crumbled, revealing the heartbreak behind it.

Faith continued talking, hoping she would finally get through to him. "Then there's Tala's sister, a doctor who told me she doesn't treat humans—but then instantly made an exception for me when I scraped my hand. They have the cutest younger cousin who curled up next to me on the love seat because she was sad she hadn't learned how to shift yet. And then there's Tala. She's—" Faith cut herself off. If she told him everything she wanted to say about Tala, her father would instantly know that she had crossed the line between pretending and caring for real. "They're people like you and me, Dad. They just want to live their lives, but you won't let them."

"Don't you think your mother wanted that too?" her father asked, his voice a rough whisper.

"We don't know if the Wrasa had anything to do with her death. There's no proof." She spread her empty hands apart for emphasis. "Tala promised to look into it, but I wouldn't be surprised if she doesn't find anything."

Her father blanched. "You told her about your mother?"

The raw betrayal in his eyes shook Faith, but she refused to avert her gaze. "I trust her."

"God, they really brainwashed you."

"No, Dad, you're the brainwashed one. You're not listening to what I'm telling—"

A hesitant knock on the door interrupted her. It was opened a few inches, and Sabina stuck her head into the office. "Is everything okay in here?"

Faith's father stood and smoothed down his tie with trembling fingers. "Yes, thank you." He glanced at his wristwatch, his expression so troubled that Faith doubted he could really read the time. "I'm late for a meeting, but we're not done discussing this," he said, turning back to Faith.

She folded her arms on her desk. "We can discuss this all you want, but nothing you say will change the way I feel. I'm done supporting HASS in any way. I've seen where your hate leads, and I will no longer stand by and let it happen. I'm going to start speaking up for the Wrasa and their rights."

His jaw dropped. "You're turning against me?"

"No, Dad. I'll never be against you. If it feels like that to you, it just proves you made hate your number one priority."

Her father looked as shaken as if an earthquake had brought down every last one of his hotels. His Adam's apple bopped up and down, either because he was swallowing hard or because he was trying to speak, but nothing came out. Finally, he stumbled to the door and slipped past Sabina as if he barely even saw her.

His footsteps retreated down the hallway, slow and as heavy as Faith's heart felt.

Faith slumped against the back of her office chair. God, what had she done? She hadn't planned on saying all of that—she'd been too afraid of losing him. But once she'd started, the words had seemed to bubble up from deep inside of her, and she hadn't been able to stop.

Sabina entered the office and closed the door behind her. "Are you okay? What happened to your face?"

"I'm fine," Faith said, even though it was a lie. She touched her cheek. The swelling had gone down, but the skin was still a little tender. "Let's just say I had an unexpected meeting with a tree."

"The MacAllister family tree?"

"No. You know my dad would never hurt me. I literally walked into a tree." Faith lifted her hand, palm-out, to show her the bandage too.

"Got it. But what happened with your dad?" Sabina crossed the room and dropped onto the chair on the other side of Faith's desk. "I've never heard you argue with him before."

"I never have before." At least not a knockdown, confrontational argument like that.

Sabina leaned forward. "Was this about…Tala?"

"Yes. No. It's not just about her. To be honest, I think it was a long time coming." She had gone along with what her father wanted for too long, simply because she didn't want to upset him.

"So Tala had nothing to do with it?"

"She had everything to do with it," Faith murmured, more to herself.

Sabina leaned her elbows on the desk and studied Faith. "Everything, huh? Last time we talked about her, you insisted you weren't in love with her and were just having fun for the moment. Is it safe to assume that things have gotten serious between you two?"

The last time they'd talked about Tala had been less than two weeks ago, yet it felt like a lifetime. "It's…"

Sabina picked up a paper clip from the desk and threw it at her. "Don't you dare say complicated."

"I was about to say: It's not what you think." Faith flicked the paper clip back across the desk at her.

"What is it then?" Sabina asked.

Faith hesitated. How could she even begin to explain the situation and everything that had happened? Should she lie or at least skip over the fake part of her relationship with Tala?

But Sabina was her best friend, and she wasn't involved with HASS. Faith had detested having to lie to her, and she didn't want to continue. She made sure the door was closed before she said: "What I'll tell you now can't leave this room, okay?"

Sabina slid forward, onto the edge of her chair. "You don't have to worry about that with me; you know that. Now spill! What's going on?"

"Everything started about a month ago, when Tala approached me out of the blue and asked me to be her fake girlfriend."

Sabina clutched the edge of the desk with both hands. "Wait! What do you mean…fake? I watched the two of you together at the bowling alley! You two had sizzling chemistry. You even kissed! That wasn't all fake…was it?"

Faith glanced away. Then she forced herself to look at Sabina, and the entire story burst out of her like champagne from a bottle someone had shaken before opening.

Well, not the entire story. For now, she left out the part where her feelings for Tala had started to feel not so fake anymore.

When she finished her tale, Sabina was gaping at her. But there were no signs of judgment on her face, only astonishment. "You're kidding! You went undercover to spy on the shifters for your father, like a CIA operative or something?"

"On the Wrasa," Faith corrected. "Yes. Only I was the world's worst secret agent. Every attempt to plant a bug in Tala's apartment failed. If I'm honest, it was probably because I wasn't trying very hard. The more time I spent with Tala and then her family, the worse I felt about lying to them."

Sabina flopped against the back of her chair. "You don't happen to have any alcohol in one of those drawers, do you? I could really use a drink!"

"Sorry," Faith said. "HR frowns on the director of guest experience getting the conference services manager drunk on the company's dime."

Sabina chuckled.

"Besides, I haven't even told you everything yet. We..." Faith nibbled her bottom lip. "We kissed. And I'm not talking about that peck at the bowling alley."

"Yeah, I saw the photo." Sabina waved toward the glossy magazine Faith's father had left behind on her desk. "You kissed to sell your fauxmance to the paparazzi."

"No. I mean, yes, that time."

"That time? You mean...?"

Faith flushed from head to toe. She nodded. "Tala kissed me last night, when we were alone. Or I kissed her. I have no idea who started it. All I know is that we ended up making out on the couch, and if my father hadn't called..." Her blush intensified.

"So... your fake relationship isn't so fake after all?"

"It was supposed to be, but..." Faith shrugged helplessly. "Tala makes me laugh and tear my hair out and melt on the spot when I watch her with Chloe."

Sabina's mouth formed a silent *Oh*. "She met Chloe? You never introduce your dates to your daughter."

"It wasn't planned, but...yes. And they both acted as if they've known each other for years. Tala made pancakes this morning and—"

Sabina let out a playful whistle. "Ooh, so she stayed the night?"

Faith fought down another blush. "Not the way you think. She slept on the couch."

"But you wouldn't have minded if she knocked on your bedroom door in the middle of the night," Sabina stated with a smirk.

Faith lost her struggle. Her cheeks heated, which was all the answer Sabina needed.

Sabina sobered. "Hey, I want you to know I support you one hundred percent. I instantly thought you two made a cute couple when we went bowling, and I still think so. I've never seen you like this over anyone, not even when you and Jon first got together. What are you going to do?"

"Hell if I know." Faith sighed. "You've seen my father when he thinks it's all fake. What do you think he would do if it were real?"

"But you want it to be real, don't you?" Sabina asked.

Faith closed her eyes and whispered, "Yes."

A few hours later, Faith was at her desk, reading guest feedback. Online reviews were always a good distraction, no matter what was troubling her.

So far, she had already found two for her collection of most ridiculous reviews:

I subtracted one star because the bed was so comfortable that I overslept and missed my flight!

And: *Room service was too fast. I barely had time to get comfortable before my food arrived.*

Faith chuckled. Somehow, she couldn't see demands for slower room service and less cozy beds making it into her action plan.

A knock on the door interrupted her just as she was reading the last review.

"Come in," she called.

The door was opened, and one of the hotel's front desk employees lingered in the doorway. "This just arrived for you, Ms. MacAllister." He crossed the room and handed her a plain white envelope.

"Thank you." She waited until he had left, then turned the envelope over. Her name was printed across it in an unremarkable, professional font. There was no return address.

She took a letter opener from the top drawer of her desk and sliced the envelope open.

Inside was a single sheet of paper, which she pulled out and unfolded.

A quick glance showed no salutation, no friendly closing, and no signature. The entire letter consisted of only three short sentences:

Your beloved mate is a murderer. She killed several humans. If you don't believe me, ask her.

She stared at the words, trying to make sense of them. *What the…?* Who on earth would send her fabricated garbage like this?

Anger surged through her. She jumped up, hurried around her desk, and pulled open the door. "Thomas?"

The front desk employee had nearly reached the end of the hallway. He turned and gave her a questioning look.

"Do you know who sent the letter?"

He shook his head. "A bike messenger dropped it off."

"Thanks." She forced a polite smile, went back to her desk, and reread the letter.

The words blurred before her eyes, but by now, they had burned into her memory: *Your beloved mate is a murderer.*

Faith gritted her teeth. That accusation was as absurd as the guest reviews she had just read. The letter had to be the work of a Wrasa hater—someone who wanted to drive a wedge between her and Tala and stop her from speaking out for Wrasa rights.

But then again, whoever had written the letter had used the word *mate*. A Wrasa-hating human wouldn't have done that. It must have been a shapeshifter. But why would one of them lie and try to turn her against Tala? Even though not all of them approved of relationships with humans, they wouldn't sabotage her support for Wrasa rights.

Unless…

She clutched the letter opener until her fingers went numb.

Unless it wasn't a lie.

What if it was true?

No. It wasn't. It couldn't be.

But wisps of doubt crept in at the corners of her mind.

Tala was a Saru—a soldier. She had agreed to fake-date Faith because her superiors had ordered her to. What if she had also been commanded to kill humans? Would she have obeyed an order like that?

Her father's warnings echoed in her head: *Shifters are cunning, manipulative creatures! They're bloodthirsty killers!*

"Nonsense," she said loudly because she needed to drown out her father's voice. Just because Tala was a soldier didn't mean she was a cold-blooded killer.

Whoever had written that letter didn't know Tala as well as she did. Sure, Tala had a tough exterior, with a single-minded focus on her job, but those layers of fierceness and sarcasm concealed a loyal heart, an unexpected playfulness, and a deep sense of compassion.

Faith flashed back to the way Tala had held her as she cried, to the softness of her touch as she had put her hand on Faith's belly to ease the cramps, to Tala's patience as she had read Chloe a bedtime story.

No, Tala wasn't capable of such horrifying acts.

The letter held no evidence, just a wild accusation from a cowardly stranger who hid behind total anonymity. She wouldn't let it ruin all the progress Tala and she had made toward understanding each other and uniting their species in harmony.

Resolutely, she stuffed the letter back into its envelope. With trembling fingers, she fed it into the shredder and watched as the tiny blades tore into the paper until the hateful allegation dissolved into thin, unreadable strips.

But as much as she tried to unsee them, the words didn't disappear from her mind. *Your beloved mate is a murderer,* kept reverberating through her head.

It was her father's influence; she knew that. Tala had done nothing to deserve her distrust, and she felt guilty for wasting a single thought on that damn letter.

And yet that glimmer of doubt remained.

Faith was determined to snuff it out once and for all. But this time, she would go about it the right way. She had learned from the incident in the forest, where she had endangered the entire pack by sneaking around behind Tala's back.

She wouldn't make that mistake again. This time, she would come right out and tell Tala about the letter. Tala would laugh—that wonderful, playful laugh she seemed to show only Faith—and say: "Boy, whoever sent that letter has an amazing imagination. Maybe they should write for a TV show."

Or maybe her golden eyes would spark with indignation, and she would be as outraged as Faith was about this attempt to sabotage their relationship…um, alliance.

Once Faith heard the truth from Tala's own lips, she would finally be able to silence her father's voice in her head, and they could move on.

Her hand hovered over her phone. Should she call Tala right now?

Before she could decide, it rang.

Faith clutched her chest. *Jesus.* What a weird coincidence! Was it Tala?

She checked the caller ID.

It wasn't Tala. It was Tala's boss—Jeff Madsen. Why was he contacting her instead of Tala?

Faith's heartbeat sped up. *Don't be paranoid,* she told herself. She couldn't allow herself to fall back into her father's mindset, assuming all Wrasa had a hidden evil agenda.

Quickly, she accepted the call.

"Ms. MacAllister." Madsen's commanding voice boomed through the phone. "We haven't talked about next steps yet."

"Uh, next steps?"

"Where to take your relationship."

Faith's cheeks burned. Her entire body did as images flashed through her mind, showing her what might have happened if her father's call hadn't interrupted the make-out session on the couch. A breathy gasp escaped her.

"Ms. MacAllister? Are you all right?"

"Yes, yes," Faith said quickly. She fanned herself with her free hand. "I'm just not sure what you mean."

"I think we can consider phase one of Operation Make-Believe Mate a success. The two of you were very convincing, so the general public believes you and Tas Peterson are a happily mated pair."

Very convincing. Right. Faith didn't say anything, afraid her husky voice would give away why they had been so convincing.

"Now it's time to build on that by having you speak out for the Wrasa Rights Act," Madsen continued.

"Of course." An hour ago, Faith had told her father she would do just that. And she would—but first, she needed to get confirmation that the letter was nothing but a baseless accusation, with no foundation in reality.

"I was thinking it might be good for you and Tas Peterson to attend the Healing Hearts luncheon this weekend," Madsen said. "It's a fundraiser supporting the creation of hospital departments that specialize in treating Wrasa. It would be a great opportunity to show your support, and it's in DC. What do you think?"

The luncheon might indeed be a great opportunity—not only to show her support but also to tell Tala about the letter on their way to the event.

Asking her about it on the phone, as she had considered earlier, wouldn't have been the best approach. She needed to meet Tala face-to-face and see the truth in her eyes. Only then would she be able to laugh it off and put it to rest once and for all.

Faith didn't give herself time to reconsider. "That sounds like a great idea," she answered.

"Good. Tas Peterson will pick you up at noon on Saturday."

When the call ended, Faith sat staring at a tiny strip of paper that had fallen to the floor next to the shredder.

Her stomach burned as she tried to come up with a way to start that difficult conversation.

How did you ask the woman you had passionately kissed if she might, by any chance, be a killer?

CHAPTER 8

On Tuesday evening, Faith had just put Chloe to bed and was folding laundry in the living room when her phone rang.

The name *Jon* flashed across the screen.

Faith's stomach tightened. She hadn't heard from him since she had basically kicked him out of her house two days ago, after they had argued about Tala, and she didn't look forward to more of the same.

But he was Chloe's dad, and she couldn't ignore him.

She swiped her finger across the screen and lifted the phone to her ear. "Hi, Jon," she said, trying hard to sound calm and friendly.

"Hey." His voice was neutral, without any of the anger and fear from their last interaction. "I thought I'd call to talk about Chloe's birthday. It's coming up next month, and I have no clue what to get her. Any ideas?"

A relieved "oh" slid out before Faith could stop it. She had assumed he wanted to rehash their argument. "Um, sure. I have some ideas. I'm glad you're calling."

"I'm not going to lie," he said. "I'm still concerned about you associating with shifters when our daughter is around, but I'm trying to be civil for Chloe's sake."

It wasn't an olive branch toward the Wrasa, but Faith hoped it could be a start. Maybe with a lot of patience, she could eventually help him see past his prejudice.

"So, any ideas what to get her?" Jon asked again.

"Actually, yes." Faith bit her lip. "I know what she wants more than anything, but you're not going to like it."

"What is it?" He groaned. "Don't tell me it's a pony. I thought we talked her out of that last year."

Faith chuckled. Her gaze drifted to one of the framed photos above the fireplace, showing her, Jon, and three-year-old Chloe petting a miniature horse. They looked like a happy family. "We did. It's not a pony." She took a breath. "She wants a Wrasa Barbie."

A resounding quiet stretched between them.

"A…what?" Jon finally asked.

"A Wrasa Barbie. It, uh, can turn into a fox."

"I'm not buying her that!" His voice hardened.

Faith had expected that reaction. "That's okay," she said as calmly as possible. "I'm not asking you to. But I'm letting you know I'm getting her one."

"Come on, Faith! Don't you see how wrong that is? I thought we were on the same page when it comes to protecting Chloe, but ever since you started associating with one of them, you haven't been thinking clearly."

Faith didn't take the bait. Discussing Tala wouldn't get her anywhere. "What's the harm, Jon? It's a Barbie."

"She can have a Barbie—a normal one. Not one of those propaganda toys."

"Propaganda?" Faith echoed. "How is it propaganda to acknowledge that shape-shifters exist?"

"They're putting ideas in kids' heads, making them think shifters are harmless and fun when they're not."

Faith opened her mouth to tell him to check out the crime statistics—Wrasa were actually less likely to commit crimes compared to humans. They had tried hard to stay under the radar for centuries, and that meant avoiding any kind of trouble with the law.

But before she could, Jon said, "Look, I didn't call to fight with you. I just want to know what to get Chloe for her birthday. You know I can't be trusted to shop by myself."

Faith's lips curled into a reluctant smile. "Yeah, definitely not. I remember the model rocket kit you got her for her first Christmas after we divorced!"

"Hey, it was really cool!"

"Yeah, maybe for thirty-year-old Jon, but not for three-year-old Chloe!"

Jon made a sound halfway between a laugh and a groan. "Lesson learned. So, what else could I get her?"

"There's this unicorn backpack that she saw the other day," Faith said. "Bright pink, with sparkly sequins, ears, and a horn."

Jon sighed. "I'm going to find pink sequins all over my condo all year long, aren't I? Maybe the Wrasa Barbie wouldn't be so bad after all. Just joking," he quickly added. "Unicorn backpack it is. Anything to make Chloe happy."

Faith hoped that would be true going forward too. Maybe someday, it would include finally accepting the Wrasa.

For a moment, a companionable silence settled between them, even though the edges of tension still lingered.

"Oh, before I forget," Faith finally said. "I was going to call and ask you if you'd be able to take Chloe this Saturday. I know it's my weekend, but something came up, and Dad's going to be working, so he can't watch her." She decided against telling him she would be going to a luncheon with Tala, knowing it wouldn't end well.

"This Saturday? Sorry, I can't. I'm going fishing, and I've already booked the cabin, so I can't cancel. I decided a few weeks ago I needed to get away for a bit. Clear my head, you know?"

Maybe some time away would do him good. A weekend away from DC and his HASS buddies might help him see how far he'd gone down the wrong path and that he needed to step away from all the hate.

"No problem," Faith said. "I'll ask Sabina." If her best friend couldn't babysit either, at least she had a reason to put off asking Tala about the anonymous letter.

"You okay?" Jon asked. "You sound…I don't know. A little strange."

"I'm fine." No way would she tell him about the letter.

"All right. Please send me a pic of that sparkly unicorn backpack, so I don't get the wrong one."

"Will do," Faith said. "Have fun with the bass and the catfish."

"Thanks." His voice softened. "Have fun doing…whatever. Good night."

"Night, Jon." Faith ended the call and slid the phone back onto the coffee table.

Fun wasn't exactly what she expected for Saturday, but if the letter turned out to be a hoax—as she suspected—at least she would be able to put her mind at ease once and for all.

CHAPTER 9

ON SATURDAY AT NOON ON the dot, Tala stood on the top step leading up to Faith's town house. As she rang the doorbell, her stomach fluttered, and it wasn't because all her senses were on high alert in case Faith's can-throwing neighbor was around.

Part of it was the anticipation of seeing Faith again, but mainly, it was the thought of somehow having to find out if she was still spying on them.

The door swung open, but instead of Faith, her best friend Sabina stood in front of Tala.

"Hi, Tala. Good to see you again." Sabina looked her up and down. "You clean up nicely."

Tala brushed one hand down her pantsuit. "Thanks," she said with a regal nod. "Um, will you be joining us?"

Sabina laughed. "No, don't worry. You'll get Faith all to yourself. I'm just here to babysit Chloe. Faith is upstairs, trying to convince Chloe to take a nap."

That wasn't why Sabina's unexpected presence had worried Tala, of course. If Faith's best friend had joined them, it would have been harder to find out the truth.

The click of heels coming down the stairs drew her attention. A few seconds later, Faith rounded the corner and walked toward them.

Her ankle-length, off-the-shoulder dress left her collarbones and the elegant line of her neck exposed. The deep-red satin was cinched at the waist, accentuating her hourglass figure. The welt on her cheek from last week had either fully healed or its faint remnants were expertly concealed beneath a touch of makeup, which gave her skin a flawless appearance. Her long chestnut hair cascaded in gentle waves over her shoulders. In the sunlight, it shimmered with a reddish glint, making it look almost like a foxtail.

Foxtail? Great Hunter, now you're losing it. But Tala couldn't stop staring, especially since every other step Faith took revealed a glimpse of her toned leg through a thigh-high slit in the dress on one side. Together with the stiletto heels Faith wore, it had a devastating effect on Tala's libido.

Tala swallowed hard. She clutched her car keys and struggled not to forget everything else—like the fact that Faith might still be working for HASS. *Shit.* Being a proficient Saru really was a lot easier if you weren't attracted to the person you were supposed to be investigating.

"Hi," Faith said softly as she stopped in front of Tala. Her smile seemed shy, almost nervous.

Did this feel too much like a real date for her too?

"Hi." Tala cleared her throat. "You look beautiful."

The loveliest blush rose up Faith's chest, and Tala could follow every inch it traveled. "Thank you. You look pretty good yourself." Faith's gaze raked over Tala and lingered on the deep V-neck of her buttonless blouse, sending a shiver through Tala.

If Faith really was still spying, at least she seemed to struggle with the same problem Tala did.

After several moments of them staring at each other, Tala remembered that Sabina was watching them.

They had to keep up their roles as mates, so she moved closer, put one hand on Faith's hip, and placed a short kiss on her lips.

The fabric of Faith's dress felt as smooth as she imagined the skin beneath it to be, and it took all of Tala's willpower not to trail her fingers over it.

Faith went very still, as if she hadn't expected to be kissed. Then she leaned into the contact, and the kiss lingered.

Their mate scent wrapped around Tala like an intoxicating embrace. Was it possible that it had gotten even stronger since she had last seen Faith on Monday? It was so potent that it even drowned out the mate scent perfume Faith had put on.

Good thing Tala had used a touch of the fragrance herself so her scent would match Faith's.

She forced herself to break the kiss, let her hand slide away, and step back so she could think clearly, even though every cell in her body ached to stay close.

It hit her again like an ice-cold wave. This wasn't just any mission, and Faith wasn't just any human target. She was her mate. The thought that she might have lied to Tala, betrayed her and her entire species…

But maybe she hadn't. Tala clung to that hope. Faith was here, dressed to the nines, ready to head out to the charity event. She hadn't made up an excuse for why she couldn't go. That was a good sign, right?

Quiet steps came down the stairs, and Chloe's popcorn-and-honey scent wafted over moments before she snuck around the corner.

When she saw Tala, her eyes lit up with a pure, unguarded joy that made Tala's heart swell in a completely un-Saru-like way.

"Tala!" Barefoot, Chloe ran forward and flung herself at her.

Tala bent down and caught her in a gentle embrace. "Hi, Chloe." She ruffled the girl's tousled curls.

Chloe finally released her from her tight hug and peered up at her. "Can you come and play hide-and-seek with me? If you shift, you can hide under the bed!"

Faith put her hand on Chloe's shoulder and gently guided her away from Tala. "No hide-and-seek, sweetie. You're supposed to take a nap."

Chloe's bottom lip stuck out in the cutest pout ever. "But I'm six, Mom!" She held up six fingers. "I don't need naps anymore!"

"You do if you barely slept the night before," Faith replied. "If you go back to bed, Auntie Sabina will read you a nap-time story."

"Okay," Chloe replied without any real enthusiasm.

"Oh, will she?" Sabina muttered, but she was grinning as she looked back and forth between Tala, Faith, and Chloe.

"Yes, she will," Faith said. "Because she'll find a box of her favorite Belgian truffles in the fridge as a reward."

Sabina's grin broadened. "Ooh, bribery. Works for me."

Faith held up her index finger in a silent warning. "Don't let her—"

"Skip the nap or eat too many sugary snacks. Don't worry, Momma. I've got this. You two go have fun." Sabina winked at them, but Tala was too tense to tease Faith about her insistence that humans didn't wink.

Faith didn't make a joke about it either.

"Come on, little one." Sabina held out her hand to Chloe.

With a dramatic sigh, Chloe took it, but when Sabina led her away, she tugged her fingers free, ran back to Tala, and hugged her again.

Swallowing, Tala put a hand on her shoulder. Great Hunter, as if the mate scent hadn't been bad enough. Now Faith's pup had to show her, too, how hopelessly entangled she had become.

She had completely lost her objectivity and would have to remind herself of that all afternoon.

Chloe let go, hugged her mom, then ran back to Sabina. With one last wave, she disappeared around the corner. "Can you read me Winston's story?" her voice trailed back downstairs.

Tala and Faith had both watched her go. Now they turned toward each other.

Faith licked her lips. "Sorry. She was supposed to be napping."

"Never apologize for a great pup like Chloe," Tala said. "Ready to go?"

Faith nodded. She grabbed a red clutch from an entryway table.

As they crossed the courtyard, Faith was strangely silent. Their usual banter was absent.

Tala peered at Faith and caught her glancing over too, then quickly away.

Was Faith merely reacting to the tension she felt from Tala?

She didn't think so. Something was off about her today. Faith fidgeted with her clutch and kept sneaking glances at Tala out of the corner of her eye—lingering looks that weren't just about admiring Tala's pantsuit or the cut of her blouse.

Tala tried to decipher what those looks meant but couldn't. It was as if Faith was trying to find the answer to a question she didn't dare ask.

"Is everything okay?" Tala finally broke the silence.

"Oh, yeah, yeah, of course." Faith nearly stumbled over the words.

That only convinced Tala something was going on.

Mirella's words came back to her—about how jumpy Faith had been when she had caught her in the kitchen.

Could that be why Faith was so nervous now too? If she had indeed planted a bug that night, she probably knew by now that it had been destroyed. She knew they were on to her.

Tala inhaled deeply, hoping to catch a whiff of Faith's scent so she could figure out what exactly she was feeling.

But Faith had put on what seemed like half a bottle of the perfume. In combination with the real mate scent, it was a double whammy that hit Tala's nose—and her heart—with the force of a sledgehammer.

Had Faith splashed on too much of the perfume by accident, or was she trying to hide her emotions from Tala, making it impossible to catch her in a lie?

The accidents were starting to pile up. Faith might have *accidentally* dropped the bug in the kitchen, then *accidentally* put on too much of the scent-covering perfume...

Tala the Saru didn't believe it for a second. Tala the woman…the mate desperately wanted to.

When they reached the narrow stairs that led down to street level, she paused to let Faith go first.

As Faith passed her, she brushed against Tala, sending goose bumps up and down Tala's body. Faith visibly shivered too.

Was she feeling the same white-hot sizzle? Something else seemed to flicker in Faith's eyes too…something that resembled the way Faith had looked at her when they had first met at the parade—as if she wasn't quite sure whether Tala was friend or foe.

Instantly, Tala wanted to reach out and comfort her. This afternoon was supposed to be a test for Faith and her loyalty, but now it was starting to feel more like a test for Tala's professionalism—and she had a feeling she was failing miserably.

She wanted to forget about this damn test and just trust Faith, and that was highly unusual for her.

As she followed Faith down the stairs, the silence between them was thick, like a fog Tala couldn't see through.

For the first time, Tala was searching for words—anything to draw Faith out. "Did I tell you my brother and his mate will attend the luncheon too?"

"Which one?" Faith's voice was high-pitched, as if she wasn't asking merely out of curiosity.

"Rey and Mirella. As you can imagine, Wrasa health care is a cause Rey is passionate about."

Faith's shoulders stiffened—a subtle reaction Tala might have missed if she hadn't spent so much time with Faith and weren't so attuned to her body language.

Why would Rey's and Mirella's presence make Faith tense up? While Rey had been an asshole for most of their visit with the pack, that didn't justify being afraid of him.

Was it because Mirella was a Saru?

Faith nodded but didn't give a verbal reply.

"A few local reporters will attend too," Tala continued. "We thought maybe this would be a great opportunity for you to say a few words in support of interspecies marriage or our rights in general. Not up on stage—afterward, when the reporters are swarming, looking for a few sound bites from attendees."

"Sure," Faith said. "If all goes well, I can totally do that."

If all goes well? Her conditional response was less than reassuring.

What had become of the woman who had passionately defended Tala to her neighbor…who had even stood up to her father on Monday? Or had it been a lie when Faith had texted to tell her about the argument she'd had with her father?

When they reached street level, Tala pointed the key fob at her car and unlocked the doors.

But before she could walk over and open the passenger-side door for her, Faith paused in the middle of the street and turned toward her. "Tala, I…"

Tala's gaze flew to hers. "Yes?"

Faith's lips parted as if she was about to finally explain.

A car honked behind them.

Faith jumped.

Tala let out a startled growl and pulled Faith out of the way.

As the car drove past, she searched Faith's face. "What is it? What were you about to say?"

"Nothing," Faith said quickly. "Let's go before we're late." She slipped into the passenger seat and closed the door between them before Tala could follow up with another question.

Tala stood still for a moment and stared at her through the window. Her heart sank. Clearly, Faith was hiding or at least not telling her something, and Tala could no longer ignore that it probably involved her spying activities for HASS.

A vise seemed to squeeze around her chest as she sank into the driver's seat. The woman next to her—her mate—had most likely betrayed her.

She couldn't take her to the luncheon like this. The risk of Faith saying something to the reporters that would harm the Wrasa's cause was too great.

Tala had thirty minutes to either convince Faith to support them…or figure out what she would do if she refused.

They drove along K Street, with only the sounds of traffic and the windshield wipers interrupting the silence. When Faith had gotten dressed for the luncheon, the early May morning had promised sunshine, but now the sun had disappeared behind thick, gray clouds, and it had started to rain as soon as they had gotten into the car. The insistent tap-tap-tap against the windshield matched the hectic beat of Faith's heart.

She glanced over at Tala for the dozenth time, trying to find a way to broach this difficult topic.

Tala looked different today.

The sleek, wolf-gray pantsuit hugged her lithe frame just enough to hint at the lean muscle beneath. The deep V-neck of her white blouse draped open whenever she leaned forward, revealing a hint of cleavage. Was she even wearing a bra?

Jesus, you need to get confirmation that she didn't kill anyone, not find out what kind of lingerie she's wearing!

Faith cursed herself for chickening out and not asking earlier—and for needing to ask at all. She hated treating Tala like the enemy she had once assumed her to be. Shouldn't she be able to brush this off as a silly note sent by a troublemaker?

But she couldn't. The letter had struck at her deepest fear, and if she wanted even a sliver of a chance to move forward with Tala, she needed to bring it out in the open.

The question was just how. Was there a way to ask Tala about the contents of the letter without sounding as if she still thought of her as a monster?

Tala seemed equally ill at ease. Her outfit wasn't the only thing different about her today. Faith had sensed it as soon as she had come downstairs and laid eyes on her.

Tension appeared to coil in Tala's body. She sat ramrod straight, her grip on the steering wheel tight. Whenever traffic allowed, she kept glancing over at Faith. Her gaze was wary, probing. Was Faith becoming paranoid, or was Tala eyeing her with suspicion?

"Is everything okay?" Faith finally asked.

"Yes, of course," Tala answered without missing a beat, but Faith could tell she was lying.

Nothing seemed okay anymore. The easy rapport they had developed was gone, replaced by the old wall of mistrust.

Once again, her father's voice in her head got louder: *Shifters are cunning, manipulative creatures.*

"Shut up!" Faith firmly told it.

Tala's head jerked around. "Um, pardon me?"

"Oh, no, no. Not you! I meant—" Heat rose to Faith's cheeks. God, she was a mess. She lifted her hands to hide her face, then realized she was about to smudge her makeup and dropped them back to her lap. "I meant…you seem a little…off today. Distant."

"Me?" Tala sent her an incredulous look. "You're eyeing me like you expect me to pounce on you or something! Even with the perfume, I can tell you're as twitchy as a cat in the middle of a wolf pack! What's going on?"

Crap, was it that obvious? Good thing she had given up her attempts at spying on the Wrasa. She sucked at this undercover operative game.

"I got a letter," Faith blurted out. *Ugh.* She hadn't meant to say it like that, but now that she had, she couldn't stop the words from bubbling out of her. "I know it's complete and utter nonsense, an obvious attempt to break us up…um, I mean…to destroy our cooperation."

Tala frowned. "What letter? I don't understand. Who sent it?"

"I don't know. It wasn't signed."

"What did it say?" Tala asked.

Faith looked away, unable to face Tala as she gave voice to this silly accusation. She watched raindrops trace erratic paths down the windshield and whispered, "That you…" The words caught in her throat, and she had to clear it before she could continue. "That you killed humans."

The car swerved for a moment before Tala regained control.

A much-too-loud silence filled the space between them.

Faith waited without breathing.

In a second, Tala would laugh at the ridiculousness of it all. Or growl at the stranger who had dared drag her name through the mud.

But not a single sound came from the driver's seat.

Slowly, Faith turned her head.

Tala had gone pale. Anguish twisted her usually composed features. Anyone else might have missed it, but to Faith, it was clear as day.

Cold sweat prickled at the back of Faith's neck. *No, no, no, no.* It wasn't true. It couldn't be true!

"Faith…" was all Tala said in a strangled whisper.

With that one word, Faith knew. "Oh my God! It's true! You killed someone."

"Faith, please, I can explain."

"Explain what?" Faith's too-shrill voice reverberated through the car. "Cold-blooded murder?"

"No! No, it wasn't like that. It… I…" Tala's knuckles blanched as if the bones were about to pierce the skin.

A roaring sound filled Faith's ears as thoughts and images crashed through her mind. "W-what about me?" she got out in a strangled whisper. "What if I refuse to keep playing your mate? If I tell the reporters my father was right all along? Are you going to—" Her voice broke, but she forced the words out. "Are you going to kill me too? And Chloe?" Her heart slammed against her ribs as she rasped out the last two words.

"What? No!" Tala winced hard. She gave Faith a look so stunned, so full of pain as if Faith had stabbed her in the heart. "Never! Great Hunter, Faith, I would never harm you or Chloe in any way. I couldn't." Her voice was choked with emotion.

She sounded so sincere.

For a second, Faith's heart betrayed her—she believed Tala. *No! Don't let her trick you again. They're master manipulators.*

"Faith, please. I can't explain it here. Let's go to my apartment and talk."

Go to her apartment? Faith let out a hysterical laugh. She might be naive but not that naive. Everyone knew what would happen if you let a killer lure you back to their place. "Stop the car!"

"No, Faith, I can't—"

"Stop the car, or I'll call the police!" Faith tore open her clutch and grasped her phone. Her hands trembled so badly that she nearly dropped it. She managed to unlock it with a few shaky swipes and pressed the 9, then the 1. Her thumb hovered threateningly over the last digit.

A helpless growl escaped Tala. "Don't. Please. You're making a big mistake, and this time, you won't be able to take it back. If you press that digit, you won't just hurt me. You'll hurt every Wrasa. My mom and dad. Sutton. Arlyn and—"

Every name hit Faith like an arrow. "Stop the car—now!"

At the next red light, Tala brought the car to a screeching halt next to a sidewalk.

Get out! Faith mentally shouted at herself. Her breath came in ragged bursts. She fumbled with the seat belt, but the clasp kept evading her damp, trembling fingers. The phone slipped out of her hand and tumbled onto the floorboard.

Shit, shit, shit!

Just as she bent to find it, the seat belt finally came free. She threw open the passenger-side door and jumped out without pausing to retrieve the phone.

Rain hit her immediately, like icy needles on her overheated skin.

"Please, Faith!" Tala shouted after her through the still-open passenger-side door. "I swear I would never hurt you. Please don't betray us!"

Faith didn't stop. She darted through the puddles and fled down the sidewalk as fast as her stilettos would allow on the slick pavement.

To either side of the street, office and apartment buildings towered over her, offering no refuge. Not a single person braved the relentless rain.

She was on her own.

Lungs burning, she skidded around the corner, into a smaller one-way street—where Tala couldn't follow in the car—and kept running until Tala's panicked shouts faded behind her.

CHAPTER 10

THE PAST FEW MINUTES HAD been a blur of wet pavement and frantic driving as Tala combed the streets, looking for Faith. She had thought about leaving the car behind and running after her, but there wasn't a free parking spot in sight, and abandoning the car in the middle of traffic would alert the police.

Tala's skin burned with the need to shift, and it took all of her willpower to keep it at bay. No time to give in. She had to find her!

The windshield wipers were struggling to keep up with the rain, which had turned into a downpour. Tala could barely see a thing—worse, she couldn't follow Faith's scent trail because the rain had washed it away.

Faith was out there somewhere, drenched, alone, and scared—of her! The expression on Faith's face right before she had fled was burned into Tala's memory. The fear, the betrayal…

She pushed the thought away. *Think, Tala! Think!* Where would Faith go?

Not back home. Tala knew that for sure. Faith wouldn't risk putting her daughter in danger.

She also couldn't call the police because she'd left her phone behind. Tala had picked it up and turned it off so it couldn't be tracked.

Where else would Faith feel safe? There was only one place—one person—Tala could think of: Peter MacAllister.

The thought of him finding out made her stomach churn. She didn't want to believe Faith would tell her father everything, but she couldn't rule it out. Faith was panicking. She probably felt betrayed, as if Tala had misled her on purpose the entire time. Maybe she would even revert back to thinking of all Wrasa as the enemy.

Still driving in ever widening circles around the side street Faith had disappeared in, Tala jabbed at a button on her car's dashboard to activate the Bluetooth, then tapped the top contact.

The sound of the ringing phone echoed through the car, making Tala very aware of every second ticking by.

"Tas Peterson," Madsen's voice finally came through the speakers. "Shouldn't you be at the charity event?"

No time for long explanations. "I need MacAllister's home address."

"Why? What happened?"

Tala's heart raced. She hesitated. If she told him everything, would he give the kill order, as he had in the past, before they had revealed their existence to humans? This time, she wouldn't follow the order. She wouldn't harm a single hair on Faith's head. But she couldn't keep what had happened from him. "Faith found out we…I killed humans. She panicked and ran."

"What?" Madsen's voice boomed through the speakers, drowning out the screech of the windshield wipers. "And you just let her go? Do you have any idea what you've done?"

Fire flared along Tala's arms. Her hands shook around the steering wheel as she struggled to control herself and not shout back. "I didn't *let* her. She threatened to call the police. What was I supposed to do? Kill her?" She roughly shook her head, even though Madsen couldn't see it. "No. I'm done with that."

"Did I say anything about killing her? Try talking to her first! Assure her you've never killed anyone."

Tala hadn't even tried to say that. Apparently, she had lost the ability to lie to Faith. "She knows me too well, sir. She saw the look on my face and just…knew."

"Then at least make her understand they weren't senseless murders!"

"You think I didn't want to?" Now she was shouting, but she no longer cared. She hadn't missed how he had phrased his answer: Try talking to her *first*. That meant he didn't rule out giving the kill order! "But if she's really still spying for her father, I had to assume that she was wearing a wire. I couldn't speak freely. That's why I suggested we go to my apartment, where I could have scanned her, but that only made her panic more."

"Find her!" Madsen snarled. "Drag her back to your apartment and offer her whatever she wants in exchange for her silence. If this gets out…"

He really didn't understand humans—or at least not Faith. "We won't be able to bribe her, sir. Not with money."

"Then offer her something else. The truth about her mother."

Tala sucked in a breath. "Do you know something I don't? I've started to look into it, but it's a case that happened over twenty years ago, and the medical examiner doesn't remember it."

"No, but I'm the council speaker. If anyone can find out what happened, it's me."

"Okay." Tala shakily blew out her lungful of air. "But Faith isn't our only problem, sir. Someone sent her a letter, saying I killed humans. Only a Saru would know that. We've got a traitor."

"Impossible," Madsen said firmly. "No Saru has an interest in turning Ms. MacAllister against us. They'd be digging their own grave."

True. Tala took her foot off the gas a little while she thought furiously. "Maybe they didn't want to turn her against us. Maybe they wanted to turn her against *me*."

"A personal vendetta?" Madsen asked. "Have you made any enemies among the Saru?"

Tala could think of only one who might bear a grudge against her: Mirella, her brother's mate.

Her future sister-in-law hadn't liked her ever since Tala had broken up with Lasandra, and that wasn't the only reason Mirella might try to split her and Faith up. She and Rey seemed to think Tala had gotten involved with Faith only to increase her chances of becoming natak.

The timing couldn't be a coincidence either. The anonymous letter had been sent only days after their visit with the pack.

But she didn't voice her suspicion. She couldn't afford to accuse the wrong person, especially since it would harm her own pack. Besides, for now, finding Faith took priority.

"If I think of anyone, I'll let you know. But first, I have to find Faith. Can you send me her father's home address?"

"I just sent it to your phone," Madsen said. "You'd better get there before she does. Peter MacAllister can never find out, do you hear me?"

"Loud and clear, sir." Especially since he was shouting. "I'll let you know as soon as I find her." She ended the call, glanced at the address Madsen had sent her, and pressed her foot on the gas.

Faith dashed down the sidewalk without taking the time to veer around a puddle. Cold water splashed up her legs. Her stilettos slipped on the slick pavement, and she nearly fell. Gasping, she caught herself against a parked car and ducked behind it to catch her breath.

Apartment buildings rose up to her right, while a row of historic brick houses stretched to the left. The neighborhood might usually bustle with activity, but now the tree-lined street lay deserted, and the broad sidewalks were eerily empty.

The rain had turned into a downpour, matching the avalanche of emotions pelting down on her.

It had all been a lie. Tala's tenderness, the bond that had seemed to grow between them… All just a trick to manipulate her. The thought sent a fierce ache through her chest. How could she have been so naive to ignore her father's warnings and fall for Tala's clever scheme…possibly even fall for her?

As much as Faith didn't want to admit it, she did have feelings for Tala—and the worst part was that they hadn't gone away, now that she knew the truth.

Her heart still stubbornly refused to believe that Tala was a cold-blooded killer. A part of her wondered if she should have stayed and listened to whatever Tala had to say. Maybe there was a reasonable explanation for what Tala had done.

But then again, what reasonable explanation could there be for killing innocent humans? If there was one, surely Tala would have explained right then and there. Instead, she had stammered something about going to her apartment—a delay tactic rather than a valid defense.

Clinging to the hope that there was more to the story was probably naive. Was she letting Tala manipulate her again?

Faith couldn't tell anymore.

She scanned the street for any signs of Tala or her car.

Nothing moved. Except for her, no one was out in this weather. She was on her own, without anyone to turn to for help.

Her feet ached, and her lungs burned, but she forced herself to keep going.

A gray awning provided a momentary cover from the rain. *River Inn*, the sign above the sliding glass doors said.

A hotel!

It was smaller than her father's flagship hotel she worked in, but the familiar sight of a lobby promised safety.

Faith veered toward it.

The glass doors slid open, and she stumbled inside.

The jarring contrast between the cold rain and the danger outside and the cozy atmosphere inside made her shiver.

Two guests—probably waiting for the rain to let up—gaped at her, and Faith was very aware what a sight she must be. Her drenched dress clung to her body. Water dripped from her hair onto the floor, and the rain had most likely turned her makeup into a smeared mess.

She felt the weight of stares on her, but she ignored them as she crossed the small lobby.

The single employee manning the front desk looked up from his computer. His eyes widened as he took in her disheveled appearance. "Ma'am, are you all right?"

Faith opened her mouth, then snapped it closed, not sure what to tell him. Should she ask him to call the police?

But something held her back. Tala had told her before that calling the police never ended well for the Wrasa. The thought of armed officers hunting Tala twisted her gut. No matter what Tala had done, she couldn't do that. Her father would probably call her gullible, but she still cared.

"Would you call me a taxi? I…had an accident and lost my phone." For now, she just wanted to get away from here, to somewhere safe, where she could think.

The front desk agent appraised her as if searching for injuries. "Do you need an ambulance?"

"No, no, just a taxi, please."

"Of course." He reached for the phone.

Faith wrapped her arms around herself, trying to ward off the chill that had nothing to do with her drenched dress.

A minute later, the front desk employee lowered the phone. "The taxi will be here any minute."

"Thank you." She walked away to wait closer to the exit.

Now she had to decide where she wanted the taxi to take her.

Home was out of the question. Despite all the doubts running through her mind, she did believe Tala when she'd said she would never hurt Chloe. But why take the risk of dragging her daughter into this?

She would go somewhere else, where she would be safe while she figured out her next steps.

Only one destination came to mind—her father's office. She knew he was there, working, even though it was the weekend.

A part of her wanted to reject the idea of turning to him for help. She had distanced herself not only from his stance on the Wrasa but also from him in the last few weeks, no longer sharing important things about her life with him.

But despite the growing distance between them, she knew one thing with unshakable conviction: he would always keep her safe.

She would decide what to tell him when she got there.

Tala bit back a curse as MacAllister's house came into view. Faith's father couldn't have picked a worse place to live. The prestigious neighborhood sat on a hill, its streets not following the grid layout that defined the rest of the city.

Clearly, only the power brokers and political elites could afford to live here. Tala had passed several embassies on her way up, and right across the street was a residence flying the French flag, with a replica of the Statue of Liberty on the front lawn. It was probably an ambassador's home or something.

Several discreet black SUVs with tinted windows were parked along the curb, and a man in a suit leaned against one of the white columns, smoking a cigarette. His posture was relaxed, but Tala didn't miss the way his gaze zeroed in on everything that moved in the vicinity.

Shit. Getting Faith out of this neighborhood without attracting attention would be next to impossible. One wrong move and the area would swarm with police, private security, and maybe even Secret Service agents.

She circled the block and examined MacAllister's austere brick mansion from all sides. Nothing moved, and the large driveway was empty.

It wasn't raining as heavily in this part of the city—barely a light drizzle. Tala rolled the window down, stuck her head out, and inhaled deeply.

The odors of rain, asphalt, and cigarette smoke filled her nostrils. Not a hint of Faith's milk-and-honey aroma or their mate scent hung in the damp air.

Even Peter MacAllister's sharp peppery scent, which she remembered well from the parade, was hard to discern, the aroma merely a faded trace, as if he hadn't been home since early this morning.

Where on earth were they? Was it possible Faith hadn't fled to her father after all?

Tala had been so sure that was where she would go.

Maybe she had. Faith had told her once that Peter had been a workaholic when she was growing up, barely leaving the office except to go to church, even on weekends. What if he was at work, and instead of coming here, Faith had gone straight to his headquarters in Arlington, while Tala had detoured to his residence?

"Dammit!" Tala slammed her fist against the steering wheel and sped toward Arlington as fast as she dared.

CHAPTER 11

THE RAIN HAD STOPPED BY the time Faith climbed out of the taxi in front of the towering glass-and-steel office building. Thankfully, she had dropped only her phone but still had the clutch with her credit card so she could pay the cabbie.

Her father's car was in the parking lot.

Faith had expected to feel relief, but instead, a heavy mix of dread, doubt, and confusion settled in her belly.

When she entered the lobby, Toby—the security guard who'd worked for her father since she'd been a child—looked up from the news program on his small TV.

He stared at her damp dress and smeared makeup for a moment before jumping up from behind his desk. "Are you all right, Ms. MacAllister?"

Faith forced a reassuring smile. "I'm fine, Toby. Just forgot my umbrella at home."

"Ah." He sat back down. "Do you want me to get you a towel?"

"No, I'm fine. Is my father upstairs?"

Toby nodded.

"Thanks." She walked past him to the elevator and made her way to the top floor.

The outer office was empty, the hum of the air conditioner the only sound. Her father had always insisted that his employees enjoy their weekend and didn't come in, even if he spent almost every Saturday working.

As she got closer, the faint tapping of her father's keyboard drifted through his office door.

She walked over, knocked softly, and opened the door. "Dad?"

He sat behind his antique oak desk. The reflection of his computer screen in the large window behind him showed an Excel spreadsheet. "Faith?

What are you doing here?" He glanced up from his work, and a look of alarm crossed his face. "What happened? Are you all right?"

"I'm fine," Faith choked out.

He got up from behind his desk, rushed to the executive bathroom adjoining his office, and returned with a towel, which he pressed into her hands. "Here."

"Thanks." Faith half-heartedly dabbed it over her arms, chest, and hair, but her attention wasn't on what she was doing. Her mind was still racing in circles as she tried to grasp what had happened and reconcile the Tala she had gotten to know with what she had found out about her.

"Tell me what happened," her father said, his voice urgent.

She hesitated. If she told him, there would be no going back. Whatever she said next had the power to change the world—to destroy Tala's life and affect all Wrasa—Tala's warm, welcoming mom, her gruff but soft-hearted father, Sutton, Arlyn, Kiera, Lasandra, Felix, Jasper the bellhop, and all the aunts, uncles, and cousins.

In the past month, she had witnessed the discrimination and sometimes even violence Wrasa were facing. If she revealed Tala's secret to the public, it would get so much worse.

Humans would treat all Wrasa like killers, and Faith couldn't believe they were.

Even Tala wasn't a monster. If she had wanted to harm Faith, she could have done it in the car.

Would that count as mitigating circumstances? Would Tala get a chance to defend herself in court? Would law enforcement, the judge, and the jury treat her fairly, give her a chance to tell her side of the story?

You didn't even give her that chance! What makes you think they wouldn't shoot first and ask questions later?

And maybe quite literally! Militias, hate groups, and people like Faith's neighbor were just waiting to take matters into their own hands.

This time, they might attack Tala with something worse than a can of Coke.

Her stomach lurched.

"Faith," her father said, his voice sharp as if he had already called her name several times without getting a reaction. "What happened?"

Please don't betray us! Tala's desperate voice echoed through Faith's mind.

"I...I got caught in the rain." What was she doing?

But she knew it was the right thing. She couldn't live with herself if she condemned an entire species.

The Wrasa deserved better—and Tala deserved a chance to explain.

"In that dress? Where were you?" Her father walked around his desk, took the suit jacket from the back of his chair, and carried it toward her. "Here, put that on." He held it out to her, still several steps away.

Before Faith could think of an answer, a sharp crack made them both flinch. The window behind her father exploded inward. Glass shards flew everywhere.

Her father staggered and went down.

"Dad!"

He clutched his arm. Blood seeped through his fingers, staining his shirt. Someone had shot him!

Faith dropped to the floor. Her gaze darted to the shattered window, trying to find out where the shot had come from, but she couldn't make out the shooter.

Her father struggled to get back up, a dazed look on his face.

"Stay down!" Faith shouted and crawled over to him. A shard of glass sliced into her knee. She bit down on her bottom lip to stop herself from crying out and kept crawling until she reached him.

"Are you hurt?" he got out between gritted teeth, his face tight with pain.

"I'm fine." But he wasn't. Faith stared at the bloodstain on his sleeve growing bigger and bigger.

She grabbed the towel from around her shoulders, wrapped it tightly around his arm, and clenched both hands around it, applying pressure.

A grunt of pain escaped him.

Faith's knee throbbed, and blood stained her fingers, but she ignored both. She had to get him to safety. "Dad, can you walk? W-we need to move!"

Her father grimaced but gave a curt nod.

Faith slung his good arm over her shoulder. With their heads down, they stumbled out of the line of fire and took cover behind the solid mahogany bookcase along the wall to her left.

By the time her father slid down and sat propped against the side of the bookcase, they were both breathing hard.

The towel had gotten loose, and Faith wrapped it more tightly around his arm, then pressed his good hand on top. "Where's your phone?"

"On my desk."

"Hang on." Crouched low, knees shaking, she dashed over to the desk.

There! Her father's phone sat next to his coffee mug.

She lunged for it, every muscle tense, expecting another bullet to tear through the broken window any second.

But everything stayed quiet as she dropped back to the floor and crawled to her father's side.

Her heart slammed against her ribs so hard that she thought she might pass out.

With trembling fingers, she entered the code—her birthday—to unlock it, tapped 911 for the second time that day, put the call on speakerphone, and wrapped her hands back around her father's arm.

The ringing of the phone seemed to stretch on forever, even though it probably lasted only a few seconds.

"911, what's the address of your emergency?" a calm female voice sounded through the phone's speaker.

"I... It's..." Faith could barely think. For a second, the address eluded her, then she blurted it out in a shaky rush. "I need help! Somebody shot my dad! Oh God, what do I do?"

"I understand; your dad's been shot," the dispatcher repeated. "What's the phone number you're calling from?"

"Uh... 202-555-78—no, wait!" This wasn't her phone. Her dad's number—what was it? Her pulse pounded in her ears as she tried to remember. "It's 202-555-46...um...12. Please, please, hurry!"

"Help is already on the way," the dispatcher said, her tone reassuring. "Can you tell me exactly where your father was hit, and if you have anything to put pressure on the wound with?"

"His arm—his upper arm! There's so much blood!" Faith's voice cracked. "I-I wrapped a towel around it, and I'm pressing down, but I don't know if I'm doing it right."

"You're doing exactly the right thing," the dispatcher replied. "Can you tell me how it happened?"

Faith swallowed, her mouth dry. "We were in h-his office, on the top floor, and someone shot through the window. The bullet...it...it went right through, and there was glass everywhere, and then my father fell, and I realized he was hit."

"Are shots still being fired?" the dispatcher asked.

Faith shook her head, jerky and frantic, then realized the operator couldn't see her. "No. Just the one."

"Is the shooter still nearby?"

"I-I don't know." She peered through the shattered window but couldn't make out anything. The world outside seemed unreal and distant. "I didn't see anyone. I think they're in the building across the street. The—the Lockridge Center. How much longer? Where's the ambulance?"

"Stay calm. They're getting close." The dispatcher's soothing voice cut through Faith's panic. "Are you in a safe location, out of the line of fire?"

Faith struggled not to hyperventilate. "I-I think so. I pulled him behind a bookshelf."

"Very good. Is he conscious and breathing normally?"

His breathing was fast and shallow, and his pupils were wide as he stared at her with an unfocused gaze that frightened her as much as the blood.

"Yes, but it's so fast! And he's still bleeding." The wet warmth of his blood coated her fingers. "I'm pressing down on the wound as hard as I can."

"You're doing an amazing job," the operator replied, her voice calm. "Keep applying pressure. Don't lift the towel. How old is your dad?"

"He's, uh, fifty-nine." Faith pressed down harder, making him groan. "Hang on, Dad. The ambulance will be here any second."

"How about you, ma'am?" the dispatcher asked. "Are you hurt?"

"N-no. I'm fine. I think." Faith could hardly even feel her own body, except for the sting in her fingers from pressing down hard.

"What's your name?" the dispatcher asked.

"Faith. Faith MacAllister."

"You're doing great, Faith. Are there any other victims you're aware of?"

"No…no, just him."

"Is there anyone else in the building?"

"Not on this floor. Toby is downstairs, in the lobby. Uh, the security guard. But I don't think he heard the shot from down there. God, I hope he doesn't come up here and put himself in danger. He's almost seventy!" She realized she was rambling and snapped her mouth shut.

"Can you call him and tell him to secure the doors until the officers arrive?" the dispatcher asked.

Faith had only ever seen her father call security by using the landline in his office. She eyed the distance between their hiding place and his desk. The few steps across the shard-littered floor seemed like an unbridgeable chasm. "Not without using the desk phone, which is right in front of the window."

"No," the dispatcher said immediately. "Stay where you are. We'll get the number and call the security guard."

Faith exhaled. "Okay."

"The officers will be there soon. I'm going to stay on the phone with you until they arrive."

Faith kept applying pressure, even though her hands started to ache.

Her father sat slumped forward. He was pale and sweating, and his breath came in shallow gasps. Faith tried not to think about how much blood he was losing.

"Please, please, hang in there," she whispered to him or to God or to both.

"Not much longer now," the dispatcher said. "Keep the pressure on. They're almost there."

Every second seemed to last an eternity as Faith crouched next to her father, hands wrapped around the blood-soaked towel.

The dispatcher kept talking to her, encouraging her and asking questions about the layout of their floor to help the police and the EMTs reach them faster. The words blurred together, but the reassuring tone helped Faith fight down her panic.

After what seemed like an eternity, the distant wail of sirens drifted in through the broken window.

"Please, please, hurry!" Faith whispered.

The sirens quickly grew louder, then cut off.

Faith strained her ears, listening for the ding of the elevator. After another eternity, the sound of heavy boots echoed up the stairwell instead.

"Police!" a deep voice shouted from the other side of the door.

"Here!" Faith shouted back, relief making her sway on her knees. "We're in here!"

The door flew open, and several officers stormed in, guns drawn. They moved swiftly, immediately taking cover so they wouldn't be in the line of fire. Two of them advanced toward the shattered window from an angle. They peeked out, then signaled to someone in the neighboring building. "Clear!"

A radio crackled. "No visual on the suspect," a distorted voice replied. "Suspect has fled the scene."

As soon as the police had given the all clear, two paramedics rushed into the room. "We've got it from here." One of them gently eased Faith's fingers away and took over applying pressure while his colleague set up their equipment.

Faith slumped onto the floor as her adrenaline slowly drained away. She whispered a "thank-you" to the dispatcher and ended the call but gripped the phone as if it were a lifeline.

Within minutes, the paramedics had secured her father on a stretcher and carried him out.

Faith immediately followed them on unsteady legs, but one of the officers tried to stop her. "Ma'am, we need a statement before you leave. Can you tell us anything about the shooter?"

"You can get my statement at the hospital. I'm going with my father." She tried to push past him, refusing to leave her father out of her sight for even a second.

The officer stood his ground. "We need details to secure the area. Did you catch a glimpse of the shooter? Any idea of who he might be?"

"I didn't see anything. Someone fired through the window, hitting my father. That's all I know. Please, can I go now?"

The officer hesitated.

"Let her ride with us," one of the paramedics called. "She needs to go to the hospital to get checked out anyway. Her knee probably needs stitches."

Faith glanced down.

The paramedic must have caught a glimpse of her knee through the thigh-high slit in her dress, which had shifted when she'd moved.

She pulled the fabric apart just enough to get a better look.

Blood dribbled down her leg from a cut right below her knee.

Amidst the chaos, Faith had barely noticed the pain while she had focused on helping her father, but now it started to throb.

Finally, the officer stepped aside and let her through.

As she caught up with the paramedics in front of the elevator, her father opened his eyes and mumbled, "It was the shifters. Tell them it was the shifters."

Tala slowed the car as the headquarters of Hearthstone Hotels and Resorts loomed ahead of her. The logo at the top of the high-rise building—an H encased in a circle—was visible from blocks away.

Two police cruisers were parked at an angle in front of the building. Their emergency lights flashed, creating red and blue reflections on the glass-and-steel facade.

The entrance had been cordoned off with yellow crime scene tape. Several people—some in uniform, some in suits—stood near the entrance.

More police cars and a SWAT van were parked in front of the building across the street.

The entire block felt as if it was on lockdown.

Oh shit! Tala immediately pulled over, into a narrow space between two parked cars, close enough to observe but far enough away not to draw the police's attention.

What had happened? Had Faith told her father everything, and he had called the police?

But half a dozen police cars and a SWAT van in front of two buildings looked like something else.

Besides, a part of Tala still clung to the hope that Faith wouldn't alert the authorities.

Not that she could blame her if she had. Faith had to be terrified and feel horribly betrayed. She probably assumed Tala was an evil murderer, as her father kept telling her.

No matter what her heart said, Tala couldn't risk sticking around.

Just as she was about to get out of there, a knock sounded on the passenger-side window.

Tala's head whipped around.

A silver-haired man in a security guard uniform stood next to her car. He motioned for her to roll down the window.

Damn. She had been so focused on the police officers that she had missed him approach. Where had he come from?

Heart racing, she lowered the passenger-side window and hastily tried to come up with an excuse for why she was there. Should she pretend to be a curious bystander who wanted to know what was going on?

"Hey, I know you!" He pointed his finger at her.

How on earth could he know her? She was sure she'd never seen him before.

"You're Ms. MacAllister's girlfriend, aren't you? The Wrasa."

Tala hesitated. But he had said *Wrasa*, not *shifter*, so he clearly wasn't a hater. "Yes, I am. Do we know each other?"

"No. I'm one of Hearthstone's security guards. My granddaughter follows you on social media. Her boyfriend is a wolf-shifter, and she's so happy to see another out and proud Wrasa/human couple that she shows me pictures of you and Ms. MacAllister all the time."

It was great to meet a human who supported his granddaughter's relationship with a Wrasa, but Tala didn't have time to dwell on it. She gestured at the police cruisers. "What happened?"

"Oh hell, I'm so sorry! Here I am, going on and on about my granddaughter when Ms. MacAllister… There was a shooting."

The word knocked the air from Tala's lungs. "What? Is Faith okay? Where is she?" The steering wheel groaned beneath her desperate grip. A burning sensation shot down her spine, then turned into a piercing ache that engulfed every bone and joint. She struggled to fight down the first signs of an impending transformation.

"She and Mr. MacAllister were rushed to the hospital," the security guard answered. "I don't know much more. My shift was over, so the police took my statement and told me to go home."

"Which hospital?" Tala rasped.

"Uh, I think someone said Virginia Hospital Center."

She had passed a sign for VHC earlier! Tala didn't wait. Without taking the time to close the window, she pulled out of the parking space, did a U-turn, and accelerated down the street. She didn't even care whether the police noticed her speeding away. All she cared about was getting to Faith, making sure she was okay, protecting her from whoever had hurt her.

The rainy streets blurred all around her as vivid images of Faith lying in a puddle of blood flashed through her mind.

No! This couldn't be happening! Faith had to be okay!

She tried to fight down her rising panic and distracted herself by focusing on the attacker. Who would shoot Faith and her father? Who had a reason to hurt them?

Madsen!

He must have given the kill order, sending another Saru to silence Faith because he knew Tala would refuse to carry it out.

A menacing growl reverberated through the car. She would skin him alive!

She stabbed at her dashboard and hit Madsen's contact.

"What in the Great Hunter's name did you do?" she snarled as soon as the call connected.

"What are you talking about?"

His denial only fueled the fire raging inside of Tala. "Don't act like you don't know! You had Faith *shot*!"

Madsen let out a low, startled sound. "Someone shot her? Is she dead?"

"I… I don't know." Tala's voice broke on the last word, her worry piercing the protective layer of her fury. "Why don't you ask the Saru you sent to kill her?"

"I did not send anyone!" Madsen's booming voice made the speakers vibrate. "If I did, I'd be more subtle than shooting her!"

Tala forced herself to drag in a deep breath, then another. He was right. Snipers drew too much attention. A random stabbing or something that looked like an accident was more the Saru's style.

If it hadn't been him, then who had shot Faith and her father?

It couldn't be a coincidence that someone had tried to kill the MacAllisters right after Faith had received an anonymous letter, revealing that Tala had killed humans.

Was the shooter the same person who'd sent the letter?

Every bit of evidence pointed at Mirella. She was in DC today, and as a Saru, she knew how to handle a gun, even though it wasn't their usual weapon of choice.

Maybe she had realized she had gone too far when she had sent the letter, endangering not only Tala but all Wrasa. Had she planned to silence Faith at the luncheon, and when Faith hadn't shown up, she had managed to hunt her down?

Tala didn't have the time to put together all the puzzle pieces. If Mirella had gone rogue, she wouldn't stop until she had killed Faith. Tala floored the gas pedal. "I have to go!" she shouted and ended the call.

Her car sped across an intersection just as the light turned red. She had to get to Faith before Mirella could show up at the hospital to finish the job!

CHAPTER 12

Faith's entire body ached with exhaustion. As the weight of everything she'd been through that day crashed down on her, she slumped against the back of the plastic chair in the hospital waiting room. The harsh fluorescent lights and the sharp odor of disinfectant made her head throb.

At least her leg was still numb from the local anesthetic. A doctor had put in a few stitches just below her kneecap.

The hallway outside the waiting room bustled with activity—nurses, doctors, and other medical staff walked past. At least one police officer still hung around, maybe waiting for her father to make it through surgery so he could take his statement.

Or maybe he was guarding her dad so the shooter couldn't try to kill him again.

Faith's pulse sped up at the thought that the person who'd shot her father was still out there and might try to harm him again.

For the first time, she was glad that Violet and Noah were keeping her company. Several HASS members had dropped by earlier. Faith had no idea how they had found out about the shooting—maybe her father's group had contacts within the police force. Everyone else had left again, but Violet and Noah were glued to her side.

Noah paced the waiting room, drawing glares from several people. Every squeak of his shoes spiked Faith's headache. "It was the shifters! They must have found out you were using your fake rela—"

"Shh!" Faith pressed a finger to her lips and sent him a warning stare. "Would you shut up about that in public?"

Noah ducked his head. "Sorry." He lowered his voice to a whisper. "I was just trying to say that they must have found out you've been spying on them, and that's why they tried to silence you and Peter."

"That doesn't make sense. Whoever the shooter was, they fired a single shot," Faith murmured, trying to be the voice of reason despite her own fears. "That's hardly the way to silence *two* people."

Noah opened his mouth for a reply.

Faith held up her hand. She couldn't deal with this right now.

Since the medical staff had rushed her father into surgery an hour ago, her thoughts had returned to the question of who had shot him again and again, but she hadn't come up with an answer.

Nothing made sense anymore—not since she had fled Tala's car.

If it had been the Saru, wouldn't they have been more likely to shoot *her* than her father, trying to stop her from telling him about the letter? At first, she had considered that she might have been the real target and the shooter had hit her father by accident, but if that was the case, surely they would have fired more than one bullet.

"Please, Noah." She sent the bulky guy a pleading look. "Speculations won't help anyone. Can we wait until we hear what the police have to say and focus on my dad for now?"

"Of course." Noah continued his pacing. After another lap around the waiting room, he paused in front of her. "Can I get you anything? Water, coffee, something to eat?"

He had asked her the same question twice in the last ten minutes. His concern was touching, but also a little suffocating. Faith couldn't remember the last time she had eaten—could barely remember what day it was. The mere thought of food made her queasy, and she knew she wouldn't be able to stomach coffee either. "No, thanks, Noah. I'm fine."

"Do you want me to call Jon?"

"I already tried calling him, using my dad's phone, but he didn't pick up," Faith said. "He said something about going on a fishing trip this weekend. I'll try again as soon as Dad is out of surgery."

She would also have to call Sabina in a minute and ask her to stay with Chloe for longer than expected. But she wanted to have some privacy for that call because she wasn't sure she could tell her best friend what had happened without breaking down.

Noah nodded and resumed his pacing. The squeaking of his shoes on the linoleum grated on her already frayed nerves until she couldn't stand it anymore.

"Actually," Faith said, "some tea would be nice."

Noah beamed, clearly relieved at having been given something to do. "Of course. I'll be right back." He hurried down the hallway.

Violet smiled at her. "Phew. Thanks. I thought he'd wear a hole in the floor with his pacing."

Faith tried to smile back, but it felt like a grimace. Her hands wouldn't stop shaking, and as she stared down at them, she detected traces of her father's blood stubbornly clinging beneath her fingernails, even though she'd scrubbed them earlier. She curled them into fists so she wouldn't have to see it.

"Hey." Violet reached over and squeezed Faith's tightly clenched fist. "He'll be okay. Peter is tough. He's been through worse."

Her touch was soothing, but it felt all wrong. Her hand was too large. Too cool.

Faith realized she had gotten used to Tala's slim hands and her higher body temperature.

How she ached to curl up in Tala's arms, the way she had in Silver Falls, and feel safe again. But Tala was the last person she could ever feel safe with…or at least she should have been.

"Did I ever tell you how I met your father?" Violet asked.

Faith looked over and met Violet's eyes. Their color matched her name. "No. Tell me," she said, eager to hear something that had nothing to do with gunshots, surgery, Tala, or this messed-up day.

"It was a couple of years ago, on Friday the thirteenth, actually. I was having the worst day. I'd gotten a flat on my way to work, right during rush hour. But I'm a modern woman, of course,"—she winked at Faith, making her think of Tala again—"so I thought: No problem, I've got a spare. I'll be on my way within minutes. Except when I went to grab the jack, it was missing."

"Ugh," Faith said.

"Yeah. I called AAA, but they took their sweet time. No one else stopped to help. Maybe I looked too intimidating." Grinning, Violet indicated her six-foot frame, wide hips, and soft belly. "Finally, this black luxury sedan pulls up behind me, and out climbs Peter, in an expensive suit and tie. He rolled up his sleeves, got a jack out of his trunk, and changed my tire."

A rush of warmth went through Faith. That sounded exactly like her dad. She could almost see him kneel in the dirt, not caring that he got grease all over his hands.

"And the best part," Violet continued, "was that he got a phone call halfway through. He put it on speaker and had an entire business conversation about some conference while he was jacking up my car, like it's the most normal thing in the world!"

They both chuckled, and Faith's headache eased.

Footsteps approached.

Faith looked up immediately, hoping to see a doctor with news about her father.

Instead, a police officer in uniform stood in front of her. "Ms. MacAllister?"

"Yes?"

"Sorry to bother you. This won't take long. I just have a quick question." He held up a clear evidence bag. Inside, something metallic glinted under the harsh light. "The Bureau of Shape-Shifter Affairs has already run the ID number through their database, but just to confirm… Can you tell me if this looks familiar to you?"

It was a silver chain with a small, round stainless-steel tag. Of course Faith instantly recognized it—it was a set of the ID tags Wrasa were forced to wear at all times.

"We found this at the scene," the officer said. "In an empty office across the street from your father's building. It's likely where the shot came from. We believe the shooter lost it while fleeing the scene."

A Wrasa had shot at them?

"I knew it!" Violet slapped her hand down on her thigh. "It was a shifter!"

Faith studied the ID tag and caught the engraving on the thin piece of metal. It was the capital letter F.

For fox-shifter.

No.

No!

Tala would never hurt her. The shooter had to be another fox-shifter.

But how many fox-shifters in DC had a reason to silence Faith and her father? How many were trained Saru soldiers?

With the Wrasa making up only one percent of the population, there couldn't be many. Probably just one.

The off-white walls of the waiting room seemed to close in on her.

A sharp pang of nausea rolled through her. Faith stumbled to her feet. "Excuse me. I need a minute," she whispered and bolted past the officer toward the nearest restroom.

Tala skidded into a parking space at the back of the hospital lot, flung the driver's side door open, and jumped out of the car. Her only thought was getting to Faith as fast as possible. *Please, please, Great Hunter, let her be okay!*

Before she could take more than a few steps, a figure lunged from behind a nearby car and tackled her.

The air was knocked from Tala's lungs as she slammed onto the asphalt. For a moment, she lay there, dazed, the weight of her attacker pinning her down.

"Stay down, or they'll see you!" a female voice hissed into her ear.

Mirella!

She had come to finish what she had started and kill Faith!

A blaze of fury ignited deep within Tala. With a wild growl, she twisted around and threw a punch as hard as she could. Her fist hit Mirella's jaw and sent her sprawling sideways.

Pain exploded in Tala's knuckles. Her entire body trembled with the effort to keep her human shape. The fox clawed for release, ready to tear into the person who had hurt her mate. She lunged at Mirella, trying to pin her down, and raised her fist to deliver another blow.

"Stop!"

It was Rey's voice.

So her own brother was in on it too? That betrayal sliced deep, but Tala couldn't focus on it now.

He grabbed her from behind and yanked her up, off his mate, who scrambled back and struggled to her feet.

"Let me go!" Tala snarled.

But Rey held firm. "What the fuck are you doing? If you touch my mate again, I'll kick your ass from here to Silver Falls! We're here to help you!"

"Cut the crap. You're here to kill Faith." She twisted in his grasp so they were face-to-face and bared her teeth in a fierce growl. "That'll happen over my dead body!"

"Kill Faith?" Rey looked as stunned as if Tala's right hook had hit him, not Mirella. "What in the Great Hunter's name are you talking about?"

With Rey standing so close, blocking her from landing another punch, the scent of his confusion was so strong that Tala could easily smell it, even through the sharp odors of sickness and disinfectant that wafted over from the hospital.

The tightness in her chest loosened a little. He was telling the truth! He had no idea—at least not about this part of Mirella's plan. "Why don't you ask your mate?"

Rey turned toward Mirella. "You don't know what she's talking about either, do you?"

"I don't. I never pretended to like Faith, but that doesn't mean I want her dead."

Tala huffed. "Right. You'd be inconsolable if something happened to her. And, of course, you also don't know anything about the letter."

"What letter?" Rey asked. "You're making no sense."

"Someone sent Faith a letter, telling her I killed humans. Which, unfortunately, is the truth."

As a Saru's mate, he might have already had his suspicions, but he still stared at her.

"But only a Saru would know that," Tala continued. "And I can think of only one with a personal grudge big enough to risk revealing it to a human. Your mate! Mirella had the knowledge and the motive! Afterward, she probably realized the consequences of what she'd done and tried to clean up her mess by shooting Faith and her father!"

"Shut up!" Rey's eyes blazed. "You've spent too much time among humans, and it's messing with your head."

"If you don't believe me, have Mirella swear she's innocent, and then take a good long whiff of her."

"I don't need to sniff her to know she didn't do any of those things!" Rey turned to face his mate. "Tell her again so *she* can take a whiff, and then let's get out of here before the police catch us!"

Mirella held out both hands. They were trembling. "Rey, I…"

A wave of exhaustion overcame Tala. Why was she standing here, discussing this, when all she wanted was to see Faith and keep her safe? "Just come clean, Mirella. Admit that you shot at the MacAllisters and—"

"No!" Mirella desperately looked back and forth between her and Rey. "I admit I sent the letter, but I swear I didn't shoot anyone. You've got to believe me!"

Tala's heartbeat thundered in her ears, and she struggled to rein in her anger so it wouldn't trigger a shift. So it was true. Mirella was behind the letter. The traitor was part of her own pack. The realization left a hollow feeling in her chest. "Do you have any idea what you have done? Faith was our best ally—our biggest chance in our fight for equal rights! You not only sabotaged that but risked exposing the Saru's secret to the world!"

"Best ally?" Mirella let out a sarcastic laugh. "If she'd wanted to speak up for our rights, she'd have done so already! She'll never take a public stance against her father."

"She certainly won't do it now, after what you did!" Tala's heart ached at all they had lost—all *she* had lost. She desperately tried not to think that she might have lost Faith for good. *No! Faith is alive. She has to be alive!*

"I didn't want to do it, but you forced my hand," Mirella muttered.

"Me?" Tala pressed a hand to her chest. "How did I force you to send that letter?"

"You're blinded by your feelings for her! First, you naively believed her when she claimed she followed us into the woods to warn us, when it's more likely she was in cahoots with her father's goons. Then you stubbornly insisted Faith couldn't have planted the bug."

Tala squinted at her. "There never was a bug in the kitchen, was there? You lied about that too."

Mirella hung her head. "It was necessary."

Tala's head spun. Faith hadn't planted a bug. She wasn't still spying on them for her father. She was fully on their side—or had been, until Mirella had messed it all up.

"Why?" Rey whispered. The protective growl was gone from his voice. Now he just sounded defeated. "Why would you do something like that, Mirella?"

"I did it for you, nemi!" Mirella sent him a pleading look. "You were there for everyone in the family for years, working hard to make sure the pack was thriving. Then Tala shows up with a surprise mate no one has ever heard of, and wouldn't you know it, the little human manages to win over everyone! After they left, all everyone talked about wasn't our twere or how we managed to unite the packs—it was Tala and her new mate and their bright future!"

Tala couldn't believe what she was hearing. "You destroyed our fragile peace with the humans because you were jealous?"

"No! I did it because you don't deserve to be natak. Rey does." Mirella clutched his hand, but Rey pulled away. "He's what's best for the pack. He was there for them every single day, including during the chaotic time right after Kelsey outed us to humans. Where were you when the pack needed you most?"

Tala's stomach churned. As much as she hated to admit it, Mirella was right about this one thing. She hadn't been there for the pack, too scared they would blame her for not stopping Kelsey.

"You didn't show your muzzle for an entire year," Mirella continued, "and then thought you could just show up and claim the position as your father's successor because you're the great peacemaker who'll marry MacAllister's daughter!"

Tala stared at her. "You risked the future of our species to secure your and Rey's personal ambitions?"

"I never would have asked you to do that, Mirella," Rey said in a rough whisper.

"But you deserve it! Being natak is the only thing you ever wanted."

Rey tilted his head. "Maybe. But if that's the price, it's too high."

"You're both blowing this out of proportion," Mirella said, her voice shrill with desperation to make them understand. "The risk is so small, it's basically zero. I didn't send Faith any evidence. All she has is a wild accusation from an anonymous letter. Even if she goes public, we can make it look like she's just bitter and out for revenge after an ugly breakup. The human press eats up shit like that."

How could she downplay what she had done? Tala gritted her teeth. "What do you think the press will write about the leader of HASS and his daughter being shot by a Wrasa?"

"That wasn't me! Do what you told Rey to do and use your nose if you don't believe me!"

Tala had avoided breathing through her nose. The hospital smell was too overpowering, even from across the parking lot. Now she carefully stuck out her neck and sniffed.

Mirella's scent was a complex mix of components, most of all desperation, guilt, and a fierce loyalty toward her mate. The only thing absent was the sulfurous odor of a lie.

She was telling the truth. She hadn't shot Faith. Which meant...

A gasp escaped Tala. Someone else was after Faith! The shooter might still be out to kill her, and Tala had no idea who they were. Mirella had been the only person she could think of.

She had to get to Faith and protect her!

Her fists clenched. The lengthening nails dug into her palms as she shoved Mirella out of the way and stormed toward the hospital entrance.

"Tala, wait!" Mirella rushed after her and clutched Tala's arm.

With a growl that promised bloodshed, Tala whirled around. "If you don't take your paw off me this second, I'm going to rip out every single finger and ram them down your—"

"Stop!" Rey thundered with the authority of a future natak. "We really are here to help you."

"No matter what you might think of me, I'm good at my job," Mirella said. "I made a lot of connections over the years—including connections in the police force. That's how we found out someone shot at the MacAllisters and which hospital they were taken to."

"We tried to call and warn you, but the call went straight to voicemail, so we rushed here, knowing that's where you'd be heading as soon as you found out," Rey added.

"Warn me of what?" Tala asked.

"The cops are looking for you," Mirella said. "They think you shot the MacAllisters."

Tala froze. "Me?" Great Hunter, did Faith think that too…provided she was even conscious? She had to get to her—now!

But Rey and Mirella blocked the way.

"Listen," Mirella said quietly. "I know I went too far. But I swear I want to help you."

"We need to get you out of here," Rey added urgently. "We can smuggle you to Silver Falls, and you can hide with the pack. I promise we'll keep you safe."

Being safe meant nothing if Faith wasn't. Tala wrenched her arm away. "No. I'm not running. I need to protect Faith."

"There are cops everywhere! HASS and security guards too!" Rey gestured toward the entrance, where a police officer chatted with someone from security. "They'll arrest you before you can even set foot inside the hospital."

"I don't care." Tala dropped her voice to a low growl. "I'll get to Faith or die trying."

Mirella bit her lip.

She and Rey locked eyes for a moment before Rey slowly nodded and said, "We'll help you get in."

Tala didn't trust Mirella one bit, but as the human saying went, she wouldn't look a gift horse in the mouth. "How?"

"They probably all know what you look like, but they don't know me." Mirella took a deep breath. "Be right back." Without another word, she strode toward the hospital and disappeared inside.

"Don't judge her too harshly," Rey said quietly. "She did what she thought was best for the pack. Best for me."

"Frankly, right now, I don't care what she thought," Tala replied, her attention on the entrance. "If Faith dies…" Her voice cracked. In the past, she would have hated to sound so vulnerable in front of Rey, but now she didn't care about that either.

"You really love her, don't you?" Rey gently touched her shoulder. "When you showed up with her in Silver Falls, I admit I thought for a second it might all be fake. Just a ploy to secure your position in the pack."

If only he knew. "She's my mate, Rey. Nothing about that is fake." Great Hunter help her, it was the truth.

He squeezed her shoulder. "We'll get you to her."

They waited in silence, his hand on her shoulder, until—minutes later—Mirella reappeared. She had traded the dress she had worn to the charity luncheon for a set of scrubs and was pushing an empty wheelchair. "Here." She handed Tala a mask. "Put this on, and pretend you're sick."

"That won't help much if the guards take a closer look at me," Tala said as she slid it over her mouth and nose. "We need to distract them somehow."

"One distraction, coming right up." Rey discarded his suit jacket and rolled up his right sleeve.

"What are you doing?" Tala asked.

"Remember how people always stare at my arm? For once, it'll come in handy." Rey led the way toward the entrance.

Tala hunched over in the wheelchair and tugged the mask up to cover as much of her face as possible. *Ugh.* The mask reeked of chemicals and synthetic materials. Having to rely on Mirella, who pushed her forward with steady hands, made her skin itch, but she had no choice.

Rey headed straight toward the security guard and the police officer he'd been chatting with. Right in front of them, he pretended to stumble.

"Whoa!" The security guard caught him, and both men helped to steady him.

"I'm so sorry! My balance isn't the best since I had the accident." Rey raised his right arm, which ended above the elbow. "I have an appointment for a prosthesis fitting. Could you tell me where to go?"

While everyone stared at his limb, Mirella pushed Tala past them and through the doors.

The stench of the hospital felt suffocating, even through the mask. Tala's nerves buzzed, and she tensed, expecting someone to shout out and point at her any moment.

But no one paid her any attention.

Mirella bent down. "Where to?" she whispered.

"Let's try the ER."

They veered to the right, and Mirella wheeled her down a busy hallway with signs pointing toward the ER and the OR.

Rey quickly caught up with them.

A whiff of something familiar hit Tala's nose.

Faith!

Was her milk-and-honey scent real, or was her imagination playing tricks on her?

But the scent seemed to get stronger with every step Mirella took.

Tala sat up straighter in the wheelchair, all senses on high alert.

Someone rushed around the corner, heading straight toward them.

Great Hunter, Faith!

Her chestnut hair was wild and tangled, and rust-red smears marred her ankle-length, crimson dress at knee-height. She walked with an awkward stiffness, one leg held ramrod straight. The metallic odor of blood clung to her, and dark shadows smudged her eyes, yet to Tala, she was the most beautiful woman she'd ever seen.

Faith was alive—hurt and exhausted, but alive! Tala wanted to howl and shout it to the sky! She gripped the arms of the wheelchair, resisting the urge to leap up and sprint down the hallway toward her.

But she couldn't blow her cover now that she had gotten so close.

As fast as Faith had appeared, she veered to the left and rushed into a restroom.

"Go," Tala said to Rey and Mirella. "Get out of here."

They hesitated.

"No," Rey said. "We won't leave you behind. We're all getting out of here together."

"I'm not getting out of here. Not before I've had a chance to talk to Faith."

"We'll wait for you right here," Mirella said. "Just in case it doesn't go well. If she thinks you shot at her and her father, she might not want to hear you out. She'll scream for help, and then all hell will break loose."

That was a risk Tala would have to take. The thought that Faith could believe she had shot at her cut deep, but she couldn't really blame her. Shots being fired at them the day Faith found out Tala had killed humans probably looked like too much of a coincidence.

Whatever Faith thought of her now, Tala had to find a way to make her understand.

"Fine," Tala said. "But don't come in. I need to earn back Faith's trust, not make her think there are now several Wrasa coming after her."

Mirella gave a terse nod. "If we see someone coming, we'll knock on the door."

"Thanks. But don't think this makes up for everything you did." She sent Mirella a fierce glare, then made sure no one was watching before jumping out of the wheelchair and pushing through the door of the restroom.

CHAPTER 13

Faith barely made it to the restroom before her stomach heaved violently. Bile rose in her throat. She pressed her clutch to her belly as she retched into the nearest trash can.

Then soothingly hot, comforting hands were there, holding her, gently brushing errant strands of hair away from her face, rubbing her back in slow, steady circles until her body calmed.

Faith leaned into the familiar warmth. Slowly, the painful heaving stopped, and she rinsed her mouth at the sink. Then her brain caught up with what her body had already sensed: Tala was here! She spun around, her heart thundering in her ears.

Tala stood in front of her. A mask covered the lower half of her face, but the look of utter relief in her golden eyes was unmistakable. "Thank the Great Hunter you're okay!" Her gaze swept over every inch of Faith's body, then paused on the thigh-high slit in her dress revealing a glimpse of Faith's bandaged knee. She furrowed her brow. "Well, more or less okay."

For a second, the same relief flooded Faith—that Tala was here, had made it through the police and HASS presence outside unharmed.

Then the events of the past few hours came crashing back—finding out Tala had killed humans; fleeing from the car; her father collapsing to the floor, bleeding; the police showing up with what might be Tala's ID tag…

She zeroed in on the V-neck of Tala's blouse. The place on her chest where the ID tag normally rested was empty.

The tag the police had found at the crime scene had been Tala's.

Faith's stomach twisted again. She tried to jump back, away from Tala, but the sink stopped her. She opened her mouth to let out an alarmed shout.

Tala leaped forward and pressed her hand to Faith's mouth. "Please don't scream." She pulled Faith into one of the stalls and pushed the door shut behind them with her knee.

Faith struggled and tried to wrench her head away, but Tala was stronger, her grip firm yet careful, as if she was reining in her strength to avoid causing harm.

"Please, Faith," Tala whispered into her ear. "I know all of this looks bad, but I swear I didn't shoot your father, and I'm not going to hurt you. I'll let go of you in a second, but you've got to promise not to scream. Please give me a chance to explain. That's all I ask for. Just give me two minutes. If you don't believe me then, I'll walk out of here and surrender to the police." The raw, pleading look in her eyes pierced through Faith's panic.

She stilled in Tala's gentle grasp and nodded. She didn't have much choice, but more importantly, she wanted to hear what Tala had to say, hoping beyond hope that Tala had an explanation that would prove her innocence.

Tala instantly took her hand away.

Faith knew she could call for help now. Violet, Noah, the police, and security would storm in within seconds. They would wrestle Tala down, draw their weapons, and if Tala—cornered and desperate—shifted or attacked, they might shoot her like a rabid animal.

No! Faith shoved the mental image away. Everything pointed to Tala having shot her father, and yet Faith didn't want to believe it—didn't want to see her hurt…or worse.

Tala pulled down the mask as if hoping Faith would be able to read the truth on her face. "Whatever the police told you, I swear it wasn't me," she said with urgent intensity. "I didn't shoot at you or your father. Please, Faith, you've got to believe me. I would never hurt you—not even by hurting your father. I wouldn't do that to you. I love you."

They both froze. For a moment, everything around them seemed to stop. Even the annoying drip-drip-drip from one of the faucets faded away.

Faith's heart gave a strong thud.

Tala touched her lips as if she couldn't believe what had just come out of her mouth.

I love you. The words seemed to echo through the restroom.

Her confession and the sincerity in Tala's eyes set off an ache in Faith's chest.

A spark of joy—small and hesitant—wanted to flicker alive inside of her, but she smothered it. This was too much—too many emotions to untangle, most of them confusing.

She couldn't deal with it right now, so she instead chose to ignore the revelation and focus on everything else Tala had said.

I swear it wasn't me.

Faith wanted to believe her so badly. But her rational mind—or maybe her father's voice in her head—screamed at her to be careful. She had seen the ID tag, laid out before her as evidence. "But your ID tag…" Her voice shook. "The police found it in the building where the shot was fired."

"What?" Tala wildly shook her head. "I was never there, Faith. I lost my tag days ago and haven't had a chance to get a replacement from the Bureau of Shape-Shifter Affairs. I know it sounds like the least convincing excuse ever, but it's the truth. When we were packing our bags, preparing to leave my parents' house, I put the tag in my pants pocket. I forgot all about it because of everything that happened once we returned to DC, and when I got home the next morning, it was gone. I thought I'd lost it when your neighbor attacked me, but I never got around to telling you."

Faith flashed back to earlier, when Tala had picked her up. Now that she thought about it… Tala hadn't worn the ID tag then either. Faith knew because her gaze had trailed over every inch of bare skin revealed by the deep V-neck of Tala's blouse.

Maybe she was telling the truth. Was it possible that Tala had lost the tag and someone else had found it and planted it at the crime scene? She stared into Tala's eyes, searching for the truth.

Tala looked away. "Or maybe I was too much of a chickenshit to tell you because…" She bit her lip. "Your necklace was lying on the nightstand next to my ID tag. In all the chaos, you forgot to put it back on before we left Silver Falls, so I slipped it into my pocket along with my tag. It's gone too. I lost your mom's necklace, and I'm really sorry."

Faith's hand went to her throat, but it was bare. Of course it was. She had chosen not to wear the necklace today because of what Tala had told her about the Wrasa's experience with Christianity and the cross. "Wait. My necklace isn't gone. I found it in the laundry room when I got home from work on Monday evening."

A rapid knock sounded on the restroom door.

Faith froze.

"That's my lookout," Tala whispered. "Warning me that someone's coming!" With animal-like instincts, she leaped up onto the toilet so her legs weren't visible beneath the stall door. Gently, she grasped Faith's shoulders and directed her around until her feet faced away from the toilet, making it appear less conspicuous.

For several seconds, nothing moved. Then the door to the restroom squeaked open, and footsteps echoed across the tiles.

"Faith?" Violet's concerned voice came from only a few yards away. "You've been in there for a while. Are you all right?"

Faith's heart started to hammer against her ribs. She could call out. One word and Violet would storm in, followed by Noah and the police.

Tala wouldn't try to stop her; she sensed that. She didn't cover Faith's mouth with her hand again. She simply stood on top of the toilet, her palms resting lightly on Faith's shoulders as she waited to see what Faith would do.

"I'm fine," Faith called back. "I just need a minute."

Tala gave Faith's shoulders a soft squeeze.

Faith's thoughts raced. She needed to buy them some time so they could figure out what was going on. Something about the ID tag wasn't adding up. If there was even the slightest chance Tala was innocent, she wouldn't betray her and put her in danger.

"Actually, if I'm honest, I'm not fine at all," she added. "I've just been sick. Guess my stomach didn't handle being shot at well."

"Oh no. I'm so sorry." Violet's voice was full of compassion. "Is there anything I can do? Do you need some water? Should I get a nurse?"

"No," Faith said quickly. "Just…could you put the *cleaning in progress* sign in front of the door? I need a few minutes to clean up and get myself together without anyone barging in on me."

"Of course." Violet's shoes squeaked on the tiles, probably as she went to the cart full of cleaning supplies Faith had spied in the corner when she'd come in. "The officer is still outside, waiting for you, but I'll tell him to come back later."

Faith exhaled quietly. "Thanks, Violet."

"Take your time," Violet said. "If your tea gets cold, at least we'll have a good excuse to send Noah back to the cafeteria."

Faith chuckled weakly. "There's that."

Violet paused for another beat, then the restroom door closed behind her.

Tala waited a few more seconds before she slid from the toilet. "Thank you. That was brilliant." She lightly brushed her fingertips along Faith's arm as if afraid she would pull away.

The touch felt warm, not threatening at all, as if her body already knew what her head wanted to believe: that Tala would never hurt her in any way. Faith gave her a tense nod.

Tala stepped out of the stall.

Faith followed her and took a moment to rinse her mouth at the sink again. "If someone framed you by planting the ID tag, does that mean… the letter…?"

"Mirella sent it. She wanted to drive a wedge between us to diminish my chances of becoming natak. She also lied to me, telling me you had planted a bug in my parents' kitchen and were still spying on us."

"What? I didn't! I'm not! I brought the bug to Silver Falls, but I swear I didn't go through with planting it! I took it home and flushed it down the toilet."

"I didn't want to believe it, but I couldn't be sure," Tala said. "That's why I couldn't talk to you earlier, in the car. First, I had to make certain you weren't wearing a wire. That's why I suggested going to my apartment."

Faith's head spun. "Jesus. What a fucked-up cat-and-mouse game! Or wolf-and-human game. So Mirella is behind it all? The letter…it was all a lie? But that look on your face when I asked you about killing humans…"

It was the same expression of anguish that crossed Tala's face now. "I wish it was all a lie," she said quietly. "But unfortunately, that part was true." She studied the bathroom tiles as if she couldn't bear to see the look in Faith's eyes. "I'm not going to lie to you. I have killed humans."

Faith had known it the moment she had seen Tala's reaction in the car, but it still hit her like a punch to the throat, robbing her of breath. "How many?" she gasped out because it was the first thought in her jumbled mind.

"Three," Tala answered in a raw whisper. "One of them pulled a gun on me."

A shiver went through Faith at the thought of Tala staring down the barrel of a gun. "Okay, that was self-defense, but what about the other two? Why would you kill them?"

"I didn't have a choice," Tala said, her gaze still averted. "I was ordered to."

"So Madsen or the council wanted them dead?" Faith asked. "But why? And why would you follow such a horrible order?"

"I'm a soldier. I can't pick and choose which orders to follow. And, in a way, it was self-defense too. Or at least we had convinced ourselves that it was and we were only protecting our kind." Tala lifted her head, torment etched on her face. "I'm not proud of it. None of us are. We're not cold-blooded murderers, no matter what your father wants you to believe."

"You killed people," Faith said, still trying to reconcile that fact with the Tala she had gotten to know—the woman who had tenderly acted as a heating pad for her and who had allowed Chloe to pet her fox form.

"I'm not trying to make excuses, but you have to understand the world we grew up in. None of us ever had the kind of carefree childhood many humans have. Even as little pups, we were very aware that one wrong step could mean our entire species would be wiped out forever. Keeping our existence secret was considered the most important thing—something to never be questioned. That's why it's called the First Law."

Faith tried desperately to make sense of it all. "First Law?"

"Our most important law that kept us safe for centuries. It required us to keep our existence hidden—at all costs."

"Including the cost of human lives?" Faith asked, even though she already knew the answer.

Tala nodded with a look of guilt, pain, and regret in her eyes. This wasn't the face of a ruthless killer. "Only as a very last resort. We thought it was the only way to prevent total extinction—a question of kill or be killed. We were in survival mode our entire lives, especially the Saru."

That sounded horrible. Faith couldn't imagine living like that. "And you never questioned it?"

"I did," Tala said quietly. A visible shiver ran through her body. "I barely slept for months every time I had to follow a kill order. The last time, I wasn't sure I could go through with it, even though that would have meant losing my rank, my position in my pack...and probably my life. Thankfully, the council revoked the kill order. But any time I thought about speaking up, fighting for change, something happened that made me fear how humans would react if they ever learned of our existence."

Faith sighed. "Your fears might have been a little exaggerated, but I can't say they were totally unfounded."

"I'm not so sure they were that exaggerated. The last time humans found out about us, it ended with many of us being tortured or burned at the stake. Even nowadays, you saw how humans treat us." Tala touched her temple, where the can of Coke had hit her. "We're just wild animals or even ruthless monsters to them."

"Not to all humans," Faith whispered. "Not to me."

Tala swallowed heavily. "Is that still true? After what I just told you?"

"I…" Faith licked her lips. "I don't want to think of you like that. Now that I've gotten to know you, I no longer see you as a monster. Even when I ran from you, a part of me wanted to turn around and hear you out."

"And now that you did?" Tala asked quietly.

"I don't know what to do with all the things you've told me," Faith replied. "This is a lot. You killed humans. Innocent people. That's not something I can just dismiss."

Tala hung her head. "I know. You don't know how much I wish I hadn't, but…I can't change it. I'll have to live with it for the rest of my life."

The guilt and remorse on her face were genuine; Faith knew that without a doubt. "I need time to process all of this."

Tala's hunched shoulders straightened. "You've got all the time you need. For now, let's focus on how to get out of this mess." She waved toward the door and the presence of police, security, and HASS beyond.

Faith nodded. "Yes, let's figure out who shot my father—and how they could get their hands on your ID tag."

And just like that, they were a team again—partners who worked together instead of against each other.

A sense of unity and connection settled over Faith, so profound and unexpected that it brought tears to her eyes. She had struggled all day with what to do, her thoughts a whirlwind of doubt and uncertainty. But despite the horrible truths she had found out about Tala, trusting her felt undeniably right.

Now wasn't the time to linger on that. She pushed back her emotions to focus on the task at hand. "Could it have been Mirella? If she sent me the letter, maybe she's behind the shooting too."

Tala shook her head. "That's what I thought, but she swore it wasn't her, and her scent confirmed she was telling the truth. Besides, she couldn't have gotten her paws on my ID tag."

"Hmm. If you slipped it in your pocket, along with my necklace, maybe it fell out when I put your pants into the washing machine."

"That would make sense." Tala paced the restroom as if that helped her think. "But how did it get from your laundry room to the building in Arlington?"

"I have no idea." Faith leaned against the sink and watched Tala's smooth movements. "It's not like anyone but me had access to my house."

Tala whirled around. "Jon!" A loud growl echoed through the restroom. "Your ex has a key!"

"Not anymore," Faith said. "I made him give it back after he let himself in without asking and then refused to leave."

"Hmm." Tala continued her pacing, her arm brushing Faith's on each pass. "Who else has access to your place?"

"No one. Well, except for Chloe. But she's six!"

Tala held up both hands. "I know, I know. I'm not suggesting she's the shooter. The only way she would ever harm a Wrasa is by cuddling them to death."

A smile tugged on Faith's lips. "Or by pelting them with dozens of curious questions. She's fascinated with everything to do with the Wrasa."

"Do you think…? If she saw the ID tag in the laundry room, is it possible she would have taken it?"

"Maybe." That, of course, still didn't explain how the tag had ended up in Arlington, but it was at least a hint of a lead. "Let's ask her. I need to call Sabina anyway."

"You don't, by any chance, know her number by heart?" Tala asked. "I left your phone in the car."

"I don't. But I have this." Faith pulled her father's phone from her clutch and scrolled through his contacts.

Tala stared. "You had another phone all along?"

"No. It's my dad's." Faith found Sabina's number and was about to tap it when Tala touched her hand.

"I'm sorry I scared you so much that you dropped your phone and felt you had to run for your life," Tala said quietly. "I wanted to tell you about the First Law before, but how do you tell your…someone something like that?"

Faith didn't know what to say. Her instinct was to make Tala feel better about it, but "it's okay" didn't seem like an adequate response to someone admitting to having killed people, so she just nodded and called Sabina.

"Hi, Mr. MacAllister," her best friend's voice drifted through the phone. "What can I do for you?"

"Sabina, it's me. I don't have my phone right now, so I'm using my dad's." Faith hesitated, but the shooting would probably make the news, and she wanted Sabina to hear it from her. "Don't panic, but…something happened. Dad was shot. He'll be fine," she quickly added, hoping it would turn out to be true. "But he's in the hospital."

A loud gasp reverberated through the phone. "What? Is he—?"

"He's fine," Faith repeated, as much to herself as to Sabina. "The bullet hit his arm. He's in surgery. Whatever you hear or see on TV, don't believe it. It's not what it looks like."

A warm touch to her back made Faith glance up and into Tala's eyes, which were full of gratitude and something else Faith refused to think about right now. She leaned into the touch.

"What do you mean?" Sabina asked.

"I don't have time to explain right now. I need to talk to Chloe."

"Uh, okay. One second." Sabina called out to Chloe in the background. "Can you come here for a second, honey? It's your mom."

"Hi, Mom." Chloe's chipper voice came through the phone.

Faith closed her eyes, fighting to make her voice sound calm so she wouldn't scare her daughter. "Hi, sweetie. Are you having fun with Auntie Sabina?"

"Mm-hmm. We took a nap and then made spaghetti, and I showed her how to play Rhino Hero, but Auntie Sabina is not as good at it as Tala. I won three times!"

"That's great, sweetie. Listen, I have to ask you something, and I promise you're not in trouble, okay?"

"Okay," Chloe said after a short pause.

"Did you happen to see a silver chain with a round metal tag in the house this week?" Faith asked. "You know, like the ID tag Mr. Randolph, the janitor at your school, wears."

Another pause, this one longer. "Yes," Chloe whispered, as if sharing a secret. "It was on the floor."

"Where?"

"In the laundry room."

Faith held her breath. "What happened to the tag? Did you take it?"

"Only for a little while. I was just playing Wrasa." Defensiveness crept into Chloe's tone.

"It's all right, Chloe. I'm not mad."

"But Dad was," Chloe whispered. "He saw me playing with it, and he said it's not for humans and took it away."

Faith swayed and leaned more heavily into Tala. "Your dad took it?"

"Yes. But I didn't tell anyone, like Daddy said."

Anger seared through Faith. Jon had dragged their daughter into this? Had told her to lie? "Chloe, sweetie, it's okay. You didn't do anything wrong." Her voice wavered despite her effort to keep it steady. "But if anyone asks you to keep a secret, you can tell me anyway, okay?"

"Okay," Chloe said. "Are you really not mad?"

"I'm not mad at you, sweetie. I promise."

"Is Tala?" Chloe asked even more quietly.

Faith glanced at Tala, who instantly shook her head. "She's not mad either."

"Oh. Okay," Chloe said, sounding more upbeat.

"I'm sorry if you were worried about that. I love you, and I'll see you soon. Can you give me Auntie Sabina for a second?"

"Love you. Bye!" Chloe's staccato footsteps echoed through the phone.

"Faith?" Sabina's voice was back.

"Hey, listen, can you stay with Chloe for longer than we'd planned? I have no idea how long I'll be here."

"Of course," Sabina said right away. "Don't worry about Chloe, okay? I'll stay for however long it takes."

"Thank you. You're the best. Oh, and Sabina? Keep Chloe away from the TV, and don't answer the door or let anyone in until I get home. Not even Jon, okay?" *Especially not Jon.*

"Um, okay. But why not even Jon?"

"I'll explain later." Faith felt as if she was on autopilot as she said goodbye and ended the call. Her hand still holding the phone limply dangled down. She turned toward Tala. Her mouth opened and closed as she struggled to find the words to explain. Her brain could barely grasp it.

"I heard everything," Tala said.

The touch to Faith's back became a soothing stroke, gentle and rhythmic, grounding her in the midst of this new, shocking reality.

"Jon," Faith finally whispered. "He took your ID tag. He shot my father and made it look as if it was you. He even made up a fishing trip to give himself an alibi!" The words sounded surreal, even though she was the one saying them. "How could he? My dad was more like a father than a father-in-law to him all these years! He could have killed him—or me—all just so he could frame you!"

"People do irrational things when they're full of hate, Faith." Shadows darkened Tala's eyes.

Faith still couldn't believe it. Jon was far from perfect, but she had always been convinced that he was a great father and a decent man. How could he be capable of this? It felt impossible, and yet the puzzle pieces all fell into place. He had the ID tag; he knew her dad would be at the office alone this weekend, and he'd grown up hunting with his uncles, so he knew how to handle a rifle.

"Okay, let's assume it was him." Getting out the words was hard, but Faith forced herself to continue. "How do we prove it? If all we have is a six-year-old's word, no one will believe us—and I don't want Chloe to be dragged into this mess."

"We'll find a way to leave her out of this," Tala said firmly. "Do you have a key for his house so we could go and look for the rifle while he's at work?"

Faith shook her head. "I had one for his old place, but he moved into a new condo two months ago, and I never got a key."

"Then we need him to confess."

"I doubt the police would bring him in for an interrogation," Faith said. "They already have a suspect: you."

Tala nodded grimly. "And the evidence that places me at the crime scene."

Faith massaged the bridge of her nose as she tried to think.

"So Jon confessing to the police is out," Tala said, sounding as if she were thinking out loud. "But maybe he would confess to your father."

"Why would he?" Faith asked. "He just shot my dad. He wants him to think it was you."

A sly glint sparked in Tala's golden eyes, and the corners of her lips curled up into a subtle, foxlike grin. "What if he thought your father already knew who really shot him?" She gestured at the phone in Faith's hand.

"Oh." It was her father's phone. If she texted Jon, he would assume it was her dad. Faith opened the messages app.

Tala leaned close and peered over Faith's shoulder to see what she was writing.

The heat emanating from her was soothing and made Faith's breath catch at the same time, her body reacting as if nothing between them had changed. With trembling fingers, she tapped out a message. *I know it was you.* Her thumb hovered over the send arrow.

Could she really do this? Should she?

Jon was Chloe's father. The man she had been married to.

And she was about to set a trap for him!

Then she thought of her father's blood seeping through her fingers and of what Jon was trying to do to Tala…to all Wrasa. If she let him get away with it, there would be more blood on her hands.

"You don't have to do this if you're not sure," Tala murmured. "We can find another way to prove my innocence."

Faith appreciated Tala's willingness to risk her freedom for her sake, but she shook her head. There was no other way. She pressed *send.*

They looked at each other.

The weight of the phone felt heavy in Faith's hand as they waited for him to respond.

Three little dots appeared at the bottom of the screen.

"He's replying!"

They leaned close so they could both see the small screen.

The three dots disappeared, as if Jon had deleted whatever he had written.

"Quick!" Tala said. "Write something reassuring! He probably thinks Peter won't forgive him if he admits to having shot him."

Genius plan! Faith added. *Now everyone will think it was the Wrasa!* At the last second, she changed *Wrasa* to *shifters* before sending the text.

This time, it took only seconds for Jon's answer to pop up.

I'm so sorry! I didn't mean to hurt you! I was aiming for the far wall, but you lifted your arm just as I squeezed the trigger. Are you okay? It was just a graze, right?

Tala pumped her fist. "Yes! We've got him."

Faith didn't feel like celebrating at all. A new wave of nausea washed over her, and she pressed her lips together to fight it down.

Tala stilled next to her. "I'm sorry." She softly touched the small of Faith's back. "I'm not happy it was him. I'm just glad we have proof it wasn't one of us because that would have destroyed all the work we've done toward equal rights."

"I get that." Faith sighed, lifted the phone again, and replied to Jon's message. *You could have given me a heads-up.* She held her breath, hoping his answer would confirm that her father really hadn't known about Jon's plan.

I thought it would be more convincing if you truly believed it was one of the monsters and didn't have to lie to the police, Jon wrote back. *And I needed Faith to believe it. Her and Chloe.*

Faith's pulse accelerated. *Chloe?* she tapped out with trembling fingers.

She's as obsessed with those monsters as her mother! Jon answered immediately. *Can you believe she wants a Shifter Barbie for her birthday? And I caught her playing with the monster's dog tag, pretending she was one of them! That's when I knew I had to do something. I couldn't stand by and let that happen. I had to protect Chloe by any means necessary.*

The floor tilted beneath Faith's feet. She dropped the phone back into her clutch because she couldn't stand to look at Jon's texts for even a second longer.

"Come here." Tala caught her as Faith swayed on her feet. She held her tightly.

Faith stiffened reflexively, but within moments, her body melted against Tala's. She lowered her head to Tala's shoulder, buried her face against the silky material of her blouse, and clutched the back of the top with one hand. "It was him," she whispered against Tala's shoulder. "It really was Jon. He shot my father so he could frame you."

Tala cradled Faith against her. "I'm sorry," she murmured. "So sorry."

And Faith sensed that she was talking about much more than just Jon.

It took a few minutes, but finally, Tala felt Faith's trembling stop.

Faith lifted her head off Tala's shoulder and took a step back. "What now?"

"You need to get back before anyone comes looking for you." They had been in here for so long, it was a wonder the woman from HASS hadn't come back to check on Faith again.

"Yeah. My father should be out of surgery soon."

Tala reached out and squeezed Faith's hand. "For what it's worth, I hope he makes a full recovery."

"Thank you." Faith squared her shoulders. "Okay, let's go show Jon's texts to the police."

"I think it would be better if you go alone, while I sneak out of here. If I just walk up to the officers, I'll end up in a jail cell until they corroborate our story." The mere thought of being trapped in a cell made Tala's skin itch.

"There could even be an officer who would shoot first and ask questions later."

Faith's fingers clenched around her clutch. "You're right. Let's not take any chances. I'll show them the evidence by myself."

Tala hated sneaking away and leaving Faith behind to fight for her alone, even now that she knew who the shooter was and that he likely wouldn't try to harm Faith.

But Faith didn't seem hesitant. Her eyes were red-rimmed, yet her expression was determined, as if she was ready to take on the world to prove Tala's innocence. "Don't worry," Faith said. "I promise you can trust me. I won't betray you."

"The thought didn't even cross my mind," Tala said. "I mean, I would totally understand if you wanted to tell the police about what I have done in the past, but—"

"No," Faith said firmly. "I still don't know what to make of all that, but I won't tell anyone. It wouldn't bring back the people you killed, and it would paint all Wrasa as cold-blooded killers in the eyes of the public. I won't do that to you."

The knot of tension that had tightened the muscles in Tala's shoulders slowly unraveled. She hadn't fully realized until now just how much she had feared doubt would creep in and ruin something she knew could be special. But it hadn't. She still trusted Faith with her life, and Faith still seemed to care about her too, even though she hadn't said a word about Tala's accidental admission of love.

Tala shoved the thought away. There was no time for that now.

"Thank you," she whispered, her voice husky.

They looked at each other and hovered in front of the door.

"Be careful, okay?" Faith said. "The police are all over the hospital."

Tala nodded. "I'll wait a few minutes and sneak out once the cops are busy checking out your evidence."

Faith squared her shoulders and reached out to open the door.

"Wait!" Tala called.

Faith turned back.

"If you run into Mirella and Rey, don't be alarmed," Tala said. "They helped me sneak in here."

"Mirella helped you?" Faith gave her a look of disbelief. "I thought she was the one who sent me the letter?"

"She was. She wanted you to break up with me to make sure I wouldn't be in a position to take over the pack. It wasn't about undermining the Wrasa/human relationship. I think she came to her senses, and now she's trying to make up for what she did."

"A little late," Faith murmured. "But better late than never."

Was that true for Tala too? If she tried to make up for what she had done, would Faith forgive her for having killed several humans? Would she ever be able to fully trust her again?

"Speaking of Mirella's letter," Faith added. "I destroyed it and didn't tell anyone about it. Not even my father."

The words hung between them like a lifeline, and Tala latched on to it.

"When I jumped out of the car, I panicked," Faith added. "My only thought was to hide in my father's office and just blurt everything out and let him take over, but I did that before, and it didn't end well. So I decided that you deserved to be heard out first."

A rush of warmth filled Tala. She could imagine how hard it had been for Faith to wrestle down her fears and avoid falling into old patterns. "Thank you."

Before Faith could reply, a stranger's scent hit Tala's nostrils.

This time, it was too late to hide.

The door swung open, and a female police officer stood in front of them, blocking the exit with her solid frame. Her musky tiger scent overpowered even the sharp smell of disinfectant and cleaning agents.

A gasp escaped Faith. She stepped between them, shielding Tala with her own body. Tala's words about officers shooting first and asking questions later probably reverberated through her mind.

Tala put a hand on Faith's shoulder and gently pulled her back. "It's okay. She's one of us. A Wrasa."

"I'm Saru Ember Lennox," the tiger-shifter said. "Manark Madsen sent me to get you out of here, Tas Peterson."

How had Madsen even known where to find her?

Probably the same way Mirella had. He had guessed correctly that she would rush straight to Faith's side after finding out she'd been taken to the hospital. *Damn.* Tala hated being so transparent.

"No," she said firmly. "That's not how we're going to do this. I've got backup right outside. You go with Faith. Keep her and the evidence safe."

Ember Lennox lifted her upper lip. "That's not what my orders say."

"I'm changing them. You're going with Faith. The future of our species depends on the evidence she's carrying, and we need to ensure no Wrasa-hating officer makes it disappear." That wasn't the only reason she wanted Saru Lennox to go with Faith. Her priority was keeping Faith safe, but she didn't need to mention that.

The tiger-shifter gave a terse nod and held the door open for Faith, who moved toward her but then hesitated. She glanced back at Tala and reached out to her.

Tala touched her warm fingertips to Faith's cooler ones, and they looked into each other's eyes.

"Be careful, please," Faith whispered.

Hurried footsteps came down the hallway toward them.

Ember Lennox wrenched Faith out of the restroom and let the door fall closed between them, severing their connection.

"Faith!" The female HASS member's voice drifted through the door. "Your father is out of surgery!"

Three sets of footsteps rapidly faded away, leaving Tala behind.

She waited a couple of minutes, then snuck out of the restroom, stepping over the *cleaning in progress* sign.

CHAPTER 14

HALF AN HOUR HAD PASSED by the time Faith had finished with the police and was finally able to step into her father's hospital room. The smell of antiseptic engulfed her as soon as she opened the door. After all the voices talking over each other and the questions hailing down on her from Violet, Noah, and the officers, it was almost a relief to enter the quiet room. She had expected beeping machines, but the low hum of the lights was the only sound.

Her father lay in a hospital bed, his face pale against the white sheets. His right arm was heavily bandaged and stiffly rested along his side. He looked so vulnerable, so different from the powerful force Faith was used to, it made her throat tighten.

When she approached, he opened his eyes. His tired gaze roved over her. "Faith," he rasped, his voice slow and rough from either painkillers or anesthesia. "Are...are you okay?"

Faith walked over to his bedside. "I'm fine, Dad. I'm not the one who got shot."

He licked his lips. "Did they catch the shifter who did it?"

"It wasn't a Wrasa, Dad." Faith gripped the metal rail of the bed. "It was Jon."

Her father blinked as if he wasn't sure whether the aftereffects of the anesthesia were messing with his hearing. "What?"

God, this was hard—even harder than she had expected. "Jon was the one who shot you. He set it up to make it look like it was Tala, but it was him."

"Nonsense," her father snapped, sounding stronger, more like himself. "That's the shifters talking. They're manipulating you. I can't believe you would take their word over that of your daughter's father!"

Faith tightened her grip on the rail. "Leave Chloe out of this, please. It's bad enough that Jon used her to frame Tala."

"You're wrong," her father said. "He didn't do whatever you're accusing him of."

Faith met his gaze. "He took Tala's ID tag from Chloe, told her to keep it a secret, and left the tag behind after he shot you, making it seem like Tala was the shooter."

"That makes no sense. Why would Chloe even have the shifter's dog tag?"

"It fell out of Tala's pocket when I washed her pants, and Chloe found it."

His brow wrinkled. "Why would you wash her pants?"

Faith's first impulse was to explain away the seeming domesticity of that task, tell him it wasn't what he was thinking. But then she stopped herself. So what if it had been exactly what he was thinking? She had to stop acting as if being with a Wrasa was something shameful. She had to be the one to change her father's way of thinking, not have him dictate hers. "Because they had blood all over them—from when one of my neighbors, a member of *Moms Against Shape-Shifters*, attacked Tala. Jon took the ID tag from Chloe and planted it at the scene, even though he suspects I care about Tala. Probably *because* of that."

Silence descended on the room.

Her father stared at her.

Faith stared back as the weight of her words hit her. For the first time since Tala had said it earlier, in the restroom, she allowed herself to think about it. Tala had told her she loved her—and Faith hadn't said it back, too stunned and confused by the entire situation.

But what she had just told her father was the truth. She did care about Tala.

No, it was more than that.

She loved her.

That was as shocking and confusing as finding out Jon had shot her father. Could she really love someone who had killed innocent humans?

But then again…how could she not love her?

Tala was so unique, so complex, so vulnerable beneath an armor of fierce strength. There was so much more to her than just the tough Saru who had killed to protect her kind. With every hidden layer Faith had gotten to know, her feelings had deepened, and now she could no longer deny the truth to herself.

"Even if he did take the dog tag, you seriously expect me to believe that Jon shot me?" her father asked.

Had he decided to ignore her declaration of affection for Tala? Or had Faith missed his reaction to it while she'd been caught up in her own revelation?

He stared at her with his brow furrowed. She couldn't tell if he was processing or just unwilling to let himself fully grasp what she had said—not just about Jon, but about Tala too.

"That's ridiculous, Faith," he added when she didn't answer. "It's crystal clear it was the shifters. They wanted revenge because I spoke out against giving them equal rights."

Of course he would cling to his hateful narrative and refuse to even consider the truth. Faith had expected it. He needed to see the evidence with his own eyes. That was why she had made screenshots of Jon's confession and sent them to Violet, Sabina, and to her own phone before handing her father's device over to the police.

She unlocked the phone she had borrowed with the passcode Violet had given her. Her fingers trembled as she held it out to him.

Her father gave it a fleeting glance. "What's that?"

"I used your phone to text Jon, letting him assume it was you."

"You tricked him? Your own ex-husband?"

"I had to. The police were about to arrest Tala."

"So what? Maybe she deserves to be arrested! How do you know she wasn't the one who shot me?"

"Because I know Tala. It wasn't her. She would never hurt me—not even by hurting you," she repeated what Tala had told her because she believed it.

"And you seriously think Jon would?" He shook his head. "How on earth did the shifters manage to turn you against your own family?"

Arguing with him wouldn't help. She waved the phone. "Read this."

Reluctantly, he grasped the device with his uninjured hand. His gaze flicked left and right as he read the messages.

"There are more," Faith said. "Swipe to the next screenshot."

He did.

When he stopped reading, he didn't say anything for quite some time. His throat worked, but it took several seconds until he could formulate words. "Jon shot me." He looked more stunned than he had the moment the bullet had hit him. "This isn't some AI manipulation, is it?"

"No, Dad. I wish it were."

He stared at the phone again as if hoping the evidence might change under his scrutiny. "He really shot me?"

Faith's chest ached at the brokenness in his tone. She took the phone from him and gently slid her fingers around his left hand. "He did. I'm sorry, Dad. I know this is hard to accept. I haven't fully come to terms with it either."

"Why would he do that?" Her father's voice came out in a hoarse whisper. "He's like a son to me."

"It's all this hate, Dad. It makes people do things that you didn't think they were capable of."

"He shot me," her father repeated as if he hadn't even heard what she'd said. "He took the shot even though you were in the room, right next to me." His face hardened. "He could have killed you! I might have forgiven him for shooting me, but I can't forgive him for endangering you."

Faith wasn't sure she could forgive him either.

Was that hypocritical? She had delivered proof of her ex-husband's guilt to the police, yet she was keeping Tala's secret. Was Jon shooting her father any different from what Tala and the other Saru had done? Both had hurt—or even killed—someone because they thought it was necessary to keep their species safe.

But that was where the similarities ended. Jon's overprotectiveness toward humans was based only on his own hateful assumptions about the Wrasa, while the Saru had rightfully felt threatened by the thought of what would happen if humans found out about their existence.

Jon had acted out of hate and with the intention to harm an entire species.

Tala had followed an order, like a soldier in a war for survival. She had never targeted all of humankind.

What she had done wasn't right. But it stemmed from the centuries-old fears of an entire species, rooted in what humans and their hatred of anything different had done to them during the Inquisition.

Faith thought she could come to forgive it—but she would no longer accept all this hate. She tightened her grip on her father's hand. "This isn't just about me or about Jon. He wanted to use your shooting to fan the flames of hatred. To make humans see people like Tala as monstrous killers. He would have sent an innocent woman to prison for what he did."

Her father's lips thinned, and a spark of defiance lit his tired eyes. "Are you sure she's innocent in all this? Who's to say she didn't—?"

"No, Dad," Faith said sharply. "This was all on Jon."

"Yeah, well, even if it wasn't a shifter this time, that doesn't mean they're the good guys. They have evil—"

"Stop!" Faith withdrew her hand from his. "This hatred has to stop. *You* have to stop."

"But—"

"You were shot because of this very nonsense, and yet you keep spewing it." Faith nearly throttled the metal rail with both hands. "Jon will likely go to prison. Chloe will lose her father! And none of that is on the Wrasa—it's all on you and HASS and this senseless hate! What else needs to happen before you stop?"

Her voice echoed in the quiet hospital room. She realized she'd been shouting and snapped her mouth shut. Her throat felt raw.

He stared up at her, slack-jawed. His shoulders seemed to sink even deeper into the pillows as if deflating under the weight of her words.

Faith bit her lip. Had she pushed too far? Too fast? He had been shot and was fresh out of surgery. Maybe this wasn't the time to discuss this.

But when would there ever be a perfect time? If she didn't confront him now, this circle of hate would continue, and HASS might escalate, with conspiracy theories about the shooting spiraling out of control.

"I trusted your judgment my entire life—sometimes more than I should have," she added more softly and took his hand again. "Can't you trust mine, just this once?"

Her father looked down at their intertwined fingers and swiped his thumb across the back of her hand. "I do trust you," he said hoarsely. "It's them I don't trust."

Faith sighed. There it was again—the same us-versus-them attitude. She decided to ignore his comment. "How are you supposed to make an informed decision on whether you can trust them when you've never even had a conversation with a Wrasa?"

"Of course I've had conversations with some of them," he grumbled.

"I'm not talking about a shouting match or barking orders at a waiter," Faith said. "I mean a real, substantial exchange. You know I'm right."

He gave a one-shoulder shrug. "So?"

Faith leaned forward as if that would help her to reach him. "I've spent a lot of time with Tala in the last five or six weeks. She's a good person, Dad."

"I know you believe that, but…" His fingers curled around hers more firmly, as if he were clinging to his resolve. "I'll never see the shifters the way you do."

"You don't have to. Just stop viewing them as monsters."

He turned his head away and glanced at the narrow gap in the blinds, where a sliver of daylight seeped in. His profile was hard, his jaw clenched tightly.

"Look, Dad. You might not like it, but the Wrasa are here to stay—and so is Tala." This really wasn't the time to bring it up, especially since she was still trying to process everything that had happened. She and Tala hadn't even talked about if and how to move forward. And yet she was done denying it. She would no longer ignore her feelings for fear of how her father would react. Maybe making this personal was the only way to get through to him. "I want her to be part of my life for a long, long time."

His head snapped back around. "What are you saying? Was Jon right? Is there something going on between you and this…this…?"

"Tala," Faith said firmly. She straightened her spine. "She has become very important to me."

He squinted at her. "I-in what way?"

Faith swallowed. He had ignored her *I care* comment before, so she had to spell it out for him. "For now, we're friends. But…I'd like us to be more. Tala told me she loves me, and I realized…I love her too."

"No, Faith," he got out in a rough whisper. "No. Not one of them. I've come to accept that you might end up with a woman, but not…not…"

"Not what, Dad?" Faith looked him in the eyes. "Not someone who welcomed me into her family? Who has been incredibly kind and patient with Chloe? Who held me when I grieved for Mom and, for the first time ever, shared how guilty I've always felt?"

He had opened his mouth as if about to argue, to scream and shout, but her last sentence made him freeze. "You…you feel guilty about…your mom?"

Faith nodded, her throat tightening. "I do. Did. Tala helped me see that I was just a child and there was nothing I could have done, even if I had gone hiking with Mom that day."

He gently stroked her knuckles. "Hell must have frozen over because for the first time ever, I agree with a shifter," he mumbled. "But that doesn't mean I agree with this…this relationship. You don't know what you're getting into."

"I think I do. You're the one who doesn't know—because you've never even met her," Faith replied. "Why don't you give her a chance and get to know her? You might find you have more in common than you realize."

Her father's thumb stilled on her hand. "No, thanks. I'm not looking for things I have in common with one of them."

"Then just…meet her. Form your own opinion."

"What if my opinion about her and her kind doesn't change?"

"I'm confident it will," Faith said. "And if not, at least your opinion will be based on who she actually is as a person, not some vague, hate-filled idea of what the Wrasa are like."

He sighed heavily. "Don't expect me to like her."

God, this was exhausting. But she knew his fears and ingrained beliefs wouldn't change overnight, so she tried to be patient. "You don't have to like her. Just stop inciting hate." She squeezed his hand. "Please."

"I'm not inciting hate; I'm merely warning humans about those monsters."

"Calling an entire species monsters *is* hate, Dad. Maybe as a first step, you could stop using that word."

He didn't answer for several seconds, then finally said, "It might be the painkillers talking, but… Okay, I'll meet her. Not right away, but soon. That's all I can promise."

Faith barely dared to move for fear that this fragile moment would shatter like thin glass and he'd take back his reluctant agreement. When he didn't, the tightness in her stomach eased. "Thank you, Dad." She bent down and carefully wrapped one arm around him in a heartfelt hug, avoiding his injured side.

His left arm came up, and he patted her back. "Don't thank me yet. I agreed to meet her, but that's all. And just to make one thing perfectly clear: if she ever hurts you in any way, all bets are off."

She straightened and held his fiery gaze with the same determination. "Then let me make one thing perfectly clear too: You're free to form your own opinion of Tala, but it won't affect mine. I can make up my own mind, and I already did."

He didn't reply, just closed his eyes—either from exhaustion or in resignation.

"Get some rest, okay?" She brushed her fingers over his and stepped back from the bed.

When only the sound of his breathing answered, she lingered for a moment longer, studying his worn, pale features, then walked to the door.

It wasn't the big breakthrough she'd hoped for. He had probably only agreed to meet Tala so he could find a reason to dislike her. But maybe it was a start.

After one last glance back, she slipped out and quietly closed the door behind her.

CHAPTER 15

Five days later, on Thursday afternoon, Tala entered the lobby of the hotel Faith worked at. Even though she knew Peter MacAllister wasn't there, she still felt as if she had crossed into enemy territory. Maybe coming here had been a mistake.

No. She couldn't keep thinking like that. If she wanted to help heal the divide between humans and Wrasa, she had to stop thinking of him as the enemy.

Besides, this was Faith's territory as much as it was her father's.

Tala could sense it in every detail.

Crystal chandeliers cast a warm glow, reflecting off the marble floor and the polished wood of the reception desk. Plush armchairs were grouped around round glass tables, inviting guests to sit and rest. Hushed conversations mingled with the low sound of piano music. The air smelled of fresh lilies, coffee, and a hint of milk with honey on a rainy day.

Tala lifted her nose and greedily inhaled their mate scent, which completely overshadowed the lingering traces of the perfume that imitated it.

The irresistible aroma guided her attention toward the front desk.

Faith stood nearby, talking to a guest, who was gesturing animatedly. She was wearing her hotel uniform. The tailored navy-blue blazer hinted at the curves beneath, and the formfitting pencil skirt showed off her shapely legs. The outfit was crisp, professional, and—to Tala—devastatingly sexy.

Tala leaned against a pillar to watch her.

Faith was clearly in her element, exuding calm authority. Her confident smile was breathtaking. She tilted her head to attentively listen to whatever the guest had to say, then waved over one of her staff members and gave short instructions.

Tala couldn't look away. She hadn't seen Faith since Saturday because she had tried to lay low until the police had arrested Jon and cleared her name. Her time had been filled with reports and a council meeting, but despite keeping busy, she had missed Faith.

That was a new experience. As a Syak, she was supposed to be a pack person, yet she had never missed anyone—at least not the way she'd missed Faith.

Even so, she was grateful for the chance to spend some time alone and process everything that had happened—and to give Faith the same opportunity. Tala knew Faith needed time to sort through the whirlwind of emotions. She respected that, as hard as it was.

Besides, she still didn't know what to say, how to face Faith after the "I love you" that had slipped out on Saturday.

She hadn't planned to say it, and certainly not like that, not in a public restroom, right after the foundation of the trust between them had been badly shaken.

But somehow, those three not-so-little words had slipped past her usually formidable guard, and once they had, there'd been no taking them back. Tala didn't *want* to take them back. She wanted Faith to know the truth—every truth—about her.

It hadn't been the right moment for Faith, though. Tala knew she had totally overwhelmed her, and she could only hope Faith wouldn't push her away.

Whether Faith could forgive her, trust her…maybe even love her was out of Tala's hands. It was completely up to Faith, and Tala had to accept that all she could do was wait.

Unfortunately, that had never been her strong suit.

Every instinct urged her to act, to fight for her mate, but this was a battle she couldn't win by sheer determination.

If all Faith wanted was to keep their relationship the way it was now— just two allies, maybe tentative friends who fake-dated for the good of their species—she would have to find a way to live with that.

Faith looked up from her conversation and directly at Tala, as if she could sense her presence. She paused mid-sentence and stared for a moment before focusing on the guest again.

While she appeared entirely professional, Tala could tell that she was distracted now. Faith repeatedly reached up to swipe back a strand of hair, even though they were all neatly pinned up in an elegant top knot. After another minute, she finished up with the guest and parted ways with a firm handshake. Her heels clicked against the marble floor as she crossed the lobby toward Tala, keeping her gaze on her the entire time. She was walking a little stiffly, not bending one knee, yet to Tala, the soft sway of Faith's hips was hypnotic.

Tala stepped away from the pillar to greet her. "Hi."

Faith's smile was less confident now, more vulnerable—as if she felt as uncertain about where they stood as Tala did. "Hey. What are you doing here?"

"I would have called or texted, but I still have your phone, so I thought I would drop it off."

"Oh. Thanks. I've been using my old one, but I'm happy to have it back." Faith swiped at a strand of hair again. "Let's go to my office."

Subtle glances from several employees followed them as they walked across the lobby together.

Faith reached over and hooked her arm through Tala's.

Relief rushed through Tala. Faith wasn't rejecting her or shying away from her touch; she was publicly claiming her in a bold, almost possessive gesture that seemed to scream: *Yes, she's with me.*

Tala surprised herself by how much she enjoyed it. She held her head high, barely resisting the urge to preen as a young wolf-shifter in a bellhop uniform stared after them.

"How's your leg?" Tala asked, walking slowly so Faith wouldn't have to strain herself to keep up.

"It's fine. But it sucks that I had to get stitches just when the scrapes from the forest were as good as healed."

Tala hung her head. "I'm sorry you keep getting hurt." A fierce determination surged through her. She would do everything in her power to ensure Faith wouldn't get as much as a hangnail in the future. No one would hurt her again—not on Tala's watch!

Faith offered a small smile, as if trying to ease Tala's worries. "It's not too bad. I'm just not supposed to bend it too much because it would pull on the stitches." At the end of a hallway, she let go of Tala's arm, opened a door, and beckoned her in.

Her familiar milk-and-honey scent hung in the air, even more intense in the enclosed space. It wrapped around Tala as soon as she entered, putting her at ease. She looked around curiously.

The office was neat, efficient, and professional, but with little personal touches such as a small plant on one corner of the big desk and a framed photo, no doubt showing a grinning Chloe. Thank-you cards from guests were pinned to a huge corkboard covering one wall.

Faith leaned against the edge of her desk, her hands lightly curling around its edge, and watched her take in the room.

Finally, Tala returned her gaze to her. "Here." She held out Faith's phone.

As Faith took it, their fingers brushed, and neither pulled back, letting the touch linger.

Tala cleared her throat and finally dropped her hand. "How's your dad?"

"He's doing well. He was driving the nurses up the wall, so they sent him home the day before yesterday." Faith chuckled. "Right now, he's busy dealing with the chaos Jon's confession caused among HASS members, but knowing him, he'll probably be back at work before the end of the week."

"Good. And you? How are you holding up?" Tala studied Faith's face. The scent of exhaustion clung to her, and Tala could tell that her tastefully applied makeup hid evidence of several sleepless nights.

Faith sighed and took a moment to set her phone down on the desk. "To be honest…it's been tough. The police brought Jon in for questioning, and he confessed. The worst part was that I had to sit Chloe down and explain to her why she won't be seeing her dad this week…or anytime soon." She looked away, then back at Tala. The salty smell of sadness clung to her, dulling the sweet scent that Tala had come to associate with her. "I know what it's like to grow up without both parents, and I never wanted Chloe to go through that too."

A sharp pang of sympathy tore through Tala. She, too, knew what that was like, even though she'd been too young to remember her biological parents.

Her fox whined, restless with the urge to comfort and protect. Gently, she wrapped her hand around Faith's wrist and stroked the soft skin there with her thumb. "How did she take it?"

"She's upset and confused. She's six, Tala. Too young to understand. To her, Jon is just her fun daddy. She can't fathom why he hurt her grandpa…or why he hates the Wrasa. Hell, I'm an adult, and I can't understand it either."

Tala's skin itched with the need to do something. "I really hate that Chloe's caught in the middle of this mess. But she'll be fine because she's got a fantastic mom and a lot of other people who care about her." She hesitated, not wanting to overstep since she wasn't sure Faith would still allow her to be in Chloe's life. Finally, she added, "Including me. If there's ever anything I can do to help…talk to her or let her pet my fox form or… I don't know. Just tell me what you need, and I'll do it. I'm here for both of you."

Faith closed her own fingers around Tala's wrist, and they stood in this mutual clasp for a few moments, like two people making a pact.

And maybe they were.

"Okay," Faith finally rasped. "Thank you."

They let go at the same time.

Silence spread between them.

Tala shoved her hands into her pockets and resisted the urge to shuffle her feet. She didn't know what else to say, mostly because she had said a little too much the last time they had seen each other.

Her unintended declaration of love seemed to linger between them like a silent echo.

Faith hadn't said it back, and Tala wasn't sure where Faith wanted their relationship to go. Maybe nowhere. After all, less than two weeks ago, they had decided it would only complicate things, and now that Faith knew the truth about what the Saru…what *she* had done, the situation had become even messier.

Faith's scent didn't give her many clues either, even though she wore only a hint of the emotion-masking perfume. It was all over the place, mostly signaling upset and confusion.

Tala decided she wouldn't bring it up. Faith had enough on her plate right now. Besides, the next step needed to be Faith's.

"I'm leaving tomorrow," Tala finally blurted out. "That's what I came to tell you. Well, that and to give you back your phone."

Faith sank onto her desk and clutched the edge with both hands. "What?"

Tala couldn't help grinning. Whatever Faith wanted, it clearly wasn't her leaving. "Just for a day or two. I'm heading to Silver Falls. Madsen demoted Mirella to the lowest rank possible. In fact, I think he had to invent a new rank just for her. But otherwise, he left it up to the pack to decide how to punish her. So now the families are getting together to debate what to do with her."

Faith's fingers twitched against the desk before she straightened. "I'll come with you."

That was the last thing Tala had expected. "Really?"

"Of course. After all, what would your pack think if you showed up without your mate?" Faith winked at her.

She made it sound like a joke, but for Tala, it no longer was, so she didn't even comment on the wink. "What about Chloe? I'd love for you to come with me, but is this really a good time for her to be separated from you?"

"Could we take her with us?" Faith asked quietly. "She's got a half day at school tomorrow, so she'll be done by 12:15. I mean, if that's not a good idea, I could ask Sabina if she'd be willing to take her this weekend. But like you said, it's not a great time for Chloe to be away from me for two days."

A lump lodged in Tala's throat, and she couldn't get rid of it, no matter how hard she swallowed. Faith had always been adamant about keeping Chloe out of everything to do with their fake relationship and away from the Wrasa. So the fact that she now, after everything she had found out on Saturday, still allowed her in Chloe's life was huge! She was even willing to introduce her daughter to Tala's family—a pack of Syak she had been terrified of in the past.

Tala didn't know what to say to that. She struggled not to let her emotions spill over. "Yes, of course we can take her with us," she finally replied, trying not to let her excitement show. "Your father might not like it, though."

Faith shrugged. "He doesn't get a say."

Tala marveled at the finality of her answer and the hint of steel in her voice. Faith wasn't asking for permission or deferring to her father any longer—she was taking control! "It's decided, then. But I have to give you fair warning."

"About what? You think the pack won't be welcoming?" Faith's scent revealed neither fear nor distrust, only a trace of mild concern mixed with curiosity.

Amazing how far they had come in such a short time!

"No. Quite the opposite," Tala replied. "My parents will instantly assume Chloe's their new grandchild, and everyone else will treat her accordingly."

Faith hesitated, and her scent fluctuated through different aromas too fast for Tala to identify them all. Finally, she flashed Tala a tremulous smile. "That's okay. Maybe it'll be exactly what Chloe needs right now."

"Yeah, I think so too. She'll probably love it so much, she won't want to come back home with us."

They both chuckled.

After a few moments, their playfulness drained away, and Tala sobered. There was something she had to know before she took Faith home with her. "What about us? Do you want to tell my pack the truth about us? Or do you want to keep pretending in front of my family?"

"Are we?" Faith asked quietly, searching Tala's eyes.

"Are we what?" Tala found herself whispering.

"Still pretending?"

Tala's mouth went bone-dry. *Come on. You're a Syak. An experienced Saru commander. You can talk about your feelings without shitting your pants!*

Just as she opened her mouth to say something, Faith beat her to it. "To be honest, I don't think I am. I don't know exactly how or when it happened… Maybe when you played heating pad for me or when you read Chloe a bedtime story, but somewhere along the way, it started to feel real to me. On Saturday, when you said…"

"That I love you," Tala supplied with every bit of bravery she possessed.

Faith nodded. "That you love me," she repeated. Her voice trembled with emotion, and her cheeks took on a rosy flush. "I was too scared to say it back. To let myself feel it."

"Because of what I did as a Saru?" Tala forced herself to ask. She needed to know.

"No. I mean, yes, that too. When I got that letter, it triggered a lot of fears about the Wrasa being killers. But I thought about it a lot over the past few days, and I realized that having killed someone doesn't make you a cold-blooded killer. While I don't take what you did lightly, I understand the circumstances that led to it. If I had grown up the way you did, I can't rule out that I would have done the same."

For a second, Tala swayed on her feet. She had always wanted to believe she was a strong Saru, a soldier who followed orders and didn't need anyone's forgiveness. But now she realized how urgently she had needed to hear those words. "Thank you," she got out in a hoarse croak. "I swear I'll never give you or Chloe a reason to be scared of me."

Faith firmly shook her head. "I'm not scared of you. What scared me was knowing if I let myself love you, it would change my entire life. Choe's life. My relationship with my father. But when I stood at his hospital bed and looked down at him, I realized my life *has* already changed—and I think it's mostly for the better. You taught me to stand up for myself and what I want. So no, I don't want to pretend anymore. I want that new world in which humans and Wrasa live together as equals, and I want this…us…to be real." Faith blurted it all out in one long stream, as if the words had lurked inside of her for some time, just waiting to be said. "I know it won't always be easy, with my father and Jon and your grandmother, plus me now basically being a single mom, but…"

Tala couldn't help the grin that formed on her lips. She barely held back an excited yip. "Easy is overrated." Great Hunter, when had she turned into this awfully mushy person?

Probably right around the time she had stopped pretending and started to actually fall for Faith.

"So…" She took a step toward Faith. The remaining foot of air between them instantly seemed to heat up. "Does that mean…if I wanted to kiss you, I could?"

Faith's lips parted, and her gaze dipped to Tala's mouth, answering the question even before she hoarsely whispered, "Yes."

Tala slid her hands around Faith's waist, pulled her forward, careful not to jar her injured knee, and kissed her.

All the lines they had drawn before instantly disappeared, and the world narrowed to the softness of Faith's lips, the eager press of her body against Tala's own, and the low moan that escaped her as Tala teased her mouth open so she could deepen the kiss.

No more pretending. No more hiding. No more holding back. Tala finally let herself go.

Faith's hands slid up Tala's back and wound into her hair.

They sank against the desk without breaking their contact even for a second.

A soft chitter escaped Tala between kisses, and Faith smiled against her lips. "God, that's so sexy. Do that again."

"Make me," Tala rasped.

Faith instantly took her up on the challenge and stroked her tongue along Tala's bottom lip.

The sharp ring of Faith's office phone sliced through the haze in Tala's mind.

They both froze, their lips a quarter of an inch apart.

The phone rang again.

Faith let out a groan, her scent clearly communicating her frustration. "Sorry. I have to get that."

On slightly shaky legs, Tala backed up a step.

Faith straightened her pencil skirt, which had slid up to mid-thigh, and leaned across the desk to reach for the phone.

Great Hunter! Tala had to close her eyes as the fabric pulled tight across Faith's ass. But she couldn't keep them closed for more than a second, the need to watch Faith too strong.

"This is Faith MacAllister." Her voice came out in a hoarse rasp. As she listened to what the woman on the other end said, she turned around and perched on her desk as if her legs felt unsteady too. "No, that's not a great solution," Faith said, her attention still on Tala. "Let me handle it. I'll be right there." She ended the call and sighed.

"Duty calls?" Tala asked.

"Yeah." Faith wrinkled her nose. "Usually, I really love my job. But right now, it sucks. Because"—she paused, and her gaze lifted back to Tala—"I love you more."

Tala's heart skittered.

"And I love that look on your face," Faith added. Her lips were reddened, her cheeks flushed, and several strands of her hair had come loose from her top knot.

Tala itched to bury her fingers in them, pull her close, and kiss her breathless again—so she did, but this time, only for a few seconds. "I love you too," she whispered before she reluctantly released her. She watched Faith rearrange her hair with unsteady fingers. "How about I pick you up here at a quarter till twelve tomorrow and we'll go get Chloe together?"

"Make it eleven thirty." Faith's voice dipped. "I want a kiss before we leave."

"I can be here by eleven," Tala offered.

Faith laughed, a sound that made warmth trickle through Tala's body. She walked to the door and, when she reached it, looked back over her shoulder at Tala. "Eleven fifteen it is."

"Oh, and don't put on any of the perfume tomorrow," Tala said as she followed Faith back to the lobby.

"Why not?" Faith asked.

Tala hesitated.

The Syak bellhop and two employees behind the front desk were throwing them furtive glances.

This wasn't the place and time to explain.

"I'll explain when we have more time." Tala lowered her voice to a whisper. "And more privacy."

That conversation was definitely one she wanted to have between just the two of them.

CHAPTER 16

"Are we there yet?" Chloe asked for the sixth time since they had picked her up from school an hour ago—five minutes late because Faith and Tala had kept pulling each other back at the office door for "one more kiss."

"Almost," Tala said from the driver's seat. "Just a bit longer."

Chloe bounced in her booster seat. "Will there be other kids?"

"Oh yeah," Tala replied. "I have four siblings and twenty-one cousins, and most of them have kids. I lost count at about twenty-four."

Faith's heart swelled at the patience with which Tala answered each of Chloe's endless questions.

"Wow!" Chloe counted on her fingers. "That's more than the kids in my class!"

"Not all of them will be there, though," Tala said. "Some of my cousins live farther away, so not everyone can make it to every gathering. But there'll still be plenty of pups…kids for you to play with."

"I can't wait. It's gonna be so fun!" But then Chloe paused. Fabric rustled as she fidgeted in her seat. "Do you think they'll like me?"

"I'm sure they will, sweetie," Faith said. "Right, Tala?"

"Of course. I mean, what's not to like about such a tasty little morsel?" Tala playfully flashed her teeth in the rearview mirror.

"Tala!" Faith swatted her. It was great to see Tala's playful side emerge, yet she didn't want her to scare Chloe.

But Chloe just burst into giggles. "Don't worry, Mom. She's joking. They won't eat me."

The confidence in her voice blew Faith away, and she could only marvel at the fact that her father's and grandfather's hate hadn't seemed to influence Chloe at all.

"Humans don't taste good anyway," Chloe added as if that were a perfectly normal statement.

"I don't know about that," Tala whispered so quietly that only Faith could hear her. "I have a feeling you'd taste amazing."

Heat shot down Faith's body. *Oh boy.* She could already tell that she would have her work cut out for her if Chloe grew up around Tala—which was what she was hoping for. She pointedly ignored Tala's whispered remark and turned around in the passenger seat to throw her daughter a stunned look. "And you know that how?"

"Don't you remember?" Chloe said. "When I was little, I got in trouble when I bit Madison. She didn't taste good."

Tala's howling laughter filled the car, and Faith couldn't help chuckling too.

"Seriously, though," Tala said, a protective snarl in her voice. "Everyone knows Chloe is your pup." She lowered her voice. "That makes her *mine* too. No one will dare treat her less than warmly, not even my grandmother or Uncle Arnold. I won't let them." She glanced at Faith, and fiery resolve flashed in her golden eyes.

A shiver went through Faith, yet it wasn't one of fear. It felt good to no longer be Chloe's only protector—and to know that Tala would protect not only her daughter but also her with the same primal fierceness.

As they passed the sign saying *Welcome to Silver Falls* and Tala carefully navigated the SUV along the winding mountain road, Chloe fell silent. She peered out the window with wide eyes, oohing and aahing over an interesting rock formation, a sparkling stream, and a deer she spotted.

Towering trees closed in from both sides, forming a canopy overhead, with only dapples of sunlight flickering through.

"Look, Mom!" Chloe called. "It's like a tent!"

"Yes, I see it." Faith remembered the panic that had gripped her the last time they had traveled along this road. How different the same drive appeared now! So much had changed in only two weeks. Faith barely felt like the same person anymore.

Back then, the looming trees had seemed suffocating, dragging her mind back to her mom's death.

But this time, with Tala's support and Chloe's excited chatter filling the car, she could breathe. There was no weight pressing down on her chest. The only thing that made her heart beat faster were Tala's occasional glances and smiles.

"Can we sleep in the forest?" Chloe asked. "Can we, Mom?"

"No, sweetie. It's still too cold at night. We'll sleep in the house." Although the thought of being in the woods, even at night, didn't scare Faith as much anymore.

Through the eyes of her daughter, the forest seemed like a magical place full of possibility, not danger, just the way it had been for her as a kid. With Tala by her side, she would hopefully be able to get back to that.

"What kind of beds does Tala's family have?" Chloe asked. "Like big dog beds?"

"Just regular beds." Her daughter's question made Faith think of Tala's old room and the bed she would likely share with Tala again.

Heat swept through her body, but she shoved the thought away. With the entire pack coming together, they would have a full house, and Chloe would most likely sleep with them. It would all be strictly platonic.

Tala's fingers brushed Faith's thigh, which definitely didn't feel platonic at all. The touch was light, cautious, as if Tala was testing the waters to make sure it was okay to do that in front of Chloe.

Damn. They should have talked about it earlier, when they had been alone in her office. Instead, they had spent half an hour just kissing. Faith couldn't work up any real regrets. Kissing Tala was thrilling and new and yet felt like coming home.

"You okay?" Tala asked, her voice pitched low.

Faith nodded and covered Tala's hand with her own to show her it was okay. "Yes. I'm good."

"You sure?"

"Yeah." Faith gestured toward the forest. "It feels different this time."

Tala tilted her head. "Good different?"

"Very good different."

"Glad to hear it." Tala stroked the side of Faith's thigh with her thumb, sending a flicker of arousal through her.

"Mom?" Chloe's voice from behind them interrupted the moment.

Tala returned her hand to the wheel, but her warmth against Faith's leg lingered.

"Yes?"

"Will you turn into an animal now too?"

"What?" Faith twisted around and peered through the gap between the seats to make out Chloe's expression. "What makes you think that?"

"Tala is a Wrasa." Chloe stumbled over the word but gave Faith a look that clearly said she was being slow to grasp the obvious. "And you are her girlfriend. Does that mean you'll turn into a wolf or a fox too? Will I?"

Tala made a choking sound, but Faith couldn't make out if it was a stifled laugh or a gasp for breath.

The sound that escaped Faith was definitely a gasp. She had been thinking about how to broach the topic with Chloe since the day before, and now it turned out her daughter had assumed Tala was her girlfriend all along!

Well, of course she had. After all, Faith had told Chloe she and Tala were dating, back when their relationship had been entirely fake, and Chloe had never had a reason to assume otherwise because Faith had tried to keep the messy details from her.

"No, sweetie," Faith finally said. "That's not how this works. Humans can't shift shape, even when they're in a relationship with a Wrasa."

"Oh." Chloe sounded disappointed.

Tala chuckled. "I think your mom is fine just the way she is, lack of a pelt and all."

"Hmm." Chloe didn't seem convinced, but then perked up again. "Ooh! Mom, if you and Tala get married, I will have a mom who can turn into a fox, like I always wanted! Or a mom who can turn into a wolf who looks like a fox, I guess."

"It's okay," Tala said with a smile. "I still think of myself as a Syak—a wolf—first, but as a wise woman once told me, I can be more than one thing."

"Hold on, you two!" Faith waved to get their attention. "We're not getting married! At least not anytime soon."

Tala's lips curved into a smirk. She leaned toward Faith and whispered, "Well, you proposed, and I said yes."

"What? When did I—?" Then Faith remembered. Tala had let Faith feed her during one of their fake dates and had posted the video on social media, so her kind considered them engaged.

"Hey! No whispering!" Chloe protested. "I want to hear!"

Luckily, they rounded a final bend, and the Petersons' house appeared to their right, distracting Chloe from the conversation.

"Is this it? Are we there?" Chloe asked.

"Yes," Tala said, obvious pride in her voice. "This is it."

The SUV came to a stop in front of Tala's childhood home, and Chloe stared at the sprawling two-story house nestled among the trees. "Wow! It looks like a fairy-tale house!"

"Let's just hope my grandmother doesn't behave like a fairy-tale witch," Tala mumbled too low for Chloe to hear.

Faith swallowed, not eager for another confrontation with Tala's grandmother, especially in front of Chloe. Even though the rest of the family had been very welcoming during her last visit, she couldn't help the flutter of nerves in her belly. When they had last stayed with the pack two weeks ago, her relationship with Tala had been fake. Now it was very real, which made her feel as if she was meeting the in-laws. Slowly, she reached out to open the passenger-side door. "Oh, wait!" She turned back toward Tala. "Are you sure you don't want me to put on any of the perfume? I packed it, just in case."

The day before, Tala had promised to explain, but with Chloe's nonstop questions, they had both forgotten about it.

Tala shook her head. "You won't need it. In fact, if you continue to wear it, you might give us away. Any Wrasa with a reasonably good nose will notice that there are two similar but slightly different scents."

"So it's true?" Faith asked. "We've got mate scent? The real one?"

Tala looked as if she was about to collapse onto the middle console. "You...you knew? How?"

"I didn't know for sure, but Jasper, the hotel's only Wrasa staff member, commented on our mate scent—on a day I hadn't put on any perfume, so I was wondering if..."

Tala nodded. "It's real. Has been since at least..." She glanced toward the back seat, where Chloe struggled to free herself from the seat belt. "Since we, um, sat on your couch."

Sat on your...? Oh! She meant the heated kiss they had shared on the couch! Faith flushed.

"Totally threw me for a loop because it doesn't usually happen like this," Tala added quietly.

"Well, nothing about us happened the usual way," Faith said.

They grinned at each other.

"Mom! Tala!" Chloe's impatient voice interrupted. "I can't get out!"

"Oops." Faith wrenched her gaze from Tala's, climbed out of the car, and helped Chloe unbuckle the seat belt.

As Chloe jumped down from the SUV's back seat, the front door swung open.

Tala's parents emerged first, then her grandmother followed. Behind her, siblings, uncles, aunts, and cousins spilled out of the house.

For once, Rey and Mirella were the last ones out. The metallic odor of fear wafted around Mirella in thick waves, making Tala's nose itch.

A cacophony of greetings drifted over, but the usual ribbing and exuberant laughter was absent. Today, the pack seemed more like a funeral procession, with a barely hidden tension hovering over the group.

A dual wave of nervousness from her human companions hit Tala's nose.

Now that Chloe was faced with so many unfamiliar people towering over her, the girl's typical fearless exuberance faltered, and she pressed herself against her mother's side.

Faith looked a little pale too, her lips forming a tight line, and Tala had a feeling she knew why.

So far, the perfume had acted as a protective shield that masked Faith's emotions. Now that she was no longer wearing it, the pack would be able to smell everything—including how nervous Faith was.

Tala's stomach twisted with the fierce need to protect them. She reached over, laced her fingers through Faith's, and gave them a reassuring squeeze.

Truth be told, Tala wasn't completely at ease either. Bringing not only Faith but also a pup home was new territory, especially since this wasn't merely a relaxed family gathering. This meeting would decide not only Mirella's future but her own too since she and Rey were still competing for their father's succession.

She tried not to let her tension show as her parents headed toward them. First her father, then her mother engulfed her in a tight hug, but half of Tala's attention remained on Faith and Chloe.

"Welcome home," her mother whispered into her ear. "It's so great to see you—and to smell how nicely you two have settled into your relationship, no longer holding back!"

So the difference in their mate scent, now that it was real, was obvious to everyone! Or maybe her mother was reacting to the fact that the perfume had made it hard to sniff out their emotions, while they were more obvious now. Even Tala had let her guard down a little, no longer controlling her chemical reactions as strictly.

As half of the pack descended on them, a low rumble threatened to rise from Tala's chest. She stuck close to Faith and Chloe, acting as a buffer.

"Why are you so tense? Relax!" Her father gave her a hearty pat on the back. "We will work this out as a pack, like we always do."

Her mother nudged his side. "She's got a new pup, Brennan. Don't you remember what it was like when Tala joined our family? You growled at my father just because he wanted to hold the baby!"

"That was different," Tala's father muttered gruffly. "Your father was a big Syak, not used to holding a little fox pup." Despite his protest, a flicker of understanding entered his eyes.

Tala's cheeks went warm—not only because of the "little fox" comment but because she realized her mom was right. She was reacting like a parent who'd just had a new baby!

Her mother shot her an amused look, then stepped around her to wrap Faith in a gentle embrace.

Faith melted into the nurturing hug, and the unease in her scent slowly faded away.

"How you are?" Tala's mother fawned over Faith. "You poor thing, I heard you were hurt."

"It's just a little cut on my knee," Faith murmured against her shoulder. "Unlike my dad, I was lucky—I wasn't shot."

"Still," Arlyn said. "I can check it out later, if you want. Make sure those human doctors knew what they were doing."

Tala warmed at the attention Faith was receiving from her family.

Sutton ran up to her, ignoring the pack's hierarchy that determined the order of who could greet whom. "Aunt Tala, I did it!" She jumped into Tala's arms. "I finally shifted! Uncle Reynard guided me through my First Change, and he said I'm learning to control it so fast, I'll be able to run with the pack soon!"

Tala twirled the teen around, even though Sutton was a couple of inches taller than her. "Congratulations, Sutton! That's wonderful. I knew you'd be a fast learner." Once she put Sutton down, she glanced over at Rey, who—uncharacteristically—had stayed in the background with Mirella.

He met her gaze with a somber expression, but when he looked at Sutton, his scent revealed nothing but pride and affection for their cousin.

Tala gave him a grudging nod. While she and her brother still didn't see eye to eye, she had to acknowledge he had done a great job mentoring Sutton through the confusing emotions and the piercing pain of her First Change—a difficult task that usually befell the pack's natak.

Chloe watched with wide eyes. At least she didn't ask to see a demonstration of Sutton's newfound shifting abilities.

Tala's mother went down on one knee to be at eye level with Chloe. "Hey there. You must be Chloe. I'm Jemma—Tala's mom. Have you ever seen how much food is necessary to feed a pack of Syak?"

Still wide-eyed, Chloe shook her head. "A lot?"

"Oh yeah. Want to see?" Tala's mother held out her hand.

Chloe glanced up at Faith, who nodded in encouragement. Then she eagerly grasped the offered hand and followed Tala's mother into the house without hesitation.

Her father's stern, weather-beaten face eased into a smile, and he patted Faith's shoulder. "I hope you took a good, long look at your daughter because that's the last you'll see of her."

A low growl rumbled through Tala's chest. "Dad! Don't scare her like that!"

"What? I meant for the rest of the day."

"It's fine." Faith softly squeezed Tala's fingers. "I know Chloe is safe here."

"She totally is," Sutton said. "I'll go keep an eye on her." She rushed after them, into the house.

Arlyn chuckled. "Keep an eye on Chloe. Right. She's just hoping to sneak some food before dinner. Teenagers are so predictable!"

"Oh, as if I didn't catch you swiping a chicken leg earlier!" Uncle Seth said.

"Can we skip the chitchat?" Tala's grandmother cut in. "We've got important pack business to discuss before dinner."

The teasing stopped instantly, and the cloud of nervousness clinging to Mirella intensified as the pack headed inside.

Tala gripped Faith's hand more tightly and guided her into the house.

CHAPTER 17

No one spoke as the pack members took their seats at the long table that stretched through the living room and the dining area. Tala's parents sat at one end, while her grandmother presided over the other.

Tala chose her usual chair to her father's right, across from Rey and Mirella. It was facing the window and allowed her to keep an eye on Chloe, who was playing in the garden with the younger cousins, Tala's nephews, and her niece. The pups' laughter provided a stark contrast to the tension inside.

When Faith sat next to Tala, a loud thud shook the table.

Tala's head whipped around.

Her gaze landed on her grandmother, who had risen from behind the table, her fist still pressed to the wood.

"This is pack business. The human has no place here!" She stabbed her gnarled finger in Faith's direction.

Faith tensed but didn't flinch or slink away. She faced the matriarch with her head held high.

Tala rose and gave the most threatening growl her five-foot-two stance was capable of. "Faith is my mate. Her place is right here, by my side."

"Mate!" Her grandmother huffed. "I have no idea how you did it, but anyone can smell that your so-called mate scent is as fake as—" Mid-rant, her nose twitched, and she snapped her mouth shut.

So she had really been able to tell that the perfume was not the real deal. It shouldn't have been possible, but Grandma had always been good for a surprise. Yet even her sharp nose couldn't contest their mate scent now.

"You were saying?" Tala barely held back a smirk.

"How?" was all her grandmother got out. She wildly shook her head and turned toward Uncle Arnold. "I swear they weren't—"

"It's called love, Grandma," Tala said quietly.

"Sit, everyone." Tala's father raised his voice to cut through the noise. "We're here to discuss Mirella's status in the pack, not Faith's, and I won't have you put Faith and Tala through the same nonsense every time they come home."

Come home, Tala mentally repeated. *Not visit.* His choice of words filled her with warmth. She waited until her grandmother had sat back down before she slid onto her seat. Beneath the table, she reached for Faith's hand and gave it an encouraging squeeze.

The room fell silent.

"The details of what Mirella did aren't public knowledge," Tala's father said, "and I can't share them with you, but Manark Madsen allowed me to tell you this much: She sent an anonymous letter to Faith, and its contents could have easily caused Faith to withdraw her support for us and the passing of the Wrasa Rights Act. Her goal was to break Faith and Tala up so they wouldn't compete with her and Rey for my succession." His heated gaze drilled into Mirella, then gentled as he looked over at Tala and Faith. "Thankfully, their bond was strong enough for that not to happen, but Mirella still took a huge risk for a very selfish reason—a risk that would have affected all of us, so I encourage you to share your thoughts on what we should do with her."

His words made Mirella flinch. She visibly struggled not to duck her head as the entire pack's attention turned toward her.

"It's our tradition to let each pack member have their say," Tala whispered to Faith. "The natak listens to everyone's opinion before making his decision."

"Let me speak first. Please." Mirella's voice shook. "Then I'll accept whatever the pack decides."

When Tala's father nodded his assent, Mirella turned toward Tala and Faith. "I'm sorry. I know I wronged you both, and I won't make any excuses for that. You're fellow pack members, and protecting you should have come before any personal ambitions and grievances. I know that now."

Tala found herself staring. She had expected Mirella to defend herself, not this unflinching honesty.

Mirella faced Rey. "I'm also sorry for dragging you into this. You deserve better." Her voice cracked, and she straightened to trail her gaze over everyone present. "I want to make it very clear that Rey didn't know what I was doing. That's on me alone. Maybe I don't deserve another chance, but if you give it to me, I'll do whatever is necessary to regain your trust."

Silence settled over the table for several seconds. Then arguments started flying back and forth, some condemning Mirella, others defending her.

As the discussion grew heated, Uncle Seth got to his feet. "I stand with Mirella. She made a mistake and was stripped of her rank as a Saru. That should be the end of it. Why punish her further when she already learned her lesson?"

"Why?" Aunt Celia shouted. "Because she brought shame on the pack and endangered everyone! How can we trust someone who acted so recklessly? She shouldn't be allowed to be part of the pack, much less one who's striving to be part of our future alpha pair!"

Gasps echoed around the room. Kicking a pack member out, making them an alai—a lone wolf—was an almost unheard-of punishment.

Rey jumped up so fast that his chair toppled over. "No!" His booming voice made several of the more submissive cousins duck. "I won't allow you to cast her out! Mirella only did what she thought was best for me and for the pack. If you won't accept her as a leader, fine. I'll give up all aspirations to become natak and let Tala take over as Dad's successor."

This time, Tala gasped too.

"No, Rey," Mirella whispered. "You can't—"

"I can and I will," Rey said, fire in his eyes. "I won't let them kick you out."

It had been years—maybe decades—since Tala had last looked up to her brother, but now she couldn't help admire him. He was ready to give up his dream and everything he had worked for his entire life…for his mate.

Just a few months ago, Tala wouldn't have understood that kind of sacrifice. Now she did because she would have done the same for Faith.

Slowly, Tala rose, put both hands on the table, and leaned forward. "I can't believe I'm saying this, but…I don't think that's the best option."

Heads snapped around. Now she had everyone's attention.

Faith leaned her shoulder against Tala's side in a gesture of silent support.

It filled Tala with certainty about what she was about to add. "I'm not saying what Mirella did was right. She was very wrong in her methods, and I haven't fully forgiven her for it yet. But she did it for the person she loves… to support his dream, and after a lot of soul-searching, I…" When Tala faltered, Faith leaned more heavily against her, lending Tala her strength. "I can see her point. Rey…Reynard deserves to be natak. He was there for the pack when Grandpa died, whenever one of the pups struggled with their First Change, when humans first found out about us, while I stayed away.

I was afraid some of you would blame me for our outing, and now I realize that staying away was just as selfish of me as it was for Mirella to send that letter."

Tala closed her eyes. She hadn't intended to say that much, reveal her own insecurities to the entire pack.

Faith locked their fingers together and squeezed softly until Tala opened her eyes again and cleared her throat.

"Anyway, I think Reynard will make a better natak, and you'd be doing yourself a disservice not to put your trust in him. Give Mirella a chance to make up for what she did and to prove herself to you."

The weight of her words settled over the room. Tala had never witnessed several dozen Syak being so completely silent. Everyone stared at her, including Rey and Mirella. Clearly, her standing up for them was the last thing they had expected.

Tala fought to keep her expression impassive as she sat back down. Faith's fingers, still tangled with her own, kept her grounded.

Her father leaned back in his chair, both hands flat on the table as he regarded her. At first, Tala read only surprise on his face and his scent, but then it gave way to respect. "I have carefully listened to everyone's concerns and opinions. But there's one person we haven't heard from." His gaze zeroed in on Faith, who sucked in a breath. "Mirella's actions affected you directly, Faith. I'd like to hear what you think."

Tala hadn't expected that, but she was grateful that her father respected Faith's opinion and openly showed that he valued it equally to the views of every other pack member. She leaned close enough that only Faith could hear and whispered, "You've got this."

Still holding on to Tala's hand, Faith rose slowly and looked at Mirella, who seemed to shrink under her glare. "I'm not going to lie. What Mirella wrote in that letter…it could have broken us up. If I had given in to old fears and refused to hear Tala out…" A visible shudder went through her, and an echo of it rippled through Tala.

Only they knew how very narrowly they had escaped that worst-case scenario.

"But I didn't." Faith's voice became stronger. "I managed to let go of all the preconceived notions once and for all, and I know Tala did too."

Tala sat up straighter and nodded.

"I feel like everyone—Tala and I, Wrasa and humans—got a second chance to redefine our relationship, so maybe Mirella deserves one too."

Mirella looked up, her expression so stunned that Tala didn't need to use her nose to know what she was feeling.

Faith and Mirella stared at each other for several seconds before Faith gave a slight nod, exhaled, and sat back down.

Tala's chest swelled. She pulled Faith's clammy hand onto her lap and held it between both of hers to warm it.

"Thank you, Faith," Tala's father said. He slid his gaze down one row of pack members and up the other. "I agree with what most of you said. Mirella made a grave mistake. But it was a mistake born out of love and loyalty. Mirella deserves a chance to prove that she has learned from it—and that she understands even love and loyalty are not enough for a leader. A natak's mate needs wisdom too."

Mirella nodded and hung her head.

"She will remain a part of this pack. As for who will take over as a natak…" He glanced from Rey to Tala. "We'll settle that when the time comes. I'm not yet ready to retire anyway."

One of the cousins chuckled, easing the tension.

Even their grandmother tilted her head in approval, perhaps mostly because she preferred Rey and Mirella as an alpha pair so the pack wouldn't end up with a human as the natak's mate.

Frankly, Tala didn't care anymore. She wouldn't allow herself to get tangled up in her grandmother's hatred.

Her father made a shooing motion. "Now take a few minutes to wash your paws and cool your heads. We'll eat in half an hour."

Tala's head spun with all the odors of strong emotions wafting around the table. She waited until the rest of the pack had cleared out before she got up. "Come on. Let's go check on Chloe."

Still holding hands, they headed toward the French doors leading to the patio and the garden.

"Just so you know: I disagree with what you said," Faith whispered, leaning close. "I think you'd make a great natak."

Fake modesty had never been Tala's thing, so she didn't bother with it. "And I'm sure I will." She lowered her voice. "I'm just not sure leading *this* pack is right for me. Maybe it's my fox side, but lately, I've felt that living full-time with three dozen siblings, aunts, uncles, and cousins might be a bit much. I've always enjoyed coming back home for a while, but I've realized that there's a reason why I never applied for a posting that kept me around more."

Slowly, a smile formed on Faith's lips. "Oh, you mean a smaller pack might fit your nature better? Let's say just three—"

"Tala! Wait!" Rey's voice interrupted before they reached the French doors.

Tala grumbled under her breath.

When she and Faith turned, Rey and Mirella hurried toward them, their hands tightly clasped too.

"Can we talk?" Rey asked quietly.

Faith exchanged a long look with Tala, who nodded. "I'll go check on Chloe," Faith said.

"And I'll catch some fresh air before dinner," Mirella added.

After one last reassuring glance back, Faith stepped onto the patio, followed by Mirella, leaving Tala to really talk to her brother for the first time in years.

Faith walked to the edge of the stone patio and inhaled deeply. The chill in the mountain air felt good on her overheated face.

During her last visit with the pack, she hadn't ventured out here, so she paused and took it all in.

A kidney-shaped pool sat off to the left, its cover tightly secured since it was only the second week of May. Wicker chairs were arranged in clusters. Hedges bordered the space, and flowering bushes added splashes of pink to the green lawn that stretched toward the forest.

A dozen kids, ranging in age from toddlers to teenagers, were darting between the bushes, chasing each other in a game of tag. The older kids kept a careful eye on the younger ones, making sure no one ventured too close to the covered pool. Their laughter rang through the crisp air, and Faith could easily make out Chloe's carefree giggles.

Her daughter wasn't standing on the sidelines, watching the others, as Faith had expected. Chloe was right in the center of the game, her cheeks flushed with excitement as she ran after one of the cousins.

After the tension of the pack meeting, Chloe's laughter was like a balm to Faith's frazzled nerves. She leaned her forearms onto the back of a wicker chair and smiled as she watched Chloe.

As an only child without any cousins, she didn't often get to play like this outside of school, and Faith loved that she got the opportunity now.

If she had been worried about Chloe playing with physically stronger, more agile Wrasa kids, she now realized that her concern had been unnecessary. Chloe seemed to keep up without any problem. She looked as if she belonged. Amazing that she'd found her place here so easily.

Mirella, who had silently lingered a few steps away, walked over. "Can we talk for a minute?"

Faith glanced back at the house.

Tala and Rey stood in the middle of the dining area, facing each other with serious expressions. She could tell by Tala's body language that she was tense but not angry or cornered. The conversation seemed to be going okay—or as okay as could be expected. There was no need for her to rush back inside. "Sure."

"I, uh…" Mirella's gaze flicked to the playing kids, then back to Faith. "I wanted to thank you for speaking up for me…and to apologize to you personally."

Faith didn't move or fill the silence with half-hearted words of acceptance. After all the anxiety Mirella had put her through, she didn't want to let her off the hook that easily, so she waited to see what exactly Mirella was apologizing for.

"It was wrong of me to send you that letter," Mirella continued. "To try to make you believe Tala was nothing but a cold-blooded killer."

Now Faith couldn't keep quiet anymore. "I think she just proved that she's anything but." She tilted her head toward the living room.

"I know." Mirella's shoulders sagged as if weighed down by guilt. "I shouldn't have tried to break you up. Your relationship… Somehow, it didn't seem real."

Faith held her breath. Had Mirella sensed that their relationship had started out as fake?

"Not the same way mine and Rey's is. I didn't see you as one of us, so your heartbreak didn't seem the same."

Ah. So Mirella didn't suspect a thing—she merely didn't like humans. Faith sighed.

"But I was on the other side of that restroom door in the hospital. I smelled your fear, your desperate hope, your love for Tala. Your emotions were so strong that I could smell them despite all the hospital odors…and I realized that your relationship and your feelings weren't different at all." Mirella looked her in the eyes. "I can't undo what I did, but I want you to know I'm truly sorry."

Faith believed her—but that didn't make forgiving her easy. "It's going to take time for me to trust you."

"I know," Mirella whispered.

Faith held up her hand, indicating she wasn't done. "But since you're part of Tala's pack, I'm willing to try."

"Thank you," Mirella croaked out, one hand pressed halfway between her chest and her throat. "Except…it's not just Tala's pack anymore. It's your pack now too."

The words tripped Faith up like a rope tangling around her ankles.

Your pack. She had a pack now! A family other than her dad and Chloe. Brennan and Jemma, Arlyn, Sutton, Rey and Mirella, even grumpy Uncle Arnold and prickly Grandma…they were her family too.

She belonged here—not as a barely tolerated outsider clinging to Tala's side but as a true pack member. Chloe had instinctively understood it right away, while Faith hadn't fully grasped it until now.

Faith exhaled a shaky breath. She hadn't realized how much she had longed for it until Mirella had said it out loud.

Mirella smiled. "You haven't thought about it that way before, have you?"

Faith struggled to form words, so she just shook her head.

"Well, it's true. Even the skeptics will come around eventually."

Finally, Faith managed to return the smile. "I guess I'd better find out Tala's grandmother's name, then."

Mirella's apologetic smile grew into a more lighthearted grin. "Or you could just call her *Grandma*, like we all do."

A chuckle burst from Faith's chest, mingling with the kids' laughter. "Let's give that a few years."

Tala had rarely seen Rey at a loss for words, but now he didn't seem to know how to start the conversation. She bit back a snarky comment, suggesting a "thank-you" might make a good opener.

Snide remarks like that had been their style of communication for years, but maybe Faith had been right. Perhaps this was a second chance for them too.

"You didn't have to do that," Rey burst out. He grunted and shook his head. "That didn't come out right. What I was trying to say was…"

"Yes?" Tala drawled.

"Thank you for not letting them kick Mirella out," Rey finally said. His tone was gruff, but his scent gave him away—he was deeply grateful. "I know Mirella messed up, but she didn't deserve to be banned from the pack." He lowered his head and rubbed the back of his neck. "If anything, I'm the one who deserves it," he added in an almost inaudible mutter.

"What?" What had he done? Tala leaned against the island separating the kitchen from the dining area as her knees threatened to wobble. Great Hunter, she really couldn't deal with yet another revelation of betrayal.

"Mirella and I talked a lot over the past few days. More than we ever have before." Rey sighed. "I wish we'd done it sooner, because it turns out I'm not such a great catch as a mate as I thought. Mirella was convinced that I didn't love her the same way she loves me. That it was just a political arrangement, a way to gain power for me."

Tala snorted. "Wolf poop. I mean, when Mom told me you were engaged to Lasandra's sister, I admit that's what I thought too. But the first time I saw the two of you together, I realized you do love her. Anyone with a nose can tell."

Rey scratched the back of his neck, looking like the teenager Tala had grown up with. "You know we tend to dismiss our noses when self-doubts creep in."

True. That was probably why it had taken her so long to notice that her and Faith's mate scent had turned real.

"Mirella thought becoming natak was all I cared about—and if she couldn't help me with that, she felt useless as a mate," Rey finished, his head lowered. "That's why she went too far, sending Faith that letter and lying to you about the bug."

Tala raked her fingers through her hair. "Why didn't you tell the pack earlier?" She waved toward the long table. "It might have helped if they had known more about her motivation."

"Because Mirella made me promise I wouldn't. She doesn't want anyone to blame me in any way."

Tala admitted to herself that she had underestimated Mirella. She glanced through the French doors to the patio, where Faith and Mirella stood, talking. Her gaze was drawn from Mirella to Faith, whose cheeks had flushed in the chilly air outside. Great Hunter, she looked good out there, as if she was where she belonged!

Finally, she forced her attention back to Rey. "Does she know you're telling me?"

Rey nodded. "As much as we both want to take over as the pack's alpha pair one day, we don't want you to give up your dream just because of our mistakes."

"My dream?" Tala asked.

"Becoming natak. Truth be told, I think you'd be a great leader for our pack."

Tala gripped the edge of the kitchen island. It was the first time he had ever said something like that to her. She flared her nostrils but couldn't detect the sulfurous odor of a lie. He really meant it! "Where's that suddenly coming from? You always acted like I'm the last person you'd ever want to lead the pack."

"I know," Rey said quietly. "Faith was right. That was a me issue, not a you issue. Let's face it, you're pretty formidable. Even with four paws, it was hard to keep up with you. With only three, I always felt like I was one step behind."

"You? I was the one always struggling to keep up! I mean, you're…" She gestured at his tall, muscular build, then at her own diminutive frame. It was about more than physical differences, of course, but her appearance reminded everyone—herself included—that she wasn't a Syak. "Plus you've always been Grandma's favorite. Dad's too. Probably even Mom's."

Rey slapped the kitchen island next to her. "Are you fucking kidding me? You're their favorite! Even Grandma admires the heck out of you."

"Right." Tala huffed. "That's why she gives me shit every time I come home."

"Yes, it is. She expected you to take over the pack one day—preferably with a Syak mate by your side."

Tala glanced outside again, just in time to see Faith smile at Mirella. "Not going to happen," she murmured, still looking at Faith.

Rey chuckled. "Yeah, clearly not. You're tail over muzzle in love with Faith."

"No. I mean…yes. She's the one for me. But that's not what I meant. Me taking over the pack is not going to happen." She lifted her hand before he could interrupt. "Not because of you or Mirella. I realized that becoming natak is no longer my dream. Maybe it never really was."

"What are you talking about? You wanted it from the time you were this tall!" He held his hand up to hip level.

"I wanted it because that's what a dominant Syak was supposed to want. If I didn't want it, I wouldn't be a real Syak. But you know what? Lately,

I realized I no longer care what others think. I don't have to out-wolf the wolves or fit into a mold to feel worthy. I have my own little pack now"—her gaze went to Faith again, then to Chloe, who was playing on the lawn—"and I can just be…me."

Rey's throat worked, but it took a while before he could form words. "I had no idea that's how you felt."

"Me neither," Tala said. "Not until very recently."

"If I'm honest, I always thought part of the reason why you were so determined to become natak was that you're convinced I wasn't good enough and couldn't cut it as the pack's leader," Rey murmured.

Tala firmly shook her head. "No. At times, I thought you were an ass, but never that you'd be a bad natak. As Faith said, it was a me issue, not a you issue."

Rey wrapped his arm around his belly and let out a deep laugh. "So we were both feeling inadequate and desperately trying to prove ourselves? Great Hunter, we really are siblings, aren't we?"

Even though she had just said that she didn't care what others thought, Rey calling them siblings made warmth spread through her chest. "Yeah, clearly, we're more alike than either of us wants to admit."

They stood next to the kitchen island and grinned at each other for a full minute.

"So you're really okay with me becoming natak?" Rey finally asked as if he still couldn't believe it.

Tala shrugged. "I'm fine with it."

He gave her a doubtful look.

"Make no mistake, brother. That doesn't mean you'll get to boss me around. I'm still an alpha and a part of this pack. I'll never be shy when it comes to sharing my opinion on what's best for the pack. If you mess up, I'll tell you to your face."

Instead of becoming defensive and asserting his authority, Rey chuckled. "I didn't expect anything less from you."

They nodded at each other.

"Come on, Reynard," Tala said with a pat on his arm. "Let's go get our mates and wash our paws before we're late for dinner."

He followed her to the French doors. "You know what? You can go back to calling me Rey."

"Oh? I thought you prefer Reynard now."

He shook his head. "I just didn't want to be Rey anymore, the little boy who got his face rubbed in leaves by the shortest pup in the pack every fall."

"I could still do that, you know?"

He growled playfully. "Dream on. I'd have you buried in a pile of leaves faster than you can say *mercy*."

"Ha! I'd like to see you try!"

"I will—provided you'll come home this fall." He gave her a probing look, and the joking mood shifted.

"I will. I have a feeling I'll be back more often from now on." It was probably a little soon to think like that, but she wanted Faith to come to love her family and Chloe to grow up with cousins. "Someone has to keep you on your toes after all."

With that, she opened the French doors and wrestled him for who got to step through first.

CHAPTER 18

Since most of the pack was home, the day had been pure chaos. Tala had hoped to squeeze in a run through the forest, leaving the stress behind as she shifted into her animal form. But she hadn't managed to slip away, and now a restless energy thrummed beneath her skin.

It didn't help that her mom had basically kidnapped Faith. While it warmed her heart to see Faith bonding with her mother and soaking up that time like a sponge, she missed having Faith by her side after being separated from her for most of the week.

Tala dropped onto the edge of the bed, took off her replacement ID tag, and tossed it onto the nightstand.

The door squeaked open, and Chloe rushed inside. She hadn't slowed down all day, buzzing around like a hummingbird on speed.

Tala grinned. The pup would sleep like a log tonight—while Tala would probably lie awake all night, as she shared a bed with Faith, intimately close but not allowed to touch.

Already in her pajamas, which were dotted with little pine trees, deer, wolves, and foxes, Chloe darted around the bed, grabbed one of the pillows, and ran back to the door.

"Hey, where are you going with that?" Tala called after her. "And isn't it past your bedtime?"

"Yes. I'm going to bed now." Chloe whirled around and ran back to her. "Jemma said I can sleep in the sunroom with the other pups! We have sleeping bags!" She gave a hop and threw her arms around Tala for a hug. "This is the best trip ever! Good night!" Then she was off again.

On the stairs, she nearly collided with Faith, and her excited voice drifted back to Tala as she repeated what she had just told her.

Minutes later, Faith entered the room, her irresistible scent instantly filling it. She didn't say anything as she closed the door behind herself and leaned against it. Her gaze met Tala's. "Chloe is sleeping downstairs, with the 'other pups.'" While her words might have been casual, her tone wasn't—and neither was the look in her eyes.

Tala instantly grasped why.

They would have the room to themselves tonight, without a little human chaperone to keep them in check.

"Yeah, I heard," Tala replied, her voice hoarse.

The air between them seemed to vibrate with an undeniable tension, the kind that made Tala's body tingle all over. But she vowed not to overwhelm Faith or rush her into anything.

"Are you okay with sharing the bed, even if we have to get cozy and share a pillow since Chloe stole yours?" Tala asked.

Faith pushed off the door and crossed the room toward Tala. "It depends," she said with a playful twinkle in her eyes. "Will I find another mouse in front of the bed tomorrow morning?"

"I can't rule it out. My fox likes taking care of her mate, you know?" It felt amazing to get to call Faith that for real. "It's like serving you breakfast in bed."

"I really prefer pancakes. I wonder if there's a way to stop your fox from gifting me mice." Faith tapped her index finger against her full bottom lip as if trying to think of a solution. "Let's see… Didn't you say shifting takes up a lot of energy?"

Tala nodded and watched her curiously. Where was Faith going with this? Her tone was teasing, but her scent intensified, carrying with it an undercurrent of something more meaningful that made Tala's skin buzz with anticipation.

"So if we were to burn a lot of energy tonight, you likely wouldn't feel up to shifting and hunting tomorrow morning, right?" Faith asked.

Tala swallowed against an instantly dry mouth. "Very likely. And I'd be further deterred from going out to hunt if I woke up snuggled up to a beautiful, stark naked mate."

"Oh?" Faith tried to keep up the playfulness but couldn't hide the hitch in her voice. "Is that a fact?"

Their gazes seared into each other.

"Since I never bonded with a mate the way I have with you, it's more like an untested hypothesis," Tala replied huskily. "Care to help me prove it?"

Faith took another step toward her.

She was so close now that her uninjured leg brushed Tala's knee. Faith's scent enveloped her, sending her senses into overdrive. Her fingers twitched with the urge to touch her, to pull her onto the bed, but she forced herself to stay still, waiting for Faith's reply.

"Well, I'm very committed to helping improve Wrasa/human relationships, so…"

Tala gripped a fistful of the sheets to hold herself back for a few more seconds. "Lock the door."

Faith sucked in a shuddery breath. "What if Chloe needs me tonight?"

"She won't," Tala said. "That's the great thing about being part of a pack—there are at least a dozen babysitters downstairs who'll take care of her."

With hurried steps, Faith went to the door, locked it, then returned to the bed.

When Tala stood, they were so close that Faith's much-too-fast breath brushed Tala's face, sending shivers down her body.

"Where were we?" Tala rasped.

"Not sure." Faith's eyes were dazed, clouded with desire. She stared at Tala's mouth and bit her own bottom lip.

Tala let out a low groan. That was so damn sexy. She instantly wanted to nibble the sensual curve of that lip.

"I remember something about a stark naked mate," Faith said, her voice as husky as Tala's.

"Ah, right," Tala got out with some difficulty. "Let's make that happen. But first…" She couldn't wait another second to kiss Faith. She slid one arm around her and pulled her tight against her body. With her free hand, she cupped her face as she claimed her mouth in a slow kiss.

She had meant for it to be tender, but it instantly heated up as Faith's soft lips opened under hers.

Eagerly, Tala stroked inside. Faith tasted like the berry crumble she'd had for dessert—Tala's favorite treat, just waiting to be devoured.

Her moan vibrated against Tala's lips. She clasped the back of Tala's neck with one hand and clutched her shoulder with the other, urging her closer and deepening the kiss.

The press of her body, her intoxicating scent, and the glide of Faith's tongue against her own washed away all thoughts except for one: She needed to feel more of her. All of her.

The layers of fabric between them suddenly felt like an irritating barrier.

With a low growl, Tala broke the kiss and trailed nips and kisses down her neck as she fumbled with the tiny buttons on Faith's blouse.

Faith's pulse pounded beneath her lips.

"That's the problem with human clothing—too many damn buttons," Tala muttered against Faith's throat. Part of her wanted to rip the blouse apart, sending the buttons flying, but she managed to control her impatience and popped them open one by one, determined to savor every inch of skin she bared. She kissed a path across Faith's collarbone, then down her chest, farther down with every button.

"Yours doesn't have that problem." Faith tugged at the hem of Tala's loose V-neck shirt and raised it higher.

Tala took her lips off Faith's skin only long enough to yank her own shirt over her head, leaving her chest bare, then her mouth and hands were back on Faith.

"No bra?" Faith gasped out. She slid her fingers up Tala's naked back, tracing her spine and her shoulder blades and teasing the sides of her breasts with featherlight caresses, which sent a tremor through Tala and made her task even more difficult.

"Takes too long to undo." She was talking about bras being a hindrance when it came to shifting, but right now, every single piece of clothing seemed to take too long to remove.

Finally, the last button slid free, and Faith's blouse parted, revealing creamy skin and a black lace bra.

Tala stared at the sexy sight. But just looking wasn't enough. Slowly, she reached up, cupped one of Faith's breasts, and stroked it through the lacy material. Faith's nipple instantly hardened against her palm.

A gasp escaped Faith. She eagerly pressed into the touch. "Take it off." The raw desire in her voice sent a thrill through Tala. "Take *everything* off."

Tala didn't have to be asked twice. She brushed the blouse off Faith's shoulders and down her arms, not caring where it landed.

Her slacks were next. Thankfully, the button gave way easily. The rasp of the zipper and both of their already elevated breathing filled the room.

Slow, slow, Tala told herself as she eased the pants over Faith's curvy hips and slid them down her shapely legs, careful not to brush against her stitches.

But the urgency burning inside of her made it hard to hold back.

Faith didn't seem to want her to either—she hurriedly kicked off her shoes and socks, stepped out of her slacks, and stood in front of her in only her bra and a pair of matching panties.

Tala's body groaned in protest as she backed away so she could trail her gaze down Faith's nearly naked form in a heated sweep, taking in the gentle flare of her hips, the soft curve of her belly, and the fair skin that contrasted nicely with the black lace of her underwear.

"Great Hunter," she whispered. "You're beautiful."

A bright shade of red spread across Faith's cheeks. She let out a throaty chuckle. "I've been wondering how often I can make you say that once we make love."

"How beautiful I think you are?" Tala murmured. "I'll say that so often, you might get sick of it."

"Never." Faith's brown eyes seemed to smolder as she took in Tala's body. "Especially since I'll tell you how gorgeous you are every chance I get too. But I meant how often I can make you gasp out 'Great Hunter.'"

So Faith had fantasized about this...about them.

Without looking away from her, Tala unbuttoned her own pants and kicked them off, along with her shoes and socks. "Let's find out," she said huskily and then bridged the remaining space between them.

"Wait, wait," Faith gasped out. Her hand went to Tala's upper chest, half stopping her approach, half caressing the bare skin there.

Tala froze. "What is it?"

A blush rose up Faith's body, and since she was nearly naked, Tala could trace its path with her gaze. "Um, is there anything I should know?"

"You mean, like STIs?" Tala shook her head. "Wrasa don't get sexually transmitted infections."

"Good. I don't have any either. But that's not what I meant." Faith's blush intensified, and Tala was equally charmed and mystified. "Is there anything I need to know about sex with a Wrasa...with you? Are there any differences?"

"Oh." Tala hadn't even thought about it. But then again, there hadn't been much thinking involved any time she had fantasized about making love to Faith. "Based on all the research I did, it seems it all works the same."

"Research?" Faith chuckled. "You mean all the steamy romances you read."

Tala nodded with a smirk. "Well, come to think of it, there is one difference."

Faith stared at her. "What you implied about Wrasa biology being different…that was a joke, right? You can't actually get me pregnant…can you?"

Tala's grin broadened. "No. But not for lack of trying."

"What's the difference, then?" Faith asked, her eyes smoldering.

"We've got superior stamina." Tala's voice came out in a seductive rasp.

Faith gulped audibly.

As much as Tala ached to touch her, she held herself back for another moment. "Is there anything I need to be careful of?"

"Just my knee." Faith pointed at the simple Band-Aid covering the stitches she had gotten last week. "It doesn't hurt; I just have to avoid bending it too much."

Tala tenderly traced the outside of Faith's thigh with her fingertips, feeling goose bumps erupt under her touch. "I'll be careful. But other than that?" Tala needed to be sure she wouldn't hurt her human mate.

Faith shook her head. "Nothing. Don't hold back, okay? I want to experience all of it."

The raw need in her voice sent a surge of arousal through Tala. Primal instincts hummed beneath her skin with a fierce need to claim Faith and give her exactly what she wanted.

She leaned in slowly and dropped her voice to a husky murmur: "Then hold on tight, nemi. Because I'm not stopping until you're incoherent with pleasure."

A soft gasp escaped Faith.

Her breath brushed over Tala's lips as she reached around to unhook Faith's bra.

Tala's breasts were nestled beneath Faith's, and the lacy edge of the bra rubbed over Tala's nipples. A low groan rumbled in her throat. With unsteady fingers, she opened the clasps and drew the straps down Faith's arms until the bra dropped to the floor.

She broke their eye contact to glance down and admire Faith's breasts—full and gorgeous, with rosy nipples that instantly made Tala want to touch them or lavish them with her mouth.

But before she could do either, Faith surprised her by shimmying her panties down her legs, as if Tala wasn't undressing her fast enough. "Yours too. I need to see all of you."

Quickly, Tala pushed her own briefs down, and Faith's burning gaze followed their path as they slid down her legs until they ended up on top of the growing heap of clothes on the floor.

A visible shiver went through Faith—either because of the cool air in the bedroom or because the sight of Tala's naked body affected her. Possibly both.

Tala couldn't wait another second to touch her. She drew Faith into her arms and took her mouth in a hot, deep kiss, leaving no doubt about how much she wanted her.

Faith wound her fingers into Tala's hair and pressed closer.

Their bare breasts rubbed against each other as their tongues brushed in a passionate caress.

Faith moaned into her mouth, and an answering sound escaped Tala.

Without disentangling her fingers from Tala's hair, Faith walked backward and drew Tala with her.

Together, they tumbled onto the bed.

Tala ended up on top but was careful not to put any pressure on Faith's healing knee.

With their mouths still locked together, they moved to the middle of the mattress.

Faith's legs instantly parted, allowing Tala to settle between them.

The way their bodies fit together, touching all along their lengths, made Tala's head spin.

When Tala's thigh slid between hers, Faith made an inarticulate little sound in the back of her throat and bucked up against her, pressing their hips together. Her arousal coated Tala's leg.

Tala's nostrils flared. Faith's musky scent made her dizzy with desire. A ripple of pleasure rushed to Tala's center as they started to rock against each other.

Faith's skin glided against her own like cool silk but quickly heated up against Tala's.

Tala wanted to slide her hand between them, touch her, take her, devour her, do everything all at once, but she refused to rush this. She wanted to make sure Faith would enjoy every second. "Tell me what you want," she asked, her voice husky.

"I want you," Faith whispered against her lips. "I want you to take control."

A ragged groan tore out of Tala. Faith couldn't possibly know how much of a turn-on that was for her! Still, Tala clung to the flimsy remnants of her self-control. "Okay. But if I do anything you don't like, tell me."

"Don't like?" Faith chuckled hoarsely. "I don't think we need to worry about that."

Tala caught Faith's full bottom lip between hers, then gave it a teasing nip. "No?"

"No." Faith rolled her hips against Tala's thigh again. The wetness against her skin proved how much Faith had, indeed, liked everything she'd done so far.

"Well, then…" With a satisfied grin, Tala paused to look down at her. She rubbed her nose along Faith's cheek, breathed her in, and reveled in the scent and the smoothness of her skin. Lightly, she nibbled the shell of Faith's ear, then trailed kisses down the side of her neck.

Faith's rapid pulse thrummed beneath her lips, each beat tugging at something primal within her.

Tala gently grazed her teeth over it.

Moaning, Faith tipped her head back to give Tala full access.

Goose bumps formed beneath Tala's mouth as she trailed it lower, across Faith's collarbone, and she followed them with her tongue.

Faith let her touch wherever she wanted, her body soft and open, her trust in Tala complete. But she wasn't passive either. With her fingertips, she traced sensual patterns along Tala's back and down to her hips, her butt, and the back of her thighs. Her hands were cooler than Tala's overheated skin but still left trails of fire everywhere they touched.

Good thing Faith had asked her to take control because if Tala had rolled over and let Faith freely explore her body, this would have been over much too fast.

Tala moved a little to the side, balancing on her left forearm so she could touch Faith with her hand too. She slid her fingers along Faith's side, skimming the outer curve of one breast, then followed the arcs of Faith's ribs down and caressed the silky underside.

Soft. So incredibly soft.

She kept her gaze on Faith's face, watching her expression as she slowly circled one nipple with a fingertip. On each pass, she made the circle smaller and smaller.

"Tala…" Her name sounded like a tortured groan—half pleasure, half impatience. The scent of Faith's excitement intensified.

Tala grinned down at her, then let out a groan of her own as Faith rasped her nails down her back, silently urging her on. A shiver raced through her body, and she dragged her thumb across Faith's nipple a little harder than she'd intended.

Faith arched up into the touch with a strangled cry.

Tala surged up in bed and smothered the sexy sound with a deep kiss. "Shh, sharp ears everywhere, remember?" she whispered against her lips. "You have to be quiet." Truth be told, she didn't care if every Syak in the house heard them, especially since the pups were all in the sunroom at the far end of the house, but seeing Faith trying to control herself was unexpectedly hot.

"Easy for you to say." Faith moaned. "My entire body already feels like it's on fire."

"Fire, hmm? Let's see if we can put out some of the flames." Tala ducked her head and quickly swiped her tongue across Faith's taut nipple. Then she drew back an inch and blew a cooling stream of air over the now-damp breast. "Is that helping?"

"Helping?" Faith gasped out. She stared at her, eyes hazy. "No. You're making it worse."

Tala drew circles around the nipple with the tip of her tongue, then licked it again. "Worse?" she whispered against the wet skin.

"Okay, maybe that's…oh…not the best w-word."

"How about we forget about words and focus on feelings?"

"Y-yes. Make me feel everything." Faith slid her fingers up the nape of Tala's neck, threaded her fingers through her hair, and drew her down to her breast.

Tala went willingly.

Their moans mingled when Tala closed her lips around Faith's nipple and sucked gently.

"Oh God!" Faith clasped Tala against her breast with both hands.

Delicious chills rippled across Tala's skin, and she groaned against Faith's nipple.

Faith bowed her back, pressing her breast more deeply into Tala's mouth. She raked her nails down either side of Tala's spine.

Pinpricks of lust shot down Tala's body. She gently massaged one breast with her hand while she worshipped the other with playful swirls and languid strokes of her tongue, interspersed with gentle sucks.

Faith's hands never left her for a second. Restlessly, she trailed them over Tala's back, down to her ass, then back up to clasp her head.

The sexy sounds Faith made sent flutters of arousal through Tala's belly. She loved the way Faith responded to her.

Soon, the subtle roll of Faith's hips against hers became a more insistent rocking.

Tala couldn't stop her own hips from pressing back down against her, but she stilled them. This wasn't about her; it was all about making Faith feel good and showing her how much she loved her.

Reluctantly, she pulled her mouth away from Faith's tempting breast and placed a string of open-mouthed kisses down the soft curve of her belly.

Pale silver lines—almost like tiny scars—stretched across it, shimmering in the intimate glow of the lamp on the nightstand.

Tala paused and lifted her mouth from Faith's skin to study them. "What are those?" she whispered against one of the faint marks.

Faith weakly lifted her head. Her already flushed cheeks took on an even darker crimson color, and her scent revealed a mix of embarrassment and frustration at the interruption. "Oh. Stretch marks."

Tala sent a questioning look up her body. "What's that?"

"From when I was pregnant with Chloe. Wrasa don't get them?" She stroked her fingers over Tala's hip. "Of course you don't," she answered her own question before Tala could. "Your body is perfection. Mine is—"

Tala reached up to press a finger to her lips. "Hush. I love them. I love your body. I love you."

"I love you too," Faith whispered against Tala's finger. She ran the tip of her tongue along its length, then sucked the digit into her mouth before sliding it back out achingly slow.

"Great Hunter!" Tala couldn't believe how erotic that felt. She replaced her finger with her lips and kissed Faith until they were both breathless.

Then she recreated her previous path down Faith's body. When she reached the silvery marks, she traced them with her mouth and her fingertips, entranced by how soft they were.

Faith gasped and squirmed beneath her.

Tala froze. "Does this hurt?"

"No. Although you are making me ache." Faith tightened her fingers in Tala's hair and tried to guide her lower.

"Ah." Tala smiled against her skin. "I'll get there. Trust me."

"I do."

The vulnerability in Faith's tone sent a warmth of a different kind through Tala's chest. She whispered another kiss beneath her navel, then followed the silvery lines down Faith's lower belly.

When she reached the trimmed patch of curls, Tala paused. Her nostrils flared as she took her in.

The heady scent of Faith's arousal filled the air and entwined with her own, mingling the way their mate scent had and creating an intoxicating aroma.

Any restraint she still had was slipping away fast. She had to taste her. Now.

The intensity of her desire almost scared her, but when she glanced up into Faith's eyes to make sure she was okay with what Tala was about to do, there was no fear, no hesitation, only trust and unguarded need.

Faith spread her legs in an eager invitation, opening herself to Tala's touch.

With a low groan, Tala slid lower and placed a gentle kiss on Faith's leg, just a few inches above the Band-Aid. Slowly, she ran the tip of her tongue up the inside of her thigh. The scent of Faith's desire lured her higher and higher.

Faith writhed restlessly beneath her. Her gasps and fingers flexing in Tala's hair urged her on.

Tala kissed over the soft tuft of curls, then hovered over her for another moment to breathe in her scent. She was nearly panting in anticipation, sending puffs of air across Faith's wetness.

"Please," Faith groaned out. She urged her closer with both hands in her hair.

Tala couldn't resist any longer. She lowered her head and ran her tongue through Faith's wet heat.

Faith's taste—sweet and tangy and as intoxicating as her scent—flooded Tala's mouth, and she hummed her enjoyment. She wanted to drown in her. "Great Hunter," she murmured against her. "You're delicious."

With a low moan, Faith tipped her hips up. "Then have more."

Tala ran her tongue over silky folds and circled her clit with slow, lazy swirls.

Faith's hips lifted off the bed. "More," she whispered again, her voice raspy.

Tala trailed her hand down the outside of Faith's uninjured leg, lifted it up, and draped it over her shoulder, leaving Faith even more open to her touch. Then she paused and looked up to make sure Faith was okay with that.

Faith gazed down at her through half-closed eyes, chestnut hair spilling over the pillow in wild tangles, lips parted, breasts heaving.

Great Hunter, she's beautiful. And she's mine. She ducked her head again and stroked the flat of her tongue over Faith's clit.

Faith sucked in a sharp breath and pressed herself against Tala.

The intimate feel of touching Faith this way made Tala's heart race. She alternated between light flicks and long swipes and went from fast to slow, then fast again, all her senses attuned to what coaxed the strongest reaction from Faith.

But it was hard to tell because Faith passionately responded to everything she did.

Tala couldn't get enough of the erotic roll of Faith's hips, the scrape of her nails against Tala's shoulders, the tugs on her hair.

Hungrily, she absorbed Faith's taste. She felt drunk on her delectable flavor and the sounds of pure sensual pleasure she made.

Faith writhed and rocked, her movements quickly growing frantic.

Tala grasped her hips with both hands and held her still so she could continue to pleasure her.

The moaned words tumbling from Faith's lips were indistinguishable, but Tala knew what she was saying—felt it in every cell of her body. It was her name.

Faith's breath was coming in ragged bursts. Her thighs started to quiver on either side of Tala's face, and Tala could feel how close she was.

Her own belly tightened in response, and she clenched her thighs together to keep her own arousal in check and focus on Faith. Gently, she caught Faith's clit between her lips and sucked.

With a sharp gasp, Faith pushed herself upward, into Tala's mouth. "Tala! I'm... I'm..." She dug her fingers into Tala's scalp, and her heel pressed against Tala's lower back.

Abruptly, she disentangled her fingers from Tala's hair. She shoved one fist against her mouth and bit down on her knuckles to stifle her cries. Her other hand flew down as if looking for some kind of tether.

Tala let go of her hip with one hand.

Their fingers instantly found each other and interlaced.

Faith surged up against Tala's mouth one last time, then her body went taut against Tala's, and she collapsed onto the bed, panting for breath.

Aftershocks of pleasure quivered through Faith. Her body felt weightless and heavy at the same time. For several moments, she couldn't move. Finally, she loosened her grip on Tala's hair, combed her fingers through the short, silky strands, and caressed her flushed cheek.

Tala pressed a soft kiss to the inside of Faith's thigh, sending more shivers through her, and gently lowered Faith's leg from her shoulder back to the bed. She looked up Faith's body, into her eyes, and licked her lips as if she had just finished the most delicious meal. Her pupils were wide with desire, her eyes wild yet tender, full of love. The golden glow of her irises seared through Faith like a living flame.

"Come up here and kiss me," Faith whispered, her voice hoarse and her lips parched from her panting. God, she hoped she hadn't cried out too loudly. She had been entirely unprepared for her body's intense response to Tala.

Tala prowled up Faith's body, pressing against her as if trying to imprint herself on Faith's sweat-dampened skin. Her hard nipples dragged up Faith's belly.

Renewed tingles shot through Faith.

Tala paused to place kisses on her breasts, throat, the corner of her mouth. Then she leaned over her, braced on one elbow, and gently brushed damp strands of hair from Faith's brow. The look on her face was so tender and awestruck that tears pricked Faith's eyes.

She reached up, cradled Tala's face between her hands, and pulled her down.

Tala didn't resist. She instantly claimed Faith's mouth in a deep kiss, holding nothing back.

Faith returned the kiss just as passionately and groaned into Tala's mouth as she tasted herself.

When they came up for air, both were breathing hard.

"That was incredible," Faith whispered against Tala's lips. That word really didn't do it justice, but her pleasure-hazed brain couldn't find a better one.

Tala hummed her agreement. "*You* were incredible. You're so, so sexy when you come. I need to do that again." She trailed her hand down Faith's belly.

To Faith's surprise, her body instantly reacted, leaning into the touch. But she gripped Tala's hand and drew it back up. "No."

"No?" Tala blinked. "You don't want that?"

"I do. But there's something I want more."

"Anything," Tala said without hesitation.

"I want to touch you." She wanted to see Tala come undone beneath her fingers.

Tala's breath hitched. "Anything," she said again.

Faith urged her onto her back, and Tala went easily. It was beyond hot to see the proud Syak become putty in her hands.

She hovered over Tala. It took a moment to find a position that didn't put too much pressure on her stitches, but then she forgot all about them as she looked down at Tala and tried to commit every detail to memory—the flush on Tala's high cheekbones, the fire in her eyes, the thin layer of perspiration that gleamed on her skin.

Then she couldn't wait any longer. She had to touch her. Now.

She trailed kisses across Tala's tight jawline, lightly nipped her earlobe, and caressed the satiny skin beneath her ear.

A shudder went through Tala, and she raked her fingers up Faith's back.

Humming, Faith continued her slow exploration. Tala's skin was feverishly hot beneath her lips as she kissed along her collarbone.

Tala's shoulders were perfection—all smooth softness and sleek strength, like the rest of her body. Faith nibbled the lean muscle, then dipped her tongue into the hollow of Tala's throat, tasting the salty skin.

A low noise escaped Tala, but she didn't try to take back control. The way she lay there, open to her touch—vulnerable yet powerful—was thrilling.

Faith glided one hand along Tala's sensitive side as she kissed a path down the center of her chest. Wherever goose bumps formed beneath her touch—which was pretty much everywhere—she lingered. "I can't get enough of you," she whispered as she let her hand drift across the slope of Tala's breast.

Tala's heartbeat thudded beneath her palm. "Good," she rasped out. "Because you're stuck with me."

"I can live with that." Faith cupped Tala's breasts. They were small. Firm. A perfect fit for her hands.

A low rumble started in Tala's chest, and the vibration skittered through Faith's body.

Keeping her gaze on Tala's face, she rubbed her thumbs back and forth across her hard nipples.

The rumble turned into a throaty groan, and Tala bowed her back into the touch.

"I love the way you sound when you're turned on—all raspy and growly."

"Then you must be"—another growl escaped Tala—"really enjoying yourself because you drive me wild."

"Yeah?" Faith bent her head and skated her tongue along Tala's nipple, drawing more of the delicious sounds.

Her hair formed a curtain around Tala's breast, and Tala reached down and brushed it back behind Faith's ears. "I want to see this."

Knowing Tala was watching her made it even more exciting. Slowly, Faith lowered her head and touched her tongue to Tala's breast again.

Tala twisted her fingers into Faith's hair and held her mouth in place.

Faith circled, licked, and sucked the taut nipple until Tala writhed beneath her.

She lifted her hand to the neglected breast, but Tala caught it and urged it down her body. "I need you to touch me now."

Faith's pulse quickened. She dragged her short nails down the firm planes of Tala's belly.

Tala inhaled sharply. Her muscles tightened and twitched beneath Faith's touch. Heat radiated off her in waves, fueling the fire within Faith.

When her fingertips brushed Tala's damp curls, she paused, almost overwhelmed by how much she wanted her. "What do you need?"

"With you, not much. Just touch me."

Faith slid her fingers lower, into Tala's slick heat. "God, you're so hot. So wet." A new rush of arousal hit her, as if Tala were the one touching her.

Tala hissed and shuddered beneath her. She pulled Faith down for a long, hard kiss.

Faith trailed her tongue along Tala's while her fingers mirrored the languid strokes. She wanted to go slow and draw things out, but clearly, Tala's body had other ideas.

Tala fisted the sheets and broke the kiss with a gasp. She muttered something in the Old Language, probably either curses or a prayer for control. "I don't know if I can hold back for long." The raw, helpless desire on Tala's face sent a rush of sensations down Faith's own body.

"Kalyani, nemi." It was more than okay, actually. As hot as it had been to let Tala take control, it was just as exciting to see her lose it. She stroked her faster.

Tala rocked against her. "Just like that."

"Yeah? What about this?" Faith watched her face as she slid her fingers lower and teased at her entrance.

Tala groaned deep in her throat and nodded as if she was beyond speech at this point.

The need in her eyes stole Faith's breath. She kept eye contact as she slowly slid two fingers inside and began a gentle stroking.

"Faith!" Tala's hips rose to meet her, driving her fingers deeper.

Jesus! Faith had never seen anything as amazing as Tala moving against her fingers.

Her face showed everything she was feeling as Faith stroked her, completely unfiltered. Tala's throaty groans and low growls unraveled her.

Within seconds, the thrusts of Tala's hips grew wild and uncontrollable.

Faith tried to pin her down by sliding her leg over Tala's.

But Tala immediately took advantage of that new position by raising her thigh and pressing the firm muscle against Faith's clit.

"Oh God!" Faith ground down against her and lost herself in the blaze of Tala's eyes.

"Wait… Wait!" Tala gasped out. She slid her hand between them, her fingertips tracing a fiery trail down Faith's belly. The angle was awkward, but somehow, she managed to enter her with a possessive growl. "Mine!"

"Yes!" The heat of Tala's fingers filled her deep inside.

Their moans resonated around the room as they rocked against each other, immediately finding a matching rhythm.

It was so hot and intimate that Faith struggled to breathe. The glide of Tala's scorching skin against her own was pure ecstasy. She stroked Tala deeper, moved herself against her fingers faster. Every thrust drove her higher and higher. Desperately, she tried to hang on as she found an angle that made Tala growl out her name.

Tala was panting. Her gaze clung to Faith, entirely transfixed.

Faith couldn't look away from her either even though it felt so good her eyes nearly crossed. Tala was so incredibly stunning. Her irises seemed to have turned an even more startling shade of gold, smoldering brightly.

The tension within Faith intensified, winding her tighter and tighter until she was trembling and gasping.

They both were.

Heat spread through her entire body, blazing along all nerve endings. She barely had enough control left to press the heel of her hand against Tala's clit on the next thrust.

"Now!" Tala gasped out. She curved her fingers and pressed upward as she surged against Faith one last time.

Pleasure slammed into Faith like a red-hot wave.

Tala tightened around her fingers. Her mouth opened in a soundless scream.

Faith slumped against her, and they collapsed onto the bed together.

Trying to catch her breath, Faith buried her face against the crook of Tala's neck, where her pulse hammered wildly.

Fingers still inside, they lay there, clutching each other until their heartbeats slowly returned to normal.

Carefully, Tala withdrew, and after a moment of regret, Faith did the same.

Tala exhaled. "Great Hunter," she whispered huskily.

A chuckle burst from Faith. "I lost count of how often I made you say that."

"Hmm. I didn't keep count either. Someone kept distracting me." Tala wiped her fingers on the sheets, then ran them through Faith's hair, untangling the messy strands.

"We'll have to do this again, then," Faith said even as a yawn escaped her.

"Definitely," Tala replied. "As soon as I can move."

Faith smiled against her shoulder. "So I wore you out despite your superior stamina? Mission accomplished! No waking up to a mouse in front of the bed."

"No. I'll find a more pleasant way to wake you up." Tala teasingly ran a finger down her spine.

A trail of tingles followed her touch.

But they were both too sated and tired to do anything else.

Tala reached for the crumpled sheet that had ended up at the foot of the bed and drew it over both of them. Not that Faith needed it—she knew that Tala's body heat would keep her warm all night.

She curled up on her side, nestled against Tala, who ran her palms over her back, her thighs, soothing now, not arousing.

"Is your knee okay?" Tala asked. "We probably did a few things that were not on your doctor's list of recommended activities."

"Hmm, probably. I lost track of that too. But it doesn't hurt." Faith found a more comfortable position for her knee, with its side resting on top of Tala's leg. Her eyes fluttered shut. "Tala?" she mumbled sleepily.

"Hmm?"

"I love you."

Tala's fingers stilled against her back. "I love you too, nemi."

It was the last thing Faith heard before she drifted off into a peaceful sleep.

CHAPTER 19

Faith slowly stirred awake and blinked her eyes open.

Morning sunlight cast a soft glow over Tala's old bedroom. The house was quiet; only the faint creak of floorboards from downstairs drifted through the door. No excited kids' voices or staccato footsteps yet—Chloe and the "other pups" had probably kept each other up way past their bedtime, so they were still asleep.

Faith wasn't in a hurry to get up either. Tala's naked body was pressed against her back, cocooning her in Tala's warmth. Even Faith's usually cold feet were toasty. The steady rhythm of Tala's breathing indicated that she was still asleep. One arm was draped over Faith's waist in a possessive gesture, her hand pressed to Faith's belly in a way that reminded her of the first night they had shared the bed, when Tala had played heating pad for her.

The thought put a smile on her face.

How far they had come since then! Of course, their relationship was still brand-new, but Faith trusted it would last. They had survived Jon framing Tala for nearly killing Faith's father. If they could overcome that, they could make it through anything.

Faith turned in Tala's arms so she could watch her sleep, careful not to wake her.

Tala's arm around her tightened, but she slept on. Her sharp, alert features were relaxed and unguarded.

Faith's heart clenched at the sight, and her fingers itched to comb through Tala's copper hair, which was tousled, with strands sticking out at odd angles from Faith running her fingers through it again and again.

The thought of the night before made Faith tingle all over.

They had certainly both been dedicated to burning as much energy as possible.

Carefully, she peeked across Tala's body and over the edge of the bed. No mouse.

"It worked, didn't it?" Tala's voice, low and gravely from sleep, rumbled against Faith's shoulder, sending shivers through her.

"Totally did."

"Good. I really like the stark-naked-mate tactic." Tala tightened her hold on Faith and opened her eyes. Their golden glow was as intense as it had been the previous night. "Morning."

"Good morning." Faith couldn't resist her rumpled appearance any longer. She pressed even closer and kissed her.

Tala responded sleepily but with a growing undercurrent of desire. "Want to make sure I have no energy left to bring you a mid-day snack either?"

"Well, the local mouse population would probably appreciate it, wouldn't they?"

"Not as much as I would," Tala murmured, her breath warm against Faith's face.

Just as their lips met again, Tala's phone buzzed on the nightstand.

Tala groaned and pressed her forehead to Faith's. "Seriously? I'm going to kill whoever that is." With one arm still wrapped around Faith, she reached behind herself and retrieved the phone. "Shit. It's Madsen. At least it's not a video call."

Faith froze. "Does he know about…?" She waved her finger back and forth between them.

"Us being in bed together?" A smirk curled Tala's lips. "I hope not!"

Faith lightly slapped her shoulder. Then her hand lingered against soft skin. "Us being together."

"Not really. I have to take this." Tala swiped her finger across the screen and lifted the phone to her ear. "What can I do for you, Manark?"

"Morning," Madsen said. "I hope I'm not interrupting."

Pressed close to Tala, Faith could hear every word he said.

She and Tala stared at each other. He couldn't possibly know what he had interrupted, could he?

"No, of course not," Tala replied, her professional Saru voice firmly in place. "I'm staying with my pack right now and taking the opportunity to introduce Faith to more aspects of Wrasa culture so she can fully understand and support us."

Faith clamped her hand to her mouth to stifle a laugh. *Aspects of Wrasa culture? Like how to prevent a Wrasa from leaving a mouse in front of the bed?* She pressed a kiss to Tala's temple, mouthed a silent "I'll leave you to talk," and gestured toward the bathroom. Chloe would be up soon, and Faith needed a shower before sitting down to breakfast with a pack of Syak and their sharp noses.

Tala tightened her arm around her as if she didn't want to let her go, but then reluctantly released her. Her fingers trailed down Faith's arm before dropping away.

As quietly as possible, Faith slipped out from under the warm covers.

She felt Tala's gaze follow her as she snuck across the room and pulled fresh clothes from her suitcase, ignoring her bra, slacks, and blouse that were scattered around the bed.

Madsen's voice still drifted faintly through the phone pressed to Tala's ear, and Tala responded with a distracted "Uh-huh."

Quietly, Faith made her way to the bathroom. When she reached it, she glanced back over her shoulder.

Tala still looked at her, her eyes gleaming with appreciation. Her free hand traced idle patterns on the sheets, where Faith had been lying a minute ago. "Uh, could you repeat that, sir?" she said into the phone. "The connection isn't the best up here in the mountains."

Faith pressed a hand to her mouth again. *Bad connection. Right.* She gave Tala one last amused smile, then stepped into the bathroom and closed the door behind her.

Tala wrenched her gaze from Faith's beautiful backside. "Yes, of course I'm listening. You've got my full attention, sir."

"I heard you spoke up for Mirella," Madsen said, his tone even, not giving away what he thought about that.

Tala gripped the phone more tightly. *Damn.* How had he found out so fast?

"And that you offered to give up your chance of becoming natak in favor of your brother," Madsen added before she could think of an answer.

Tala suppressed a sigh. Madsen wouldn't understand. He was the most dominant natak in the world. Giving up a position of power was not in his nature.

"I'm impressed," he said, his voice softening the slightest bit. "You put your pack first, ahead of your own ambition. Only a true alpha would do that."

Tala nearly dropped the phone. For as long as she had known him, there had been a constant tension between them. She had always believed no matter how hard she worked, no matter how good she was at her job, he would never fully accept her as a fellow Syak. But now respect reverberated in his tone, and she didn't know what to say. Finally, she settled on, "Thank you, sir."

"You're going to make a fine leader, even beyond the small units you've commanded so far," Madsen continued. "Which is why I decided to promote you. I've got a new job waiting for you."

The room spun around Tala. A new job. A promotion.

She should have been ecstatic. A few months ago, she would have been over the moon. But now all she could think about was that a new job would likely take her to a different state—away from Faith and Chloe.

So far, she had avoided thinking about the day when that would happen because it had seemed far in the future. Now that day might be right around the corner.

"Manark," she said as respectfully as possible, trying to keep a tight rein on her emotions. "My current mission isn't over yet. Faith and I still need to keep up our fake relationship until the Wrasa Rights Act passes."

Madsen snorted. "Fake relationship. Please. I wasn't born yesterday."

Oh shit. "You know about…Faith and me?" Tala barely kept her voice from cracking.

"Of course I know," he said in a haughty tone. "It's actually one of the reasons why you're getting this promotion. You've gained new insights into humans, and that'll come in handy for your new posting."

Tala let her head flop back onto the pillow. "So," she got out after a few seconds of silence, "what's the new job?"

"The FBI finally admitted they're out of their depth handling Wrasa-related cases. They have no clue about our culture or the way we think. That's why they're in the process of establishing a new agency, the FBSI."

"FBSI?" Tala repeated, her head still reeling.

"The Federal Bureau of Shape-Shifter Investigation. It will pair human agents with our Saru soldiers to handle cases involving Wrasa, whether as victims or as suspects. The agency will have two department heads, one human, one Wrasa. I want you to lead on our side."

Not too long ago, Tala would have hated having to work so closely with humans, but now it sounded like a new, exciting challenge. "Where would that assignment be, sir?"

"You'll be mainly stationed in DC."

"Oh." All tension fled Tala's body. She would get to stay in DC—with Faith!

Madsen chuckled. "Nice job perk, right?"

"Right," Tala said, even as she wrinkled her nose. Madsen knowing about her and Faith and casually commenting on their relationship would take some getting used to.

"There's something else," Madsen said, all traces of humor now gone from his voice. "I have news about what happened to Ms. MacAllister's mother."

Tala's pulse quickened. She sat up against the headboard. "What did you find out, sir?"

"Call me once you're back in DC, and we'll set up a meeting between the MacAllisters and the forensic technician who assisted with the autopsy. It's only fair they hear it first." Madsen ended the call without giving Tala a chance to reply.

Tala's hand with the phone flopped back to the bed.

The door to the bathroom opened a few inches, and Faith peeked through the gap. "Are you done?" she whispered.

When Tala nodded, Faith stepped back into the bedroom.

Tala's attention was immediately drawn to her.

Faith was fully dressed. Her hair was still damp and her face flushed from her shower. Her natural milk-and-honey scent mingled with a hint of lavender from the shampoo she had used. She was wearing a formfitting sweater and a pair of soft-looking jeans that molded to her shapely legs—legs Tala had kissed and nibbled the night before.

"Everything okay?" Faith sat on the edge of the bed and studied her with a concerned expression.

Tala gazed up at her and for a moment forgot what she had wanted to say. How was she supposed to think straight when Faith was looking like that? "You're beautiful."

Faith bent down and kissed her, her lips forming a smile against Tala's. "That's not what Madsen said, is it?"

A playful growl rose from Tala's throat. "It'd better not be!" Then she sobered. "No. He called to tell me about my new job."

Faith's features paled beneath the shower-induced flush. "New job? I thought he would let you stick around for a while, at least until I had a chance to make a public statement in support of Wrasa rights."

"No. Apparently, that'll just be a side hustle from now on. But don't worry," Tala added quickly. "I'll stick around. The new job is with the Federal Bureau of Shape-Shifter Investigation."

Faith frowned. "The Federal Bureau of Shape-Shifter Investigation? I never heard of it before."

"It's a new agency," Tala said. "And it's in DC."

The milk-and-honey scent Tala loved so much grew sweeter, as if someone had added an entire bucket of the most delicious honey as Faith's joy scented the air around her. "In DC?" she repeated in a whisper.

Tala nodded with a big grin of her own. "According to Madsen, I'm highly qualified to work with human agents since I recently gained new insights into humans."

"New insights, hmm?" Faith trailed one finger down Tala's arm. "Like what?"

Tala could barely think when Faith was touching her. "Like humans don't wink."

Faith chuckled. "So… I'm merely a side hustle now?"

Tala pulled her closer, into her lap, and nibbled Faith's neck. "Mmm. No. That's just what Madsen thinks. You'll always be my main hustle."

Faith slid her fingers into Tala's hair and tugged her head up for a kiss.

Tala let out a satisfied yip against Faith's lips. If only she could start every day like this. Well, maybe down the road, she could, now that she was staying in DC.

But there was one thing she couldn't keep from Faith, even if it might spoil their relaxed morning.

She reluctantly broke the kiss. "Madsen also said he had news about your mom."

Faith stilled in her arms. A trace of anxiety soured the sweet scent of her happiness. "What did he find out?"

Tala curled one hand around Faith's thigh and rubbed soothingly. "I don't know yet. He said he'll set up a meeting with the forensic technician who assisted with your mother's autopsy when we're back in DC."

Faith slumped against her.

Ugh. Tala hated leaving her hanging like this. She wrapped both arms around her and held her close. Every instinct screamed at her to tell Faith it would be all right, but she couldn't—not when she had no idea what Madsen's investigation had revealed.

They sat holding each other for a while, until footsteps pounded up the stairs.

Tala lifted her head. "Chloe's coming. We'd better unlock the door before she knocks it down." Reluctantly, she slid out from beneath Faith and padded to the door.

"Uh, Tala?"

Tala turned. "Yes?"

Faith slowly dragged her gaze down Tala's body, leaving goose bumps in its wake. "You're naked."

A glance down her own body confirmed it. Tala smirked. "So?"

Faith pushed off the bed and walked toward her. "Maybe you don't have as much insight into humans as Madsen thought."

"Oh, right. I forgot that you're a bunch of prudes."

Faith pressed herself against her and whispered into her ear: "I'm not a prude."

Her warm breath sent shivers through Tala. She slid her hands beneath Faith's sweater to caress her skin. "Care to prove it?"

Chloe rattled the doorknob from the outside. "Mom? Tala? Jemma is going out to collect eggs for breakfast. Can I go with her?"

"Later," Faith whispered to Tala and pinched her ass. "Now go shower."

With a grin, Tala sauntered to the bathroom.

CHAPTER 20

"ARE YOU OKAY, DAD?" FAITH asked for the second time in ten minutes.

"I'm fine," he said, as he had the first time.

His answer didn't reassure her at all.

He'd been sitting in the armchair next to her couch, tapping the fingers of his uninjured arm against his knee, since he'd arrived. He hadn't spoken much.

Neither had Faith.

She was grateful for Chloe, who sat cross-legged on the couch next to her and kept up a steady stream of chatter about school.

Her father's gaze drifted to the front door every few seconds.

Faith's did too, but she wasn't only waiting for Dr. Langston—the witness Jeff Madsen had found.

Tala was picking Dr. Langston up from the airport, so they would arrive together.

Just the thought of Tala steadied her nerves. She wanted…needed Tala there while they finally learned what had happened to her mother.

This meeting picked at a wound that had never fully healed, and Tala's calm, familiar presence would be like a soothing balm, even though the prospect of introducing Tala to her father made Faith's stomach churn.

He had promised to be civil. But would he be able to keep that promise? What if he lashed out?

She knew Tala had dealt with worse, but this was different. She wasn't just meeting another human who disliked the Wrasa—she was meeting Faith's father.

How weird that they had never actually met, when Tala had become so important to her.

Even at the Wrasa Pride parade that had started it all, they hadn't directly interacted with each other.

Faith just hoped today wouldn't end with the same kind of confrontation as the parade had.

"...and Mrs. Chapman said we could bring our pet to school!" Chloe excitedly waved her new favorite stuffed animal—a little fox, oblivious to the tension in the room. "But, Mom, we don't have a pet. Can I take Tala? She could shift into her animal form and show off her pelt. All the other kids would be so jealous!"

"No, Chloe," Faith replied. "Tala isn't a pet."

Chloe huffed with almost comical exasperation. "I know that. But she could pretend. She would get a lot of treats."

That made Faith smile despite her growing nervousness. She glanced at her dad to see how he would react to Chloe's clear hero worship of Tala.

His jaw muscles tightened, but he didn't say anything.

The doorbell rang, sparing her from having to answer Chloe's request.

Chloe scrambled off the couch and raced to the door. "Tala's here!"

"Hold on, sweetie! Let me check first." Faith reached for her phone and checked the video feed of the ring camera.

Tala stood at the front door in her usual proud, erect posture—shoulders squared, chin up. But even through the ring camera app, Faith could see the tightness in her lithe frame.

Behind her loomed a tall figure who could only be Dr. Langston.

"It's Tala with Dr. Langston." Faith pushed off the couch, smoothed her damp palms over her slacks, and followed Chloe into the hall.

As soon as Faith unlocked and opened the door, Chloe launched herself at Tala.

Tala caught her with ease and twirled her around. "Hey, pup."

Faith's father had followed them into the hall as if he didn't want them to be alone with two Wrasa for even a second. Now he stood stiffly behind Faith, brow knitted as he watched Tala and his granddaughter interact.

After a few seconds, Tala put the girl down and turned toward Faith.

She wore dark jeans, a white sweater, and a sleek black leather coat that made Faith weak in the knees.

A flutter went through her stomach as those golden eyes met hers. "Hi."

"Hi." Tala didn't move, leaving it up to Faith to decide how she wanted to greet her in front of her father, yet the warmth in her eyes was like a comforting touch.

Faith felt her father watch them as she stepped closer and embraced Tala.

The familiar heat engulfed her, draining some of the tension from her muscles.

"How's the knee?" Tala asked quietly, concern softening the sharp edges of her alpha demeanor. "Sorry I wasn't able to take you to get the stitches out this morning."

"It's fine," Faith replied. "The doc said it's healing well."

Her father cleared his throat, clearly not comfortable with the length of their embrace…or the fact that a Wrasa was hugging her at all.

Tala's fingers twitched against the small of Faith's back, but she left them there as she ended the embrace and faced Faith's father. Her features were composed, betraying none of the nerves Faith knew she was feeling.

"Dad… This is Tala. My girlfriend." Faith added it even knowing it would make her father cringe. She was done putting his needs before her own—or Tala's.

Tala's lips twitched into a surprised smile, and Faith realized it was the first time she had ever introduced Tala as her girlfriend.

Her father seemed far less pleased. He compressed his lips into a razor-sharp line.

"Tala, this is my dad, Peter MacAllister."

"Mr. MacAllister. Nice to finally meet you." Tala's tone was calm and respectful, but she didn't flinch under his scrutiny. She held his gaze, steady yet not confrontational, and offered him her hand.

Faith's father didn't tell her to call him by his first name, nor did he reach for her outstretched hand.

"Oh." Tala switched to holding out her left hand instead of the right.

But Faith knew her father's hesitation had nothing to do with his healing right arm still resting in a sling.

He stared at Tala's offered hand as if she were a dangerous predator who'd unsheathed her claws.

Faith wasn't sure he would take it, but then he reluctantly gave Tala's hand a brief, stiff shake.

A quiet exhale escaped Faith.

Then she remembered the silent presence behind Tala. "Dr. Langston. I'm so sorry. Please come in."

She would have recognized her as a bear-shifter even if Jeff Madsen hadn't mentioned it.

Dr. Langston looked as if she would knock over a wall if she accidentally ran into it. Her broad shoulders and towering frame filled the entryway, yet her kind brown eyes softened her imposing appearance. She closed the door behind herself and tucked thick, brown hair back behind her ears while clutching a duffel bag with her other hand. "Hello. I'm Dr. Marion Langston."

"Thanks so much for coming all the way from Denver, Dr. Langston. I'm Faith MacAllister, and this is my father, Peter, and my daughter, Chloe."

"Marion, please."

They all shook hands, and Faith's father watched with a stony expression as Dr. Langston's large hand gently engulfed Chloe's small one.

Chloe stared up at her with big eyes. "Are you a doctor like the ones on TV?"

"Not quite," Dr. Langston said, her deep voice soft. Thankfully, she didn't explain that she worked in a morgue.

"Sweetie, it's time to go upstairs and play in your room for a bit," Faith told her daughter.

Chloe pouted. "But I want to stay with you, Tala, and Grandpa!"

"Chloe, we've talked about this. You will see them later. I said you could say hi to Tala if you promised to go upstairs while the adults talk. Come on. You can grab my tablet and play *Way of the Turtle*."

Her daughter heaved an exaggerated sigh. "Okay." Almost in slow-motion, she trudged to the stairs.

Faith's heart raced as she led the way into the living room.

Twenty-two years of uncertainty were about to end. In a minute, she would find out what had happened to her mother. At least that was what she hoped.

Faith's father and their visitor each chose an armchair on opposite sides of the coffee table, while Tala sat next to Faith on the couch. She slid an arm around Faith and pulled her against the soothing warmth of her body.

Peter's jaw clenched tightly as he watched them, but Faith ignored his disapproving glare.

Tala's presence, her quiet confidence, made her feel everything would be okay, and she needed that right now.

"So, what is it that you shifters have kept from us all these years?" Faith's father asked before she could find a more diplomatic way to start this difficult conversation.

"Dad!"

Dr. Langston lifted her hand. "It's okay. I know this isn't easy." She turned toward Faith's father. "I wasn't too pleased that I couldn't share my observations during the investigation either. As Manark Madsen probably mentioned, I was the forensic technician assisting the medical examiner who examined your wife's remains. I smelled something on her, but I couldn't report it because no human and none of our standard tests would have detected it."

Peter squinted at her. "So you did hide something from us?"

"I didn't hide it," Dr. Langston said calmly. "I just couldn't speak up without giving away that I was not the human I appeared to be."

"What did you smell?" Faith finally had to know.

"Monkshood. It's a highly toxic plant. If ingested, it's deadly."

Faith's father shook his head. "My wife was an experienced hiker. She never ate anything she found in the forest unless she knew it was safe."

"She didn't necessarily have to eat it," Dr. Langston replied. "If she brushed against it and had an open wound somewhere, like a little cut or an abrasion, it would have gotten into her bloodstream and killed her. Even if she touched it without having an open wound, she would have experienced symptoms like dizziness and nausea."

"But the autopsy report said she died of a head trauma," Tala said, her arm still firmly wrapped around Faith.

"That's right. I believe she did," Dr. Langston said. "My best guess is that she accidentally touched monkshood, got dizzy, and had a catastrophic fall down the side of a steep hill."

Faith's father leaned forward, clutching one armrest with his uninjured hand as if struggling to stay in his seat. "You really expect me to believe that my wife just happened to come into contact with some toxic plant?"

Dr. Langston faced him with a calm expression. Apparently, either Madsen or Tala had prepared her for that reaction. "I know it's hard to accept. But sometimes, there is no villain. Just a lot of bad luck."

"Why should I believe a word you say? If shifters were involved in my wife's death, you'd never admit it."

Dr. Langston held his gaze, steady and unwavering. "With all due respect, I have no reason to lie. If I had something to hide, I could have simply told Manark Madsen that I didn't remember the case. After all, it's been more than two decades."

"Then why do you supposedly remember?" Faith's father asked.

"Because I wanted to give the family—you—closure so badly, but I knew I couldn't." Dr. Langston's voice was tinged with regret. "That's something I carried with me all these years."

"She's telling the truth," Tala cut in. She flared her nostrils as if she was analyzing Dr. Langston's scent.

Dr. Langston lifted her hand as if taking an oath. "I swear I am. The only wolves involved in your wife's death were in the plant's name."

Faith sent her a questioning look. "What do you mean?"

"Monkshood is also called wolfsbane because it's so toxic the ancient Greeks and Romans used it to poison the arrows or bait they used to hunt wolves. Quite a few Syak in their wolf forms were killed with it too."

Faith put a hand on Tala's knee. Too many people had died on both sides to keep the Wrasa's existence hidden, but her mother wasn't one of them. Her death wasn't the result of a dark sinister plot or a gruesome murder. Just an accident.

Silence settled over the living room.

Finally, Dr. Langston cleared her throat. "Do you have any questions for me?"

Dozens of questions swirled through Faith's head, but there was only one that had lingered in her mind for years, never quite letting go.

Was she ready to hear the answer?

Tala covered Faith's hand on her knee with her own and gave it an encouraging squeeze as if sensing her inner struggle.

Faith steeled herself. "If I had been with my mother that day—" Her voice cracked, but she pushed on. "Could I have saved her?"

"Don't put this on yourself," her father said hoarsely. "You were just nine years old! You're not to blame in any—"

"I need to know, Dad." She sent a pleading look to Dr. Langston, who responded with a compassionate expression.

"Your presence wouldn't have made any difference." Dr. Langston's voice held no doubt. "Even if you had cell phone reception in the middle of the forest, your mother's head injury was too severe. You might have even met the same fate as your mother if you had brushed against the monkshood too. And if you'd tried to keep her from falling, her greater weight might have dragged you down with her."

Tala squeezed her hand again, anchoring her in the present. "There was nothing you could have done, nemi," she said quietly.

Faith nodded slowly and took a freeing breath. That ache in her chest remained. She would always grieve her mother. But it felt different now—less raw and sharp.

She intertwined her fingers with Tala's and dared to ask the second question on her mind. "Did…did she suffer?"

"I don't think she did," Dr. Langston said without hesitation. "From what we found, the head trauma would have been fatal or at least knocked her unconscious right away."

Her mother hadn't suffered—hadn't endured hours of agony from the poison. That was one small mercy.

Tala rubbed comforting circles on her back, and Faith leaned into the soothing touch.

She glanced at her father. "Do you have any questions for Dr. Langston, Dad?"

"What about the teeth marks on her bones?" Faith's father asked. "How do you know she wasn't hunted down and killed by a predator?"

"My best guess is that they came from a large canine and occurred postmortem. No Wrasa would have bitten her."

He snorted. "Why would I believe that?"

Dr. Langston calmly met his gaze. "You might not believe in our decency, but you should believe in our noses. When your wife's body was found, merely faint traces of the poison remained, so only a Maki like me could detect it. But on the day she died, any Wrasa would have smelled it. They would have known biting her would be a death sentence." She paused, then quickly added, "Not that we make a habit of biting humans, even without the poison."

Faith had believed in the Wrasa's innocence for some time. Still, hearing conclusive evidence made her slump against Tala with relief. Maybe this would finally get through to her father.

When no more questions came, Dr. Langston rose from the armchair. "If you need more information or want me to take a polygraph, you can reach me any time through Manark Madsen." She shook Faith's hand.

Tala hesitantly let go of Faith and stood too. "I'll drive you to your hotel."

"It's fine. I prefer to walk," Dr. Langston said as if she could smell Tala's reluctance to leave. "The hotel is just a few blocks from here, and it'll be good to get some fresh air and stretch my legs."

Tala walked her to the door, leaving Faith alone with her father.

Now they knew. Finally had some closure. And it felt very different from what Faith had expected. There was none of the lightness she had anticipated—no weight lifting off her shoulders.

After a few moments, she realized why that was: She'd already accepted her mom's death as an accident. Hearing the exact mechanics was only a confirmation.

But she did hope it would make a difference for her father.

He stood and went to the window, staring out but probably not seeing a thing.

Tala returned and gave Faith's arm a gentle squeeze. "I'll go check on Chloe."

Faith nodded gratefully. She walked over to her father and touched his shoulder. "Dad…"

"I don't believe it, Faith," he said hoarsely, but his defeated tone indicated that the truth was finally starting to sink in.

"I do. Even if I didn't trust Dr. Langston, I trust Tala and her nose. She can smell a lie, and she would have told me if there were any."

He turned his head to look at her, as if probing the strength of her conviction. His eyes were bloodshot. "I don't know, Faith. It doesn't make any sense. Literally. It's all so senseless. I was sure there was something more behind it—that she had seen one of those creatures shift and had been killed to silence her. But now it's supposed to have been just a silly accident? Just walking too close to some stupid plant?"

The agony in his voice made Faith's chest hurt. "The way she died doesn't make her life senseless, Dad."

His Adam's apple bobbed up and down as if he was swallowing down tears. "No," he finally got out. "Her life was anything but. She brought you into this world."

Tears formed in her own eyes, and she did nothing to hold them back. "Can you focus on that and finally let go of your hatred against the Wrasa, now that you know they didn't kill Mom? Please, Dad. I already lost one parent to poison; I don't want your own hate to poison you too."

He flinched. "Dammit, Faith, you're not fighting fair."

"I'm fighting for my family—and that includes both you and Tala. It's what Mom would have done."

"I know you're right. She would have told me the same damn thing." He sighed, then smiled wryly. "You're so much like her, it's eerie. Including that stubborn streak and the way she had with people. If she were here right now, she would already be best buddies with your shifter friend, inviting her on a hiking trip." He pointed upstairs, where Tala was with Chloe.

"With Tala, my Wrasa girlfriend," Faith said firmly.

He heaved another sigh. "Yeah. With Tala." He reached up with the hand not resting in the sling and massaged the bridge of his nose. "This isn't easy for me. I…I need to rethink everything I've firmly believed ever since the shifters revealed themselves. It's going to take time."

"That's okay," Faith whispered through a tight throat. "You don't have to do it alone. I'm right here."

He roughly scrubbed the back of his hand across his eyes as if trying to hide tears. "I don't want to lose you too."

"You won't," she said firmly. "Just promise me you'll try."

His throat worked, and then he finally got out: "I'll try."

Faith let out a long, shaky breath. The rush of air released a pressure that had built up inside of her for months. "Thank you, Dad."

She leaned her head against his shoulder, and they stood together in silence until Chloe came clomping down the stairs. "Tala says we're ordering pizza!"

"I said you can ask your mother," Tala shouted from halfway down the stairs.

At the mention of pizza, Faith's stomach growled its enthusiastic approval. She hadn't managed to eat anything since breakfast. She turned toward her father. "Are you staying for dinner? I need someone who'll share a pepperoni-and-jalapeños pizza with me, and Wrasa are spice wimps."

"Are not," Tala grumbled.

"Are too," Faith shouted back.

Her father hesitated.

Chloe grabbed his hand. "Please, Grandpa! You can read me my bedtime story after dinner!"

"All right," her father finally said. "I'll stay."

Faith bit back a grin. She couldn't wait to see her father's face when Chloe introduced him to Winston, the wolf who loved to read—and when he realized how many slices of pizza Tala could devour.

Chapter 21

Being trapped in a grand ballroom full of mostly human attendees was Tala's idea of a nightmare, especially now, at the beginning of June, when the night air carried the promise of summer and the urge to run under the stars in her fox form called to her. The constant clink of glasses, the smell of expensive perfumes and colognes, and the flashes of cameras sent her sharp senses into overload.

Still, there was no place on earth she would rather be tonight.

Apparently, the same was true for DC's rich and famous. The ballroom was packed with CEOs, politicians, lobbyists, high-profile attorneys, and even a few senators and members of Congress.

Faith's father, however, was absent. He wasn't yet ready to throw his full support behind the Wrasa Rights Act, at least not publicly. But he had offered to babysit Chloe while they were at the gala, and that was good enough for now.

Pup steps, as she had reminded Faith.

At least most other prominent human figures in the city seemed to be here, all dressed up in expensive suits and glittering evening gowns.

Tala's table felt like an island in a sea of human power and influence.

Griffin's six-foot-two frame towered over the others. She had just returned from the buffet, where she had secured the best morsels for her human mate, Jorie.

Next to them was Jeff Madsen, who was deep in conversation with Kelsey and Rue.

Tala had no idea what they were talking about. She barely noticed anything going on at their table.

Her full attention was on the stage, where Faith was now walking up to the podium, back straight, head held high, as applause rippled through the audience. Her teeth were tugging on her full bottom lip, though. The tiny tell might have gone unnoticed by the crowd, but it revealed Faith's nervousness to Tala.

The emerald-green gown Faith wore hugged her gentle curves. The spotlight cast a soft glow over her, bringing out the reddish glint in her chestnut hair. Her mother's silver chain rested around her elegant neck, the cross replaced with a tiny paw pendant Chloe had given her for her birthday.

Tala's chest swelled with pride and admiration.

My mate!

Her heart beat faster as Faith adjusted the microphone. She could almost feel the crackle of her nervous energy.

Stay calm, nemi, she willed silently. *You'll do great.*

She had told Faith so repeatedly, but, of course, Faith knew how important this evening was.

Faith's gaze swept over the crowd and immediately found Tala, who gave her a reassuring smile.

"Good evening," Faith said into the microphone. "My name is Faith MacAllister—but you probably knew that already. Most of you are very much aware of who my father is—and likely who my ex-husband is too."

Tala had heard Faith's speech before, when Faith had practiced it at home, but the direct, courageous opening stunned her every time.

"A few months ago, I would have been the last person who would have been asked to get up on this stage and give a speech in support of Wrasa rights." Faith paused and flashed a smile, disarming everyone with her honesty. "Well, maybe the second-to-last person. My father probably deserves the dubious honor of having been the Wrasa's biggest enemy. He was convinced they had not only killed my mother but were also planning to eradicate the human race."

A murmur went through the ballroom.

"I would like to think my own attitude toward the Wrasa wasn't that bad, but truth be told, it was impossible not to be affected by his hate." Faith gripped the podium with both hands, but her voice gained strength with every word. "I was convinced the Wrasa were dangerous, enemies to be feared, a threat to everything we hold dear. But then I met Tala Peterson."

She looked at Tala again.

Memories of their tumultuous beginnings flashed through Tala's mind, and she sent Faith a gentle grin.

"At first, she seemed to be exactly what my father had warned me about. But the more time I spent with her, the more I realized that the Wrasa were nothing like my father made me believe. They're no different from humans—some are selfish, some bitter, but most of them are kind and loyal. They weren't the enemy. They were people. Just like us."

Applause started at a few of the tables, but Faith held up her hand, and silence fell again.

"I didn't just fall in love with Tala; I grew to love her entire pack and Wrasa culture." A smile chased away the remnants of nervousness on Faith's features. "I even came to appreciate the occasional mouse left as a gift in front of my bed."

Laughter rippled through the room where Wrasa sat, while a few humans exchanged puzzled glances.

Jorie reached over and nudged Tala's shoulder. "I can empathize. Between my cats and Griffin, I'm not sure how there are any mice left in all of Michigan."

"She's exaggerating," Tala grumbled. "I left her a mouse exactly once. Okay, twice." But other than that, the stark-naked-mate tactic was still working nicely four weeks after they had first tried it.

"Mostly, I learned one thing over the past few months: Hate and prejudice can be passed down like a family heirloom"—Faith touched the necklace she wore—"or it can be stopped. Here and now. By all of us."

She paused to let her gaze trail over the attendees until she once again made eye contact with Tala.

"I'm asking all of you to do what I did—look beyond your fear, beyond the things you assumed, the stories you've been told, and the walls you've built. Look beyond all of that and see the Wrasa for who they really are: just people, like you and me. People with hopes and dreams. People who've been hurt and forced to live in the shadows. People who deserve to be valid members of our society, with the same rights and protections as anyone else."

The Wrasa in the ballroom sat a little straighter.

"If you're not ready to do it for the Wrasa, do it for yourself. Life is better for all of us when we can live it without fearfully glancing over our shoulders. I want my daughter to have a future where love and understanding triumph over hate and division. That's what I want my mom's legacy to be. The Wrasa Rights Act is a step toward that future, and that's why I'm asking you to support it. Thank you."

The room erupted into applause, the sound rolling over Tala like thunder. Cameras flashed.

Faith smiled, nodded, and waved, yet through it all, her gaze never left Tala's.

The noise and chaos faded into the background as Tala stared back at her. She put one hand over her heart, which felt as if it was about to burst with pride and gratefulness. Great Hunter, she wasn't just in love; she was in awe of this woman!

Neither of them glanced away as Faith stepped down from the stage and made her way back to the table.

Faith returned to the table, still buzzing with adrenaline and the thundering applause.

Tala immediately stood, pulled her close, and kissed her softly. "You were amazing," she whispered against Faith's lips.

"My speech didn't rate a *Great Hunter*?" Faith asked with a teasing grin.

Tala laughed. "Oh, pardon me, I meant to say: *Great Hunter*, you were amazing!"

As they took their seats at the table, Jorie leaned over. "No *Great Hunter* from me, but I thought your speech was fantastic too. Even better than I remembered from my dream."

What a strange remark. Faith eyed the slender Asian-American woman next to her. Jeff Madsen had made the introductions earlier, but Faith couldn't remember what role Jorie played in Wrasa society. Was she even a Wrasa?

Her mate, the imposing Griffin, clearly was. Earlier, as they had entered the ballroom together, other attendees had crowded inside and accidentally jostled Jorie. Griffin had lifted her upper lip in a threatening snarl, making everyone jump back to give them space.

Jorie wasn't as easy to figure out. Faith's best guess was that she was a high-ranking Saru or maybe a council member—because all Wrasa treated her as if she were royalty.

"Better than you remembered from your dream?" Faith repeated. "What do you mean?"

The Wrasa at the table traded meaningful glances, then they all looked at Jeff Madsen.

He finally gave a slow nod.

Tala glanced at the surrounding tables as if to make sure what she was about to say couldn't be overheard. Luckily, the background noise of conversations was loud enough so no human would be able to listen in. Still, she leaned closer before saying, "I had permission to tell you sooner, but then Mirella sent you that letter, and your father was shot, and I haven't found an opportunity to tell you. And, truth be told, had no idea how to tell you."

"To tell me what?" Faith asked.

"Jorie is a maharsi—a dream seer. She sees glimpses of the future and the past in her dreams."

Faith struggled not to stare open-mouthed. "Like an oracle or a prophet?"

Tala nodded. "Humans would probably call her that, but for us, dream seers have always been an integral part of our culture and society, not just mysterious figures no one had ever met. They helped us make decisions in all aspects of life—relationships, careers, political disputes, and more."

Faith's first impulse was to find it strange that someone would base important decisions on someone else's dreams. But she reined in her knee-jerk reaction and told herself not to be so judgmental. After all, many humans read their horoscopes on a daily basis or sought guidance from religious leaders.

Maybe having dream seers wasn't so different.

"Wait, you said *helped*—past tense?" She gave Tala a quizzical look.

"Centuries ago, maharsi were accused of being witches by humans. Many were burned at the stake, to the point they almost became extinct." Instead of Tala, it was Griffin who answered. "My grandfather was believed to have been the last one…until we realized that Jorie—a human of all people—is a dream seer."

Faith's gaze darted to Jorie. So that was why all Wrasa treated her as if she walked on water! Faith needed a minute to gather her thoughts. "So you had a dream vision about this evening? About my speech?"

Jorie's shaggy bangs fell forward, into her eyes, as she nodded. She brushed them back. "Actually, I had several dream visions about you." She, too, spoke quietly and leaned closer so no one could overhear her. "Didn't you ever wonder why we asked you to be Tala's fake girlfriend and were confident you'd agree to something so ridiculous?"

"Oh yeah!" Faith let out a self-deprecating chuckle. "I was convinced it was all part of a nefarious plan."

Jorie shook her head. "There was nothing nefarious about it. I knew you'd agree to our plan because I saw it in a dream."

Heat crept up Faith's neck, and she prayed her discreet makeup was hiding her blush. "Did your dream also tell you why I agreed?"

"Yes. I knew you were spying for your father. But I also knew you'd stop at some point."

"Wait a minute," Tala whispered harshly. She put both hands flat on the table and leaned forward, toward Jorie. "When the council told me about Operation Make-Believe Mate, you said you didn't know why Faith would agree to fake-date me—that it hadn't been part of your dream vision."

"I couldn't tell you the truth," Jorie said. "I needed you to start trusting Faith, and if you knew from the start that she was spying, you never would have relaxed around her even for a second."

A roaring sound filled Faith's ears. "So you saw…everything? My entire life up to here…and the future too?"

"That's not how dream seeing works," Jorie replied. "I only get glimpses of someone's life, bits and pieces that are often hard to understand without context. And the future isn't set in stone, so all I'm seeing are hints of one *possible* future. That's why I couldn't tell you about this." She gestured back and forth between Faith and Tala.

"You knew this would happen? That our fake relationship would turn real?" Faith's voice came out in a squeak. She swiveled on her chair to stare at Tala. "Did you know too?"

Tala put her hand on Faith's leg beneath the table. "No. At least not from the start. I only found out after we kissed for real and I realized we had developed mate scent."

"If we'd told you from the start, it could have changed the course of events leading us to this future." Jorie gestured toward the podium, where Faith had given her speech in support of Wrasa rights. "The moment you two realized you belonged together for real was meant to happen naturally, not because of a dream seer's vision."

For a few seconds, everyone was silent, only the hum of conversation at other tables buzzing around them.

Faith's pulse raced as she took it all in. "So all of this…us"—she touched Tala's shoulder, then her own chest—"was destined?"

Jorie tilted her head. "In a way. But it wasn't inevitable. The choices you both made brought you here."

Tala reached for Faith's hand at the same time Faith grasped hers. As the conversation around them continued, they looked at each other.

One corner of Tala's mouth lifted up into a tentative smile. "Seems like a mouse in front of the bed isn't the only surprise life with a Wrasa has in store. I hope that doesn't change what you said in your amazing speech."

Faith didn't even have to think about it. She understood why the Wrasa hadn't made the existence of dream seers public so far—humans didn't exactly have the best track record when it came to accepting religious beliefs that differed from their own. "Never. No matter what brought us here, it feels like I'm exactly where I'm supposed to be."

"In a ballroom full of rich humans?" Tala asked with a lopsided grin.

Faith shook her head. "At your side."

"Ditto." The noise around them faded away as Tala pulled her closer and kissed her.

EPILOGUE

AFTERNOON SUNLIGHT FILTERED THROUGH THE leaves, showing off their vibrant yellow, orange, red, and brown hues.

Cheerful birdsong filled the air, a small creek gurgled up ahead, and gravel crunched beneath their hiking boots as Faith and her daughter followed the fire road downhill through the forest.

Wolves darted through the underbrush to the left and right of the path. Faith couldn't always see them, but she knew they were there—silent, swift shadows that kept them safe. Only Tala stuck close to them, her white-tipped tail wagging as she led them farther into the forest.

Faith marveled at how different this felt compared to that night in the woods six months ago. Back then, she'd been terrified of the forest and the wolves. Now she felt nothing but peace, as she had when she'd gone hiking with her mother as a child.

"There's Uncle Rey!" Chloe called, pointing to a flash of black fur. "And Aunt Arlyn! And Sutton!"

She was getting really good at the spot-the-wolf game she had invented. There were more than thirty wolves out here, but after spending nearly every weekend with the pack for the past few months, Chloe could identify them all with just a glimpse of fur through the bushes.

They followed the path around a sharp bend. The sound of rushing water became louder as they passed the small waterfall hidden behind trees to their right.

Usually, that was where they went when they came here, but not this time.

"We're going this way today," Faith told Chloe.

As they neared the familiar intersection where the fire road met the old, overgrown trail, she noticed something different.

Six months ago, that trail had been hard to climb, with fallen branches, thick undergrowth, and brambles hindering every step. Now someone had cleared it, making it wide enough for a human to pass easily.

Warmth filled Faith's chest. The pack had done it for her. Tala had told her they had searched the area for wolfsbane to make sure it was safe, but she hadn't mentioned they had also cleared the path to the ritual spot.

"Are we going up there?" Chloe asked with wide eyes.

Faith nodded. "It's a bit of a climb, but we can do it."

Tala in her fox form led the way, and Faith followed, keeping a firm grip on Chloe's hand, in case she slipped. Together, they hiked along the path winding up the side of a hill.

The wolves moved with them. The feeling of being surrounded by their pack eased the heaviness on Faith's chest that increased the closer they got.

Finally, the path leveled out, opening into a small clearing—the pack's secret ritual spot.

This was where her mother had died…or at least where she'd been found.

Faith swallowed down the lump in her throat and pointed at a majestic oak. "Leave the backpack with the clothes by that tree over there and then come over here." She put down her own, much bigger backpack, which held more clothes, and took Chloe's hand as they waited, facing in the other direction.

Groans and the cracking of bones filtered through the trees as Tala and her closest family members shifted back and quickly got dressed. Others remained in their wolf form, guarding the pack from the edge of the clearing.

Leaves rustled, then Tala joined them, while her parents, Arlyn, Rey, and Mirella formed a semicircle behind them. Tala was barefoot but otherwise fully dressed. The sunlight that fell through the canopy lit up the burnished copper of her hair. The strands mirrored the colors of the fall leaves.

Tala took her hand.

The heat of her skin swept up Faith's arm, and she leaned into her, grateful not just for her warmth but also for her support.

Chloe tugged at her sleeve. "Can I give her the rose from Grandpa?"

When Faith nodded, Chloe carefully knelt down and placed a single red rose on the carpet of leaves. "Happy birthday, Grandma!"

Faith's chest tightened as she knelt beside her daughter and laid down her own bouquet—asters, her mom's favorite. The ache of grief resurfaced, but now it was tempered by fond memories and the joy of being supported by family.

Tala stepped behind them and put a hand on Faith's shoulder.

Chloe looked over. "Do you think Grandma knows we're here? Can she see us from heaven?"

"I'm sure she knows and loves her flowers," Faith said.

But Chloe wasn't satisfied with that answer. She glanced up at Tala. "Do you think so too?"

Tala knelt down between them so she was at eye level with Chloe. "Wrasa believe that when someone we love dies, they don't really leave us."

Chloe tilted her head, curiosity gleaming in her eyes. "What do you mean?"

With a smile, Tala tucked a strand of hair behind the girl's ear. "We believe that they're in the trees, giving them strength. That when the wind blows through the leaves, they're whispering to us. That when the sun shines on our face, they're giving us a hug. They're everywhere in nature."

"Oh." Chloe's small brow furrowed, then eased into a big grin.

Faith caressed Tala's shoulder. "That's beautiful, nemi."

"I'm hugging Grandma back." Chloe stretched her arms toward the sun. "Look, Ammakki."

Faith had heard the word quite often around the pack. It was the word for *Mom* in the Old Language. But Chloe wasn't looking at her—she was looking at Tala.

Tala gasped and swayed on her knees. "Um… I swear I didn't teach her that."

The wide-eyed expression on Tala's face made Faith laugh. She stood and gently tugged Tala up with her. "She probably heard the 'other pups' use it for their moms and thought it was an appropriate title for you."

"Are you okay with that?" Tala asked.

"Of course! Are you?" Faith searched Tala's face. During the past few months, Tala had gradually taken over more of a parental role, especially now that Jon's trial had started, but they hadn't explicitly talked about it yet.

"I'm honored," Tala whispered. "I just don't want to step on your toes."

Faith took her hand and squeezed it. "You're not." She winked at Tala. "Chloe has always wanted a mom who can shift into a really cool animal."

"Yeah!" Chloe shouted. "Does that mean you're moving in?"

Tala's hand twitched in Faith's. "Um, I don't know. Does it?" She searched Faith's eyes. "You do remember what it means in our culture, don't you?"

Of course Faith remembered. Moving in together meant getting married.

"Finally!" Tala's mother called from behind them. "I've been waiting for your *twere forever*!"

Tala hushed her without looking away from Faith. "She hasn't answered yet, Mom."

After the way her first marriage had ended, Faith probably should have hesitated. But there was no doubt in her mind. She imagined having Tala there to share pancakes in the morning and going to sleep in her arms every night...and it felt right, like a missing piece finally falling into place.

"I do remember," she said, her voice hoarse. "And with everything it means, I'd love to have you move in—as long as our no-mice-in-front-of-the-bed deal still stands."

"Good luck with that," Tala's father mumbled, but they both ignored him.

"I'll hold up my end of the deal if you hold up yours, nemi," Tala said, a passionate gleam in her golden eyes.

Faith squeezed her hand again. "Gladly."

"I guess it's settled, then," Tala said, a happy yip in her voice. "Now that it looks like the Wrasa Rights Act might pass, we could even—"

A low howl rose at the edge of the clearing, interrupting her. It was echoed by another, then another, until an entire chorus resonated through the trees.

The sound sent shivers through Faith, but it wasn't fear—it was the primal feeling of being connected to something powerful.

She loved that they didn't have to shush the wolves. Here, in their ritual spot, they didn't need to fear humans hearing them since most hikers avoided the area. What a wonderful thought that her mother was the guardian angel that kept humans from this place, giving the pack a safe space to shift and run in their animal forms!

Chloe tipped her head back and let out a howl of her own.

Her human pitch stuck out from the rest of the pack, but Tala just chuckled and shrugged. "Syak come in all forms." She leaned in and kissed Faith. "And so does family."

If you enjoyed this novel, check out the other books in Jae's shape-shifter series, especially *True Nature*, the novel in which we first meet Tala.

GLOSSARY OF WRASA TERMS

While I don't think it's necessary to read this glossary to understand the Wrasa terms I use in this novel, I decided to create one anyway to help you navigate the world of my shape-shifters.

You can also find the glossary on my website: www.jae-fiction.com/glossary-of-shape-shifter-terms/

Alai – "Wanderer." Basically a "lone wolf." Slightly disparaging term for a Kasari or Syak who lives alone and is not part of a pride or pack.

Ammakki – "Mom."

Antapi – "Both." Hybrid shifter whose parents belong to different shifter subspecies.

Appo – "Dad."

Arin – "Heart." Pet name, the Wrasa equivalent of "sweetheart."

Ashawe – "Sharp." Coyote-shifters.

Kalyani – "It's okay."

Kasari – "Saffron-colored." Lion-shifters.

Kanme – "Plaything." Fling; unlike a mate, the relationship isn't serious.

Maharsi – "Great seer." Dream seer; someone who gets glimpses of the future, present, or past in their dreams.

Maki – "Large." Bears-shifters.

Manark – "Noble one." Title of a councilor of the High Council.

Mutaline – The hormone that controls shifting.

Natak – "Lord" or "master." Title of a pack or pride regent, might also be known as an alpha.

Nederi – "Under." A subordinate, often used to refer to a lower-ranking member of a pack or pride. Sometimes also referred as an "omega."

Nemi – "Jewel," "treasure," or "precious one." An endearment comparable to "darling." Only used with one's mate.

Parwese – "First." Title of the high king of the Allied Prides, regent of the Kasari.

Puwar – "Fire." Tiger-shifters.

Rtar – "Red." Fox-shifters.

Saru – "Hunter." A shape-shifter law enforcement unit that guards their secret existence. Saru is also the rank of simple Saru soldiers.

Se-asrai – "One body." Humans.

Serska – "Sister-in-law."

Skiyo – "Shade" or "shadow." A root vegetable dish that looks like lasagna but tastes like earth to humans.

Sleme – "Flame." Wrasa funeral rite (cremation).

Svayampar – "Marriage."

Syak – "Together." Wolf-shifters.

Tas – "Commander." Rank of a Saru officer.

Twere – "Door" or "transition from one phase to another." A three-day celebration akin to an engagement party.

Wertsiya – The Wrasa's High Council.

Wrasa – "Living being" or "creature." The species of shape-shifters.

Yasi makamar – "Night run." A ritual that is part of the twere. The families of the people getting engaged run together in their animal forms at night.

Other Books from
Ylva Publishing

www.ylva-publishing.com

True Nature
(The Shape-Shifter series)

Jae

ISBN: 978-3-96324-360-8
Length: 394 pages (141,000 words)

CEO Rue has no idea that her adopted son Danny is a wolf-shifter or that his beautiful tutor Kelsey isn't there to teach him algebra.

When Danny runs away, the race is on to find him before his first transformation. In the frantic search, Kelsey and Rue unexpectedly find something else: each other.

A gripping lesbian paranormal romance about family bonds and being true to yourself.

Good Enough to Eat
(The Vampire Diet series)

Jae & Alison Grey

ISBN: 978-3-95533-242-6
Length: 223 pages (64,000 words)

Robin is a vampire who wants to change her eating habits. To fight her cravings for O negative, she goes to an AA meeting, where she meets Alana, who battles her own demons.

Despite their determination not to get involved, the attraction is undeniable.

Is it love or just bloodlust that makes Robin think Alana looks good enough to eat? Will it even matter once Alana finds out who Robin really is?

Pinned by Love

Elaine J Daniels

ISBN: 978-3-96324-975-4
Length: 182 pages (55,000 words)

Monster Wrestling's top villain Iris is a harpy who craves a championship. She's forced to work with her hated rival, Lena, a minotaur who wins fights and fans with ease.

Slowly, they see each other's realities: the pressure of perfection on Lena and Iris's childhood dream. Will this ruin their rivalry?

A fun enemies-to-lovers lesbian romantasy.

The Power of Mercy
(The Superheroine Collection)

Fiona Zedde

ISBN: 978-3-95533-854-1
Length: 113 pages (37,000 words)

To her family, Mai Redstone is weak. When she becomes Mercy, a rooftop-climbing chameleon with at least nine lives, she finds her power. But when Mercy is called in by police to a murder case, her whole world threatens to crumble. The dead man made her childhood a hell. She is torn between giving the murderer a medal and finding the killer for her family. Mercy is a blade that can cut both ways.

ABOUT JAE

Jae grew up amidst the vineyards of southern Germany. She spent her childhood with her nose buried in a book, earning her the nickname "professor." The writing bug bit her at the age of eleven. Since 2006, she has been writing mostly in English.

She used to work as a psychologist but gave up her day job in December 2013 to become a full-time writer and a part-time editor. As far as she's concerned, it's the best job in the world.

When she's not writing, she likes to spend her time reading, indulging her ice cream and office supply addictions, and watching way too many crime shows.

CONNECT WITH JAE
Website: www.jae-fiction.com
E-Mail: jae@jae-fiction.com